PRAISE FOR RACHEL VAN DYKEN

"*The Consequence of Loving Colton* is a must-read friends-to-lovers story that's as passionate and sexy as it is hilarious!"

—Melissa Foster, *New York Times* bestselling author

"Just when you think Van Dyken can't possibly get any better, she goes and delivers *The Consequence of Loving Colton*. Full of longing and breathless moments, this is what romance is about."

—Lauren Layne, *USA Today* bestselling author

"The tension between Milo and Colton made this story impossible to put down. Quick, sexy, witty—easily one of my favorite books from Rachel Van Dyken."

—R.S. Grey, *USA Today* bestselling author

"Hot, funny . . . will leave you wishing you could get marked by one of the immortals!"

—Molly McAdams, *New York Times* bestselling author, on *The Dark Ones*

"Laugh-out-loud fun! Rachel Van Dyken is on my auto-buy list."

—Jill Shalvis, *New York Times* bestselling author, on *The Wager*

"*The Dare* is a laugh-out-loud read that I could not put down. Brilliant. Just brilliant."

—Cathryn Fox, *New York Times* bestselling author

INFRACTION

ALSO BY #1 *NEW YORK TIMES* BESTSELLING AUTHOR RACHEL VAN DYKEN:

Fall
Eternal
Strung
Capture

The Renwick House Series

The Ugly Duckling Debutante
The Seduction of Sebastian St. James
An Unlikely Alliance
The Redemption of Lord Rawlings
The Devil Duke Takes a Bride

The London Fairy Tales Series

Upon a Midnight Dream
Whispered Music
The Wolf's Pursuit
When Ash Falls

The Seasons of Paleo Series

Savage Winter
Feral Spring

The Wallflower Series (with Leah Sanders)

Waltzing with the Wallflower
Beguiling Bridget
Taming Wilde

The Dark Ones Saga

The Dark Ones
Untouchable Darkness
Dark Surrender

Stand-Alones

Hurt: A Collection (with Kristin Vayden and Elyse Faber)
Rip
Compromising Kessen
Every Girl Does It
The Parting Gift (with Leah Sanders)
Divine Uprising

INFRACTION

PLAYERS GAME

RACHEL
VAN DYKEN

SKYSCAPE

To everyone going through the storm—there will always be a sunrise. Joy comes in the morning.

—Hugs, RVD

Prologue

MILLER

"Our secret, right?" Her worried gaze was not setting me at ease, not in the least. Already my body rejected the idea of keeping secrets, especially from her brother, my best friend, the first-string quarterback for the Bucks, the guy I was supposed to block for and catch balls from—the same one who, years ago, had locked his sister in their house so she missed prom. *That* dude.

"Right." She licked her lips, shuffled out of the bedroom, and snuck back onto the couch. My body felt her absence.

I shouldn't have kissed her.

She shouldn't have kissed me back.

And she sure as hell shouldn't have crawled onto me.

Damn it, I sure as hell shouldn't have let her!

Maybe it was me. My fault. Maybe I was still torn up over the fact that my childhood best friend—the girl I thought I was still in love with—was currently engaged to Sanchez, our wide receiver and basically the only guy in the universe who was hard to hate despite being a cocky shit.

I slammed the pillow with both hands and then shoved it to the floor.

Kinsey crept back into the bedroom. "Sorry, I forgot my um . . ." She pointed to the floor, blushing, and then smacked herself on the forehead. "Underwear. I had underwear. I can't find them. We need to find my underwear, Miller!" A sheet flew into the air, followed by a throw pillow.

I dodged. "Stop panicking." Why, why did she have to be so gorgeous?

I tossed the remainder of the sheets while she looked under the bed. Jax had texted that he was coming by to talk to me, and if he found her in my bedroom, there would be bloodshed and absolutely no words shared between us. The guy literally told me that he would poison any guy from the team who dated her, and when I called his bluff, he showed me the search history on his phone for graphic ways to get away with murder. The guy was either psychotic or just really took his sister's sex life way too seriously—or both.

Well done, Miller, get traded to the Bucks, and after the first championship season you decide to fuck Jax's sister! Stellar plan!

"Found them!" she shouted triumphantly, thrusting a lacy pair of panties into the air like a trophy while my body went rock hard over the graphic images those panties conjured up. Images of my hands on her body, my mouth sucking her dry. I gulped. Yeah, I was getting poisoned today. No doubt about it. Especially since the moment I stepped toward her, Jax's voice filled the large penthouse.

"Miller, you in your room? Where's Kins?"

She hid on the other side of the bed while I quickly met him at my bedroom door. "Kins? Hell if I know, maybe you should put a bell on her? Better yet, one of those tracking collars they give dogs?"

"Good plan." He rolled his eyes. "Look, I know you were up late last night getting drunk off your ass." It was my turn to roll my eyes.

We won the championship. THE championship. Of course I'd gotten drunk off my ass. "But, I have a favor to ask."

"Sure." I shrugged, mouth dry. I'd do anything to get him out of my room. "Whatever you want, man, it's yours."

"Great." He sighed in relief. "It's just, one of Kinsey's exes moved back and the guy's bad news—so I need your help."

"Want me to kill him?" I offered, completely on board with the idea but pissed at myself for thinking I had some sort of stake or claim on a girl that days ago I wasn't even pining over or thinking about.

God, she smelled good.

"Miller?"

"Huh? Yes?" I blinked. Shit, what else had he said?

"Anyway, I think if we just pack her shit, things will go faster."

"Faster," I repeated slowly.

Jax leaned in. "You still drunk, man?"

On his sister? Hell yeah, I was. "Nope, totally stone-cold sober." And hard, still hard. That too.

"Our grandma's been missing her anyways, so this is the perfect plan. I just don't have time to pack up all her crap and try to convince her it's a good idea."

"Am I the packer or the talker?" I tried not to flinch when he stared me down like I was on medication.

"Dude, that's the favor. Seriously, not drunk, not even a little bit? You guys are close. Convince my crazy sister to go to Europe for the summer so I don't have to worry about that little shit getting into her head while we're training for the preseason."

I gulped. "What makes you think she'd listen to me?"

He stood taller, his dark brows furrowed together, before he gave me a light shrug that basically conveyed he had no fucking clue that his sister was half-naked, in my room, probably still burning from the memory of us clawing at one another the night before, and that I was contemplating murdering him to do it again. "Because you're friends."

3

Friends.

I'd never hated that word more than I did then, and not because of the meaning behind it, but because I was lying to Jax, my good friend, a guy I respected, one of our team captains, my quarterback, because the hand he was shaking had just run down his sister's naked body—and craved it more than it freaking should.

"Okay," I choked out, hating the fact that the damn word even existed in the English language. "You know, maybe I'm not feeling so well. I think I'll lie down before I talk with her."

"Thanks." He nodded. "I'm out to get some breakfast."

I watched him leave.

And waited for the inevitable.

"So, friends, huh?" came Kinsey's voice, and then those damn panties were tossed at my face, followed by one pillow and another and another, until all the pillows were on my side of the room. What the hell was with that woman and pillows?

"Best of." I turned and tried my best at a cocky grin.

She didn't fall for it.

"I'm not going." Hands on hips, she stared me down. "Besides, I hate my ex. Jax has nothing to worry about."

"When Jax worries, the team worries, because the team needs him not to suck, ergo, why not go to Europe for the summer? You'll be back in time to get your cheer squad in shape for the season and everyone will be happy."

Everyone but me.

I left that part out.

"Everyone?" She licked her lips as insecurity flashed across her face.

"Shit, Kins, you know what I mean."

"So I should go?" Her voice was thoughtful but her eyes did that flashing thing they did when she was seconds away from either smacking her brother in the face or going for someone's dick by way of a kick. "Yeah, Miller?"

I wanted her to stay.

I wanted to find out what was between us before it slipped away.

I craved what we'd shared. Hungered for some sort of tangible emotional connection.

What I didn't need? Another broken heart.

Lame.

Stupid.

Weak.

Whatever.

I was done with relationships.

Done with the pain that came with them and the helpless feeling that always happened after they were over.

"Yeah, Kins." I swallowed the sudden dryness in my throat, the ache in my chest, and the hurt look in her bright eyes. "I think you should go."

Chapter One

KINSEY

Seven Months Later
Two Weeks Before Preseason

"You're being ridiculous." Jax, my brother, "America's Quarterback," and all-around Mr. Perfect with his baby-blue eyes and curly brown hair, wasn't even looking in my direction!

I snapped my fingers in front of his face. With a sigh, he pressed pause on the TV remote and slowly looked at me. "You're beautiful."

"I gained ten pounds."

He shrugged. "Where?"

"Where?" I repeated. *"Where?"* I was about to say it a third time when a knock sounded at the door.

"Good, Miller's finally here." Jax shot up from the lounge chair and answered the door while I stood immobile and nearly stopped breathing altogether.

Miller.

Freaking MILLER was here?

I hadn't seen him since Vegas.

I had actually *avoided* him like the plague until I left for Europe, only to find out that he'd been dating nonstop since I'd left! Not that I'd stalked him, or paid attention to social media, including gossip sites, tweets, and stupid hashtags about his biceps. Nope, not even the ones that said he was the hottest tight end with a tight end made for sin. I especially ignored those, for obvious reasons. I'd seen that tight end up close and personal—they had no idea the type of sinning a girl would do when faced with that—and his perfect lips. I shivered then mentally strangled myself until my mental self lost all consciousness.

Hold it the hell together, Kins.

I'd been able to do it for years!

I'd been constantly surrounded by football players and good-looking men with enough muscles and money to keep any irrational human occupied.

He was just like *every* other stupid football player I'd ever known—I mean other than my brother. At least Jax kept it in his pants and didn't wear his arrogance on his sleeve like a Cub Scout badge.

Miller's badge would probably say something like "Most orgasms given by a smile." And it'd be right.

"How was your run?" Jax asked all casual as the scent of Miller filled the air. I didn't want to inhale, I didn't want the memories that came with his scent, memories of our stolen kisses, the way his mouth met my every need before I even knew I had it.

"Great." His voice was as sexy as ever, with a hint of a velvet rasp that drove me completely insane and made my legs weak right along with my self-control. My obsession with Grant Sanchez had never been this bad; that had been lust, nothing more. Which was why I'd never acted on it and was happy when he started dating Emerson, my teammate and now my friend.

I finally glanced up.

Our eyes locked. How long had he been staring at me?

I gulped.

He mimicked my movement, only for some reason it looked like his throat moved in slow motion. That damn throat, all smooth, muscular. Right. Like he had a reason to be nervous or even upset. He was a serial dater who'd basically told me to my face, mind you, after having sex with me *twice*, that I should flee the country and go to Europe for the summer!

Not the best way to make a girl feel secure. Add that to the fact that I'd gained ten pounds because Europeans ate a lot of bread, and I'd left the country with a broken heart mixed with the fury of a woman scorned. I was completely ready to throw myself off a cliff or at least put a paper bag over the pillowy half of my body that, since returning to the States, refused to drop the pounds I'd gained.

"So what's up?" Miller finally snapped his attention back to my brother, and again I was invisible. "Your text said family emergency."

All the hairs on the back of my arm stood on end. Family emergency?

Jax looked uncomfortable as he ducked his head and then ran his hands through his curly hair. "He made the practice squad."

"He?" I parroted. "Who is *he*?"

"*He* did?" Miller clenched his hands into fists. "That's bullshit."

"That's what I said." Jax swore. "I even went to Coach and explained that he'd be bad for team morale, that the reason he couldn't stay in the league was because he was a selfish asshole who'd rather take all the glory than throw a damn pass, but he wouldn't listen. Coach said that his stats were good and he was cheap, and after losing a few players after the championship, we should rebuild with players that don't cost as much as us shitheads."

I smiled at that.

Jax, Sanchez, and Miller were three of the highest-paid players in the league. It made sense that they'd try to find good players for less money, not that they needed it since those guys won games with their eyes closed, but whatever.

"Who's this guy you speak of?" I wondered aloud. "Because both of you seem pretty pissed about it, and neither of you is the type to get your panties"—Miller arched a brow in my direction as I finished in a hollow voice—"in a, um, twist." Cough, slap chest, cough. Why was he here again?

"Are you getting sick?" Jax was at my side immediately.

"Nope." I couldn't meet Miller's eyes for fear that I'd confess everything to my brother and get one football player murdered and another locked in a prison cell to rot. "Anyway, this guy? Who is he?"

The room was silent.

And then a tension filled the air so thick that I nearly felt like choking. Jax was looking at me with anger, and Miller—pity.

Oh no.

"No." I stood on shaky legs. "No."

"I tried, Kins."

"Andy." The ex that Jax had sent me away from, it seemed, was staying. "How has he not gotten hit by a car yet? Or been chased off the earth by angry husbands and ex-girlfriends? Been eaten by dogs? Swallowed by a whale—"

"He's not Jonah," Miller interrupted.

I gave him a heated glare and threw my hands in the air. "So, he's here. Big deal. I'll avoid him, he'll avoid me, and all will be right in the universe. If you boys will excuse me, I'm going to go see a man about a nap."

"She has a man in there?" Miller asked Jax.

"It's the only kind I let her have, especially after Andy."

"The stuffed kind?"

I was already stomping away when I heard Jax call out my name. Gritting my teeth, I stopped and turned. "Seriously, Jax, I'm exhausted."

Miller's gaze raked over me like I was the only hot meal he'd seen after surviving a ten-year blizzard. I shivered and tried to hold it together, and by hold it together I mean I tried not to run in his general direction and trip against his mouth.

"You guys are going to date," Jax announced.

Miller's stunned expression did not give me hope that he was already in on the stupidest idea of all time ever.

"No," we said in unison then shared a glare.

"Why would you even suggest that?" Miller's voice was eerily calm, his blue eyes wild. "Isn't the point to keep guys away from your sister? Me included?"

Jax sighed, "I trust you." His eyes searched Miller's. "You know Anderson's bad news. Look, I've thought it through—"

"I won't do it." I crossed my arms. "Jax, you can't just control everything around you. Stick to football. You're good at that. And I'm a grown woman!"

"You're twenty-two," he pointed out in a haughty voice that sounded eerily like my father's when I had too much eggnog at Christmas. "And I don't want to worry about you. If he sees you with Miller, he'll back off, especially since he wants a spot on the team. He wouldn't jeopardize that just for a chance to—"

I gasped.

Miller slapped him in the chest.

"A chance to what?" I took a step toward both guys, itching to give them matching black eyes. "Sleep with me? Is that what you were going to say? That I'm not even worth jeopardizing his career over? Thanks, Jax, you really know how to make a girl feel good!"

"God, for the last time, you're not fat!" Jax yelled.

Miller held his hands up as if he wasn't sure what to do.

"And you're dating!" Jax shoved a finger in my direction. "I trust Miller, he wouldn't touch you! And I need to focus this year. I just—"

"Jax." I softened my voice. "What's this really about?"

I'd never seen my brother so stressed out. His face betrayed his thirty-two years for the first time since he'd started with the league.

"I can't worry about one more thing." He stared down at the ground and his body trembled before he tugged at his hair and swore.

"One more thing on top of winning?" I reached for him. "Help me understand, because you're acting more psychotic than normal."

Tears filled Jax's eyes, he paled and blurted in a hushed tone, "Dad . . ." He sucked in a breath. "He has cancer."

And just like that, my world went from bright colors to gray. "Wh-what?"

"Mom asked me not to tell you while you were in Europe. She didn't want to worry you and—" Jax's voice cracked.

I had grown up with a brother who never wavered.

Who never cried.

Who always gave me the impression that, just like my dad, he was sent to earth to be some kind of football superhero.

I needed strength now, because I was never that person in the family. The pillar—*my* pillar—was currently crumbling before my eyes, and I didn't know how to make it better.

It felt like a bomb had just been dropped in the room.

For more reasons than one.

I searched Jax's eyes and what I found there made me want to protect him for a change.

It wasn't a question.

Not at all. But before I could answer Miller spoke up for us both.

"I'll do it." Miller's raspy voice filled the ache in my chest enough to cue my body to breathe. "We'll date. It's one less thing for both of you to think about. Consider it done."

And just like that.

I was officially dating the tight end for the Bellevue Bucks, the guy who'd slept with me then shoved me out of the flipping country, my brother's teammate and best friend—Quinton Miller.

Chapter Two

MILLER

I was fucked.

No other way around it.

The words fell from my mouth before I had a damn chance to stop them. But the minute they were released into the universe and I saw Kinsey's pale expression color enough that I wasn't afraid she was going to pass out, I felt better.

The best I'd felt in months.

Because I'd saved her.

And the last time I'd seen her?

I'd screwed her over.

Both times by way of her brother.

Shit, this season wasn't starting so well.

"Great!" Jax exhaled and then breathed in and out again. He slapped my back and gave it a semi-awkward rub before jerking away and scratching his head. "I, uh, I appreciate it, Miller, I just—"

"Don't mention it." No, seriously. Don't. Because every time the name Kinsey rolled off his damn tongue, my entire body buzzed with awareness and my eyes searched for her.

"Tell me more about Dad," Kinsey pleaded, her lips pressed into a thin line before she crossed her arms and rubbed them.

Jax hung his head. "Not now, Kins."

Her hands balled into tiny fists.

Unfair—that she was still gorgeous, that my mouth burned to graze hers, that I wanted to devour every single word that dropped from her luscious lips even if they were filled with bitterness and resentment. Her eyes were glossed over with worry—and even then she was still beautiful. Kinsey. The one girl that was off-limits—the one girl I couldn't seem to get enough of.

The type of woman that made a man feel at his best—even when he was at his worst.

Tears filled her eyes and then she stomped toward me.

I wasn't sure whether to back up or just let her hit me, get it over with, and pray to God that she didn't expose what I'd done. If Jax ever found out, I'd be dead, and it would be on her conscience.

"Fine." She poked my chest with one of her fingers. Her face was softer than normal, a bit more round. The weight she'd gained (not that I'd ever admit to her that I could tell) looked good on her, like she was finally healthy, gaining that ass she'd been comically obsessed with ever since my best friend Emerson joined the cheer squad and showed her how to survive off things that weren't just green.

Like bread.

Pasta.

Life.

"But he's not allowed to touch me." She licked her full lips. "At all, especially—"

"Whoa!" Jax shook his head and then laughed so loudly that I was actually offended. "Miller? He knows I'd kill him and bury the body. It's why he's the only guy who can do it—he's the only guy who would know to look the other way if you're running around doing a naked striptease."

Kinsey glared. "I was a kid."

"Doesn't matter." Jax shrugged. "Naked is naked. Go take your nap."

"No." She crossed her arms. "I want to know more about Dad."

And that was my cue to leave.

I awkwardly checked my phone. Damn it, I would kill for a text message or missed phone call—even if it was from Sanchez. Then again, he hadn't come up for air since proposing to Emerson a few months ago.

I briefly rubbed the spot on my chest that still burned after being rejected and then remembered—I was over it.

Not fully.

But getting there.

Just not as fast as I would have liked, especially since I was constantly surrounded by their inability to not scream while having sex.

I think Sanchez did it to piss me off.

And since I was their neighbor.

I was in hell.

Of course this led to me staying with Jax a few times a week, which led to this current bad life decision.

He'd trusted me.

Let me into his life.

Something he'd never done with any other teammate except Sanchez.

And all without knowing that I'd seen his sister naked—and she sure as hell wasn't six at the time.

What the hell train of thought just occurred?

I blinked and saw Kinsey shaking in Jax's arms. I missed a pivotal part of that conversation, I was still trying to figure out if it was a good thing or bad when she sniffled against his chest and then shoved away from him and ran into her room.

Slamming the door behind her.

15

Her luggage was still strewn around the living room, even though she'd gotten back last week.

And for the last seven days, Jax had asked me to come over.

I'd said *hell no* in my head and lied, told him I was busy, when I was really avoiding his sister like the plague.

And not because she was this psychotic clingy sexually frustrated cheerleader, but because I was legit afraid that I'd forget about Jax, and all the reasons I wasn't allowed to touch her, and just fuse my mouth to hers until I passed out from oxygen deprivation.

"She took that well." Jax hung his head, shoving his hands in his pockets. "I can't win with her."

Emotional heart-to-hearts—especially about things like cancer or impending death—weren't my thing. It's not that I couldn't tap into that part of my heart, but I wasn't ready to, because a part of me wasn't ready to acknowledge that I still had a lot of shit still locked up on the inside that was trying to pry its way out. Talking reminded me of my own pain and I hated it. Besides, what the hell kind of encouragement did I even have to give? When I knew nothing. And it seemed like the worst possible idea to try to offer him hope—when I sometimes felt like I had none.

And Jax? Well, he was the type of guy who had his shit together and on lockdown; he'd see right through my lame attempts at trying to make him feel better.

"She's been out of the country. That's a lot of news to dump on her first week back, man, and my dad wanted her to have that time— Kinsey needs that time, she deserves it."

Something about the way he said that made me pause.

She deserved it?

Jax's jaw clenched.

Silence overtook the room.

He was still staring at the door with his laser vision like he was waiting for it to open or maybe disappear altogether. "My dad should be fine."

"That's good news."

"One more round of chemo," he said in a hollow voice.

"How long does that take?" I had a feeling he wanted to talk. And I felt like a bastard for thinking of every excuse in the book to bolt.

Still staring at the door, Jax gave a noncommittal shrug. "A month, maybe two. We'll be playing the Pilots again." He gave me a serious nod and popped his knuckles. "Good quarterback, strong special teams, heard they picked up that dickhead Silva."

"Silva can kiss my ass." I felt my body visibly relax. Football I could talk about. Slowly I made my way toward him then stepped directly in his line of vision. "Besides, he's only fast when he's not out partying all hours, and we all know that his discipline is total shit."

He nodded, staring through me, toward the door . . . toward his sister. Damn it.

"God. Football. Family—Kinsey." He gulped, finally locking eyes with me while a muscle ticked down his neck. "That's how I deal with shit. They don't usually mix, man. I have to compartmentalize to concentrate, then I feel like a complete dick for having to do that. I just, I can't look at the whole picture all at once. It's the same with plays, I have to look at each possible outcome then back at the whole picture and dissect. And with my dad, that means—"

"You look at the end."

"Yeah." His voice cracked. "I do."

My heart splintered a bit.

I knew what it was like to lose a parent.

There were no words in the English language to describe how much life it sucked out of a person—how it still hurt, years later, how you still heard that person's voice and woke up running into the kitchen only to realize that they weren't ever coming back.

I looked away. "I got you, you know that, right?"

"Yeah, man." He finally seemed to snap out of it. "I know."

"And I'll take care of Kins, at least that's one box you don't have to open, alright?"

Because I already opened, plundered, plunged, thrust—holy shit on fire, I was going to burn in hell.

"You deal with what you gotta deal with and I'll help with the rest."

"He broke her heart," Jax added. "I'm not letting that happen again."

"You gonna lock her in her room again?"

"If I have to." He was dead serious, poor Kins.

"I will literally suffocate you in your sleep" came Kinsey's voice as she sauntered out of the room in spandex shorts tight enough to give me a heart attack and a tank top that left nothing to the imagination. "I'm going to go to the stadium to lift."

"The hell you are!" Jax roared.

Here we go.

She swiped a few tears. "It's how I de-stress!" She grabbed her keys. "And we start practice in a week, I need to lose this!"

She slapped her ass.

I swear the hardest moment of my life occurred when I looked toward the ceiling rather than in the direction of the sound of her hand hitting spandex, though I probably lost points with God when I replayed the image of me doing the exact same thing until my palm was sore.

"I can't go with you." Jax gritted his teeth. "I have film to go over."

And just like that, all eyes fell to me.

And when I say *all*, Kinsey glared and silently gave me enough threatening looks to get her point across while Jax pleaded.

Couldn't win either way.

"I should, uh, lift too."

"Gee, maybe we can have a bro-sesh and I can spot you." She rubbed her hands together. "Oh wait, you can lift ten of me. Just let me do my thing, and you can go do what dumb football players do."

"Oh yeah, what's that?" I took the bait.

"Look pretty." She winked at both of us.

"Jax, she called us pretty."

"Don't fight it." She jerked the fridge open and grabbed a water bottle. "And if you're coming to babysit, then I at least get to drive."

"Okay."

"Your car." She dropped her keys on the counter and held out her hand. "Come on, give them up, baby. Or wait"—she tapped her chin—"I think I need a better nickname for you . . ." Her eyes looked evil. I didn't like the look, well, most of me didn't, other parts were on board, treacherous bastards. "Chicken Waffle."

"You can't call him Chicken Waffle."

"I'm not." She grinned. "He can be the chicken, I get to be the waffle."

The door nearly slammed her on the ass on the way out.

"Better go after her." Jax sighed. "She's had five tickets."

"That's not so—"

"In the last year."

I groaned.

And followed her out.

Chapter Three

KINSEY

I told myself not to look at him directly in the eyes—something about his blue eyes against his mocha skin made girls like me turn to mush and say stupid things like "We should hang out sometime." When I had no business hanging out with him at all, ever.

Especially outside of our friend group.

At least he was a much-needed distraction from the fact that my dad was going in for another treatment tomorrow, and that he was most likely going to be sick all day, and that he didn't want to see me.

Because he was so sick, so weak, he thought it would traumatize me.

It was so unfair.

And yet I couldn't yell at him, because he was sick.

I sent him a frustrated text only to get a heart back, like everything was fine in the world, when really he was getting injected with chemicals that were slowly killing off all the good parts inside of him.

I gritted my teeth.

"It's a push start." Miller's voice interrupted my thoughts. "You have to push the button, Waffle."

I would not laugh.

Or smile.

Or give him even a hint that him using my ridiculous made-up name actually made me feel better.

"Try not to be such a chicken, Chicken." I put on my seat belt, pressed my foot against the brake, and started the car. A very gorgeous Mercedes-AMG SUV that felt like driving a really heavy tank that somehow still knew how to go fast.

"Oh, the things I could do to you, baby," I whispered.

"The hell?" Miller jerkily put on his seat belt while I took the corner of the parking garage as if we were starring in the new *Ocean's* movie.

"Mmmm . . ." I nodded, running my hands down the wheel as we took another turn and then accelerated out of the garage down the street toward the first green light. I pressed down on the pedal harder. I could have sworn I heard Miller praying.

"Didn't know you were Catholic," I murmured at the next stoplight.

"Just converted."

"God bless you." I grinned, finally checking him out of the corner of my eye. He was gripping the seat belt buckle with one hand like he was afraid it was going to pop out and holding the car door with the other. "Miller, it's a tank, you aren't going to fall out."

"With the way you drive, I wouldn't be so sure," he said through gritted teeth.

I rolled my eyes and continued getting lost in my thoughts all the way to the stadium, pulling to a screeching halt in the semi-empty lot and turning off the engine with a deep sigh. "That was fun."

"Fun," Miller repeated in that deep voice. "Fun is going to the movies, having a drink, happy hour, football, championship games." He snatched the keys from the middle of the console. "That was *The Fast and the Furious* without body doubles and stuntmen."

I shrugged. "Speed makes me feel better."

"Next time we're walking," he grunted, slamming the door after him like I was the offending party when he was the one who clearly didn't believe in the safety of his own vehicle!

"There won't be a next time, Chicken." I shrugged. "I'm more of a solo act. This whole dating thing is only to make sure Anderson Dickhead Harris doesn't bark up the wrong tree and get his nuts cut off."

"Are you the tree in this scenario?" Miller grinned.

"Don't get too excited. Wouldn't want your nuts to get caught in the line of fire too, Miller. You've seen my brother throw, he's very accurate."

"That's funny." He snorted and slammed his hand against the door when I tried to jerk it open.

Fine. I'd bite. "What is?"

"You."

"Why am I funny?"

Why was he so hot?

Why?

How was it fair that I gained weight?

And he gained muscle?

"You realize it would take one text to Jax." He held up his phone with his free hand. What the heck did the guy eat for breakfast? The other hand was still pressed against the door, most likely with all 225 pounds of him backing it up. "Or one phone call—and possibly a drunken confession that you seduced me in Vegas—and this would all be over."

My eyes narrowed into tiny slits. "I didn't seduce you."

"Didn't you though?" He tilted his head while a cocky grin spread across his face.

"I didn't." I opened then shut my mouth, only to open it again as fuzzy memories resurfaced. "We both went in for that kiss."

He leaned in until our faces were nearly touching. "Hmm, and whose bed were we in, Kins?"

My mouth went dry. Even the way he said my name was sexy, I could feel the low vibrations of his voice charge the air like electricity.

"Whose bed?" He cupped his ear with his free hand. "Because I'm pretty sure it wasn't yours . . ."

"I did not seduce you." I just had to repeat that, didn't I? Out loud? Making all of my girly parts relive every single moment of his touch and press replay, pause, then replay, then a heck of a lot of pauses during certain, um, moments. "I was tired, the couch was uncomfortable, you had a bed, and you were passed out from drinking every shot skanks threw at you."

"You and Emerson gave me shots," he said in a deadpan voice.

Damn it! I forgot about that part.

Sure, Kins, you remember the sex but not the moments leading up to it? The sober ones where you plied him with alcohol?

"It doesn't matter," I argued. "Jax would still kill you, and he's going through enough right now and I know you well enough to know you'd do anything for a friend. Besides, Jax would lose focus and you guys wouldn't make it back to the championships, and all the world would know it's because you couldn't keep your cock in your pants!"

"I'm Chicken, not a rooster."

"Really? With that? Right now? That's what you're going to go with?"

He shrugged, "See ya inside, Waffles. Try not to hurt yourself on the elliptical. I think one of the girls left some magazines for you to look at while you get your sweat on." His eyes heated as his gaze raked me over until it landed on my ass. "Then again, maybe just do some squats. I'd hate for you to lose all those gains."

"Look at my ass again, and I'm grabbing whatever pokes me first and snapping it."

He barked out a laugh as I shoved past him. Even though I wanted to hide in the shadows, I wanted every reason to inflict violence on the guy for staring. I put a little extra swing in my hips.

And when I turned around.

He was covering his eyes.

I hated that I was disappointed.

Almost as much as I hated that he actually had self-control when all I really wanted to do since his scent enveloped me in the car was call a truce then make out like teenagers.

"See, Miller? That's teamwork right there!" I called back, nearly running into a closed door before sprinting into the workout room and dropping my stuff on the first bench I saw.

My breathing was labored.

And I couldn't decide what was worse, the fact that I was that attracted to him, or the fact that in those few brief moments I'd forgotten all about my dad's sickness on top of all the reasons I'd stayed away from football players to begin with.

Lights were on.

Loud techno was pumping.

But I didn't see anyone else in the room, which left me and Miller. Alone.

Which basically meant my babysitter was going to either have to lift, or be bored out of his mind while I did everything but hit up the cardio machines.

"You sure you can lift that?" Miller's voice sounded behind me while I loaded one of the bars with a ten on each side.

"You sure you can count that high?" I countered, shoving the collar on each end. The barbell was sixty-five pounds, hardly my max for cleans.

I did a few Russian deadlifts to stretch my hamstrings, and was disappointed when I didn't notice Miller anywhere.

Great, the babysitter had all but abandoned me.

An annoying inner voice reminded me that I'd basically asked him to, but still.

I gave my head a shake and did a set of eight cleans.

"Your form is shit." Miller suddenly appeared in the mirror behind me holding a water bottle, and I almost dropped the bar on my feet. "Your pull is way too fast from the floor."

"Do you mind?" I snapped.

"No. But you should. And your back is going to hurt like hell tomorrow, right along with the biceps you keep using rather than a good shrug with your shoulders, but if you don't want my help . . ." He popped the top off the bottle and sat down on the bench next to me. "I'll shut up."

I started my next set.

Painfully aware that he was watching me.

I slowed my pull and shrugged harder.

When I finished, Miller was clapping. "Was that so hard?"

"Actually, it was easy." I winked.

"Waffles, was that a moment? Are we possibly . . ." He paused. "Bro lifting right now?"

"Maybe one day we'll be swole mates." I started my next set to his laughter as he walked over to the bench and started warming up.

I'd be lying if I said my eyes didn't have this annoying habit of constantly checking to make sure the bar hadn't hit him in the teeth.

What? He had nice teeth.

Pecs.

Skin.

Focus.

I took a deep breath and pushed thoughts of Miller away. All that mattered was getting my aggression out—in a safe manner that wouldn't have me using Miller as a stress reliever.

And Dad.

Dad mattered.

We spent the next hour working out in silence.

And when Miller was finished, he not only brought me a towel but handed me a chilled water bottle and then his keys.

"Don't kill us," he joked. "I really do want another ring."

"That impressed with my lifting skills?" I teased, snatching the keys out of his hand.

"Nope." He let me walk ahead of him. "But I just spent the last hour watching your ass in spandex . . . I think a little congrats are in order—though I'll have to stop calling you Flat-ass in my head."

Most girls would probably be offended.

Instead, I walked a little lighter on my feet as I skipped out of the building and made my way to his car.

But my happy attitude was severely short-lived.

Because just when I was feeling better about the horrible way the day started, Anderson Dickhead Harris waltzed toward me.

"Kinsey." He eyed me up and down, slowly, not casually, but like he knew what I looked like without clothes on and wanted to make sure I was aware that was exactly what he was thinking about.

I sucked in a breath.

Then felt a steel arm wrap around me.

I exhaled.

I held on.

I shouldn't have.

In all the moves I should have made that day—I should have run away from the temptation—I knew it in my body, in the way a sense of foreboding washed over me.

But my heart?

It had other plans.

It was too weak to run.

Stay.

So I did.

Hold on.

I did that too.

Cling.

A sense of calm washed over me.

Chapter Four

MILLER

He was six feet two inches and around two hundred pounds and one of the biggest asses I'd ever met in my entire life.

I didn't care if he shit golden footballs and came with a promise of winning every single championship from here on out—I'd still hate him, I'd still want to remove his head from his body and hand it to the kicker with instructions to let it soar.

"Miller." He always nodded, never shook my hand, never once used any sort of acknowledgment that showed he had good manners. Just a head nod, a quick clip of my name, and football talk.

It was either football.

Or girls.

Mainly the one girl that he just couldn't shut up about, the girl that got away. Funny, since she seemed to have found herself in my arms . . . and my bed. Bastard.

The very girl that I was trying not to squeeze to death. The same one who, if her shaking was any indication, wanted to crawl up me like a tree and hide.

Hell.

"Where's Jax?" The combination of his blue baseball hat with his brown eyes made him look like a spoiled little golden boy. The truth? He was a walking, talking douche who needed to get put in his place—I still had no clue what Kinsey ever saw in him other than the fact that he was a manipulative little shit, and she'd been trying to piss off Jax a few years ago because she was tired of being on such a short leash.

More protective than he was now, if that was even conceivable to imagine.

"Jax?" I repeated. "Who the hell knows? Probably going over film or some shit." I shrugged, pulling Kinsey tighter against me, and then in a move I knew would get us to the point faster and out of the damn parking lot, I mentally apologized to Kins, Jax, God, my own damn lusting body, and reached for her chin. Her skin was soft everywhere, my finger tilted that mouth toward mine and sealed our relationship with one hot open-mouthed kiss.

She snaked her arms around my neck, her mouth parting with a moan before scratching those nails up my head in a way that sent all the wrong signals to all the right places.

Full breasts plastered against my chest, and because I could, because I was a bastard who clearly had no self-control, I gripped her ass with my right hand and squeezed.

Kins gave a little yelp, then bit down on my lower lip before I chuckled against her mouth then whispered, "Sorry, I couldn't control myself."

At least that was true.

We were both panting, her face was flushed, that gorgeous pale face with those fully kissed lips and deep-blue eyes.

By the time I faced Anderson again, his smile was cool, his eyes narrowing more and more by the second. "I can't imagine Jax is happy with this." He wagged a finger between both of us then rested that same finger on his chin before touching his ball cap and giving it a nervous tug over his eyes.

"Well . . ." Kinsey gripped my hand. A woman that tiny should never be able to squeeze as hard as she was squeezing. "Jax is kind of the one who set us up, right, Chicken?"

I pinched her ass again, hoping she'd release my hand; if anything it made her squeeze harder. "That's right, Waffle Cakes, I've actually never seen your brother happier."

She gulped and her eyes flickered before she pasted on a smile. "So true."

"Uh-huh." Anderson nodded again. Damn it, enough with the cocky look and the nodding! "Well, that's great. I'm happy for you, Kinsey. And Miller, I should warn you that she's a handful." He moved to walk past us and lifted his hands in the air. "But I'm sure you're probably already aware of what it takes to keep her in line."

"The fuck?" I started charging toward him but was stopped by a small hand on my arm.

"I'll take it easy on him," Kinsey replied to Anderson with a brave smile. "Let's go, baby, I'm driving."

"You gave her keys?" Anderson's eyes widened until I thought they were going to pop out of his head. "To *your* car?"

"She's a great driver," I lied as visions of our trip and dismemberment taunted me.

"Whatever, man, you must have it bad if you think that. She nearly ran over my grandma."

Kinsey turned her head and whispered, "Probably because Grandma's a whore."

I barely kept my laugh in before Anderson nodded one last time—presumably just because he knew how much it pissed me off—and went into the facility.

By the time I turned around, Kinsey had already started the car.

"That went well." I buckled up.

She hit the accelerator so hard that I was suddenly thankful for air bags, and when she didn't say anything, I tried to engage in conversation, but was met with a speeding tyrant every time I tried. So I stopped.

I let her enjoy the silence.

The speed.

And didn't even argue when she pulled up to my apartment building and parked in my spot—one I hadn't even realized she knew was mine.

Still silent all the way to the elevator.

And to the penthouse.

"You know where my hide-a-key is too?" I grumbled behind her, only to shut my mouth when she reached under the mat, then under the mat under the mat, and pulled out the hot pink key, sliding it into the lock and letting herself in.

"Who are you?" I slammed the door behind me. "I've never shown anyone that hiding spot."

"First of all, it's a shit hiding spot." She flipped her dark long hair over her shoulder. "Second, you showed Emerson, so you basically showed me."

"I didn't show Emerson shit!" Did I? Damn it, Sanchez probably told her. The man told Em everything.

"You did." She gave an exasperated exhale, and made herself at home, going into my kitchen, grabbing some Gatorade—my Gatorade—and then flipping off her sneakers and grabbing the remote.

Confused as hell, I looked around and then finally joined her on the couch. "Are you moving in or something? Because I gotta be honest, Kins, I like my naked time and I'm pretty sure if you don't participate it's against the rules. Also, I want to stay alive, and if Jax ever found out you were in my apartment he'd kill me."

"It's not like we're having sex." She shrugged.

"What?" I jerked my attention back to her. "It doesn't matter! We're alone! You're forgetting last season when he nearly shoved me off a building for standing next to you at the bar!"

"He was kidding." She waved me off and clicked "On." "*Ballers*!"

"Oh really? Is that why he said 'I want to kill you'? Because he was kidding?"

"You were new to the team last year. He was being his overprotective self. Besides"—she leaned her body back against the couch cushions—"he trusts you now, remember that part of the conversation? Where you probably replayed visions of me naked in that hotel bed and nodded your head at him like you're actually worthy of that same trust?"

I glared. "Wrong." I jerked the remote from her hand. "He can trust me."

"Can he?"

"Are you asking for him or for you?"

She looked away, crossing her arms. "I'm not going to say anything to Jax, that's not what this is about."

"Then, care telling me what this is about? Because a few hours ago I was under the impression that the only time we're faking anything is when we're out in public, and now your feet are on my coffee table, your sweat is currently mixing with my brand-new leather couch, and you stole my favorite flavor of Gatorade."

Right, because that kiss had been fake, lying bastard.

She grabbed the bottle of fruit punch flavor and chugged half of it before handing it to me. "Chill, Gator police, there were two left."

"That's not the point!"

"Then what is? I'm trying to watch TV here."

"You have a place!" Was she really this dense? I'd known her for over a year, had seen her naked, and not once had I ever gotten the whole crazy vibe from her. "Kins?"

With a sigh, she hung her head. "If I sneeze wrong, Jax stops and drops everything and forces me to call the doctor. Swear to all that's holy, one time he actually said, 'Your cough sounds different, I think it's swine flu, we're going to the ER.'"

I whistled. "Shit, Kins, that's some next-level brotherly affection."

"He's protective." A smile teased her mouth. "And I love him for it. I think it's because I was actually really sick when I was little—not the point." She held up her hand like she didn't want me to ask questions. Like it wasn't my place to be curious. "The point is, if I go home right now, he's going to see right through me"—she rolled her eyes—"and I don't want to lie to him. Not with everything going on. Because I know him the way he knows me, Miller. He's going to kill himself trying to figure out if it's Dad or if it's you or if it's Anderson, and then he's going to play like shit because when he should be thinking about football, he's going to be thinking about all the things he can't control but wishes he could." She finally exhaled. "So I'm here, in your crazy fancy penthouse apartment, because I need a minute, alright? Can you give that to me?"

Too shocked to answer right away, I took a few breaths then finally nodded. "Yes. On one condition."

Her eyes locked with mine, and though I wasn't as practiced as Jax since he had twenty-two more years of knowing Kinsey, I saw the fear, the slight hesitation. Because as much as I liked to think I didn't care about her. I did. I really fucking cared. And it all started the minute she and I became friends and then made a stupid-as-hell decision to kiss each other, then peel each other's clothes off and—the point? I started to notice details.

And every detail was important.

From the way she carried herself, to the way her face lit up when she talked about football.

To the irritated look on her face when she was too tired to fight.

And when she was turned on . . .

Her cheeks blushed and she bit her lip when she was turned on.

Those were dangerous realizations to have.

Just another reason I let her go.

And another reason I should again.

"I need you to take a shower."

She blew out a shaky breath. "Are you saying I smell?"

I leaned in and sniffed. "Like salty waffles with a bit of dirty sports bra on the side."

She crooked her finger and then brought my shirt to her face. "And you smell like a chicken that crossed the road and got hit by a semi carrying a special order of shit, and yet, here I am, ready to forgive you for it. Some friend you are."

I licked my lips.

Automatic response to her nearness and the fact that I was a liar, she didn't smell bad, she smelled perfect, like one perfect mistake away from being even sweatier, in my bed, with my hands on her.

The door to my apartment swung open.

"Fuck, does everyone have a key?" I whispered under my breath.

"Why is she sniffing your shirt?" Sanchez grinned, rocking back on his heels before winking at Kinsey and then shaking his head at me. I expected a high five next, followed by a "So what's he like in bed?"

Thank God Emerson intervened and smacked him in the stomach.

"Thanks, Em." I slowly moved away from Kins, putting enough space between us that we looked like friends, not seconds away from screwing against the couch.

"You guys are dating?" She spread her arms wide.

Sanchez narrowed his eyes. "You both flinched."

"Muscle spasm." I coughed. "We just got done lifting."

"Wow, I feel like I just got cheated on." Sanchez shook his head slowly. "If you benched, we're through."

"Nah, I save that for you," I said in a sarcastic voice.

"My man." He held out a fist. "And you don't get spasms, I'm not buying it."

"I do ever since she drove my car, nearly killed us and buried me in it."

"You let Kins operate heavy machinery?"

"Ever since I held him at gunpoint." Kinsey made a little gun motion with her hand and shot in my direction.

"Yeah, I don't buy it." Sanchez and Emerson matched poses, making me nervous as hell. How did they even know anything? It had been hours ago, not days, and it's not like either of us went to social media.

"And Jax? He's just okay with this? He knows?" Emerson started walking toward us. "He tried to kill you last year."

"Thank you! I said the same thing." I glared at Kinsey before shrugging. "He is, uh, encouraging . . . it."

"It?" Sanchez grinned. "What exactly is *it*? Like how big is it? How pleasing? Does it like—"

I flipped him off.

He stopped talking and then burst out laughing. "Holy shit, does he know you guys slept together?"

Damn it, the only reason Sanchez even knew was because he'd seen her naked in my bed and made an assumption. A correct one, but still an assumption.

"Say it louder, Sanchez, I don't think the East Coast heard you!" Kinsey jumped to her feet. "And no, he doesn't KNOW about that, which is why your friend Miller here is still breathing!"

"And yet you're dating?" Emerson was clearly having trouble putting the pieces together.

Shit. I didn't want to lie to my best friends, the people who literally helped me make it through one of the hardest years of my life—even though they were partially the cause of it.

"Look." Kinsey reached for my hand. "You can't say anything about the sex."

"I'm so confused." Sanchez pulled out a chair and sat. "But he knows you're dating?"

"We're taking it slow." Even as the words tumbled from my mouth, I wanted to choke myself to death. Going slow? Really, man? "It's the only way that Jax would give me permission."

If Sanchez's eyes got any wider, they'd pop out of his stupid-ass head. "You asked . . . for permission?" As much as I wanted to tell Sanchez what was really going on, he'd ask too many questions I wasn't prepared to answer.

"Guys!" Kins saved me by grabbing my hand and, for once, not squeezing it so hard that I winced in front of them. "This is a good thing. Just be happy for us."

Emerson still didn't look like she was buying it. "Look, we are, it's just, I mean how long has this been going on?"

"Since Vegas," Kins offered. "We kept in touch over email, texts"— her face flushed with the lie—"that sort of thing."

The lies kept piling on.

And with that.

The guilt.

Because in order to forget her, I had to cut off all contact when she was in Europe.

I'd never sent any texts.

I'd never emailed.

I hadn't called.

It was as if what we had done never happened—it was bad enough that I helped pack her shit and pretended I wanted her to go by not meeting her eyes when she called out my name. I just turned and walked away.

(Then)

"Miller." Her voice was shaking. "Don't you—"

"—you should probably pack some stuff into your carry-on," I grumbled. "It's a long flight, I'm sure you're first class but—"

"—Miller." *I really needed her to stop saying my name, because each and every time she did, my resistance wavered, and my desire to keep her by my side increased. All I wanted to do was lock her in the room and figure out what the hell was going on between us and why my body was reacting with such a violent need to kiss her again.*

Nothing good would come from ruining the only other friendship I'd ever had with a girl. God, I was such a dick.

I just had to kiss her.

I just had to see her naked.

I squeezed my eyes shut. "Kins."

She walked over to me, her eyes clear. As she blinked up at me, waiting, her stance was cautious, closed off. Already she was protecting herself from what she probably assumed was coming.

Rejection.

"This will be good for you," I finally said. "Yeah?"

Please say no. Say. No.

Instead she hung her head, then walked off and whispered, "Sure."

I'd been a dick on purpose.

I wasn't ready for a relationship, not after all the shit last year with Em. Hell, I wasn't even sure I had a functioning heart anymore—or if I was capable of giving Kins what she needed.

God, that entire situation with Em had been so painful that the possibility of reliving it was the most terrifying thing I could imagine. Emerson had decided we were done before I even knew there was a chance for reconciliation—and I couldn't bear the thought that Kins would do the same thing, so I did it first.

With Kins the relationship part would be too easy.

To date.

To like her.

To love her.

To lose her.

So, yeah, I felt guilty. Guilty that I was lying, yet confused as to why it felt like I was lying to myself more.

"That's . . ." Em frowned. "Awesome!"

"You're frowning," I pointed out.

"Well, it's just, I mean I'm not trying to make this about me, but why didn't you guys say anything? Why all the secrecy?"

"I think you know the answer to that, Curves." Sanchez gave me a knowing look. "And I think, given your history with dipshit over here . . ."

I rolled my eyes and shook my head.

"You should cut him some slack."

Emerson's face fell. "I'm so sorry, I didn't think—"

"No worries," Kins interrupted her with a cheerful smile. "So, just curious, but how did you guys find out?"

Sanchez held out his phone. "It's all over social media. A picture of you guys in the car surfaced and then one where you guys were seriously making out in the parking lot."

"How the hell would anyone get that? The only guy there was Anderson and we were talking to him the whole time."

"Except when your tongue was down her throat, it seems." Sanchez widened the picture. Damn, we looked good together. *Keep yourself in check, Miller.* "Look at the angle, it had to be that dickface."

"Up top for name calling!" Kins held out her hand to Sanchez, and surprisingly he returned her high five. Those two were always at each other's throats, so not only was their current behavior a welcome change it also took everyone's focus off the fact that I was grabbing her ass in the picture, and I'm pretty sure that Jax's exact words were "you won't touch her."

And just like that, my phone started to ring.

With Jax's name popping up on the screen.

Sanchez barked out a laugh. "Put it on speakerphone."

"Hell no!" I jerked my phone out of his reach and hit "Ignore."

"This is the absolute best. Almost better than that time Emerson chose me over you and agreed to marry me." He was teasing, but I still wanted to punch him in the face. "What? Still too soon?"

"You're a jackass," Kins hissed at him.

"I'm *her* jackass." He pointed to Emerson, who grabbed him by the arm and started dragging him back toward the door. "What? Where we going?"

She whispered something in his ear.

He shoved her out the door, and it slammed behind them.

"Wonder what she said," Kins mumbled.

"Probably something kinky. It's Sanchez we're talking about and there's really only three ways to distract him—football, sex, cookies."

Kins shrugged and stared at the door. "Huh, not a bad way to live."

My phone started ringing again.

Panic washed over me.

I had no clue if he was pissed or just wanted to know why the hell I felt the need to put my hands on his sister's ass and my tongue down her throat.

"You look freaked out." Kins grabbed the phone and hit "Ignore," then placed it on the counter. "Give it a few minutes, we'll shower—"

"And when you say—"

"Stop." She placed her hand on my chest and shoved. "Don't you think you're in enough trouble right now? If Jax finds out you're any-where near me or the shower while I'm in it, he's going to castrate you."

"It was one kiss."

"Are we looking at the same picture?" She tapped my code into my phone with the speed of someone who had my birthday memorized and then enlarged the picture. "It looks like we're having sex with our clothes on."

Our bodies literally had no space between them and somehow she'd wrapped half of hers around mine as though she was hanging on for dear life.

"Back up, how do you know my pass code?"

"Your birthday's March seventh. God, it amazes me how stupid guys are sometimes. You're too busy with football to change your code, you're just like Jax."

I gripped her by the hips and shoved her against the counter. "Say I'm just like your brother again, and I'm joining you in that shower to prove just how much I'm not like him, got me?"

Her eyes flashed before she gulped and gave a jerky nod.

"Good . . ." My body had other ideas, ones that didn't involve letting her step one foot away from me. But she was worth more than that, more than sex, more than the only thing I was willing to give her. "Down the hall, first door on the right, fresh towels in the wood basket, and if you use my body wash I'll hunt you down."

"Seriously?" She snorted. "Your body wash?"

"I'm weird about my shit."

"Color me shocked. You gonna get your granny panties in a twist if I accidently grab your razor too?"

"Touch it and I'll know, Kins."

"What are you, some sort of neat freak?"

"No, I just like my things to stay my things."

"Oh, so you never learned sharing? Remember, you sit in the circle and pass cookies around." She stood on her tiptoes and patted me on the cheek. "Don't worry, I won't steal your cookie, Miller, not even if you force it down my throat."

I groaned.

She slapped my ass.

And I nearly broke the countertop with my fingers as she skipped off with a backward wave.

Chapter Five

Jax

The bastard wasn't answering his phone.

Of fucking course.

I looked at the picture again. I couldn't stop looking at it—everyone in the world could see my sister attaching herself to Miller like she was under the impression she needed his lungs to aid her in her next oxygen fix.

The call went to voice mail again.

With a growl, I slammed my hand against the granite countertop and glanced back at the TV. There wasn't a chance in hell I could watch last season's tape and take notes.

Options.

I took a calming breath, in through my nose, out through my mouth, repeated the process five more times before I calmly took a seat on the couch and let the soothing sound of the clock in the background pass time.

The silence buzzed.

I clenched my fists.

My fault.

I'd told them to pretend to date.

I needed to stop jumping to conclusions. Calm the hell down, and think about what could possibly possess two people who, this morning, looked ready to kill one another, to kiss—like that.

I closed my eyes.

Then snapped them open and grabbed my phone again, this time looking at the angle of the picture. Someone had been there.

Another teammate would look the other way or give Miller a high five, either that or start writing his obituary.

But Anderson.

Asshole Anderson was devious enough to take a picture, and post it wherever he could, in order to what? Get Miller in trouble? Get me kicked off the squad after I figured out who took the photo and kicked his ass? The season hadn't started. Management already had their hands tied up with bigger dilemmas than their star player kissing one of the cheerleaders.

Jealousy?

Or maybe, he was trying to call their bluff?

Maybe he didn't believe they were in a relationship, God knows he was aware of how I felt about Kins dating a football player.

And if he didn't believe it.

He wouldn't stay away from her.

I fell back against the couch and groaned.

I refused to take the chance that all of my focus would be taken away from football and Dad—and onto the slight possibility that Anderson would ruin her life again.

My chest clenched.

And my thoughts jumbled, focusing in on dark memories of carrying Kinsey when she was a child into the house, the blood, her screams. And years later, when she was dating Anderson, the emptiness on her face was haunting. The controlling bastard should be in prison.

I took my sister's life, her heart, seriously. Some might say too seriously. But those people could go to hell, because they didn't know her like I did—they didn't know her pain, they didn't share it.

Because I'd been there to pick up the pieces all those years ago.

When she'd been abandoned.

Lost.

Hurt.

When he'd verbally abused her until the girl I knew no longer existed.

When she'd been a shell of the woman she was now. Watching everything she ate like it was out to attack her—when she stopped coming to holidays altogether because the guy was such a sadistic controlling bastard that he refused to let her see her family for fear we'd tell her the truth—he treated her like a slave, and made her thank him for it.

I hated how much of myself I saw in him.

And the preseason started in two weeks.

Two. Weeks.

I unlocked my phone and dialed Miller one more time.

"Yo." He sounded out of breath.

"Yo?" I repeated. "Yo? That's how you answer the phone after shit like that picture hits the media? Yo?"

"Oh, I'm sorry, were you expecting me to answer it with an explanation? You asked me to do this, and at the first sign of actual dating you're barking up my ass?"

He was too defensive.

The arms on my hair stood on end.

I decided not to touch it.

Because if I knew anything about my friend it was that he was only defensive when he was hiding something.

I just hoped to God it had nothing to do with my sister.

"Look"—I cleared my throat, tried to sound more relaxed—"I've been thinking—"

"When are you not thinking?"

I chuckled. "For someone who just had his tongue down my sister's throat, you're not in such a good mood. I wonder why that is?"

"Not because I enjoyed it. That's for sure," he said quickly.

"Oh?"

"Hell no! She's your sister, man. Now what were you thinking?"

"Dinner."

He paused and then, "You called me because you're hungry?"

"Yes, Miller, I called you so you'd bring me food." I rolled my eyes. "No, I thought it would be . . . fun." I choked on the word. When was the last time I even had fun? "Fun," I repeated, forcing myself to sound more relaxed even though my free hand was clutching the couch cushion with such force my fingers were going numb. "For us all to go to dinner."

"Us?"

"You, me, Sanchez, Emerson, Kins . . . You know, all of us."

He was hesitating. Why the hell was he hesitating? There was talking in the background.

"Is someone there?"

"NOPE!" he yelled. "Sorry, had to turn the TV down, so loud and annoying . . ."

"Okay . . ."

"So dinner . . ." He coughed and then coughed louder.

"Dude, are you getting sick? You better not have given Kins anything!"

"Glad you care more about her than me, that hurts, man."

"She's blood." I paused, winced, and then added, "You're replaceable."

"Noted."

"Dinner?" Was that the third time I'd said it? I'd lost track.

"Sounds great, but you're bringing a date."

I froze. "The hell I am!"

"You'll be going stag, and I guarantee that Kins won't agree to go with me unless you bring a date. You know how she's been lately, trying to matchmake you."

"She's ruining my concentration and she knows it!"

"Fun." Miller snorted. "You can barely say the word without scowling, may as well try having it, all-American quarterback Heisman Trophy winner."

My throat went dry. "You know I hate it when you bring up that shit."

"Real friends show friends their trophies."

"Repeat that slower and tell me how it sounds, Miller, I'll wait."

He barked out a laugh. "Man, just bring someone!"

Sweat started pooling on my forehead. I didn't date. I couldn't. Women didn't date guys like me. They wanted to fuck them, get the starring role in the next movie they were after, suddenly get pregnant, and then laugh all the way to the bank. In all my time in football, there hadn't been one single situation where I'd felt comfortable enough to ask a woman out without being fearful of her having the wrong intentions.

"I don't have time to find a date," I mumbled. "It's already two, and you know I like to eat early."

"God, you're such a grandpa, you do realize there's something other than the early bird menu, right?"

Of course I knew, and I had money to do whatever the hell I wanted, I just didn't want to get stuck in a crowd where all the women did was stare, hike up their skirts, write their numbers on napkins, or just corner me and ask for sex. I wanted something real.

Something like my parents had.

A pang so jarring, it sucked my breath away, hit me square in the chest. "Miller . . ."

He must have noticed the change in my voice, because he quickly added. "Let's at least do five thirty, send out a group text, and maybe you'll get lucky and between now and then, someone will show up on your doorstep."

"Hate to break it to you, friend, but I'm not really into paying for dates, or strippers, or prostitutes."

"Ah, you like them for free?"

"Bastard."

"Jax?"

I stared up at the ceiling, chest tight with anxiety over the very idea of taking a girl out on a date. I hadn't dated since college, and that had been a complete disaster. Girls hit on me so much and in such cheap and desperate ways that my focus on football sharpened, because it was the only thing that gave me peace, the only thing I could trust wouldn't just stay because a big paycheck was coming.

"I've got her."

I exhaled.

And then did it again. "I know, man, I'm sorry I'm acting so crazy, I don't know what's wrong . . ." I knew. I just didn't want to admit it.

My dad's body was dying with each dose of chemo.

And there was nothing I could do to stop it.

To keep the hero from fading into nothing.

Or stop fearing that this might cause Kinsey to break down physically and emotionally like she did in the past. Knowing Miller had her back gave me a tiny bit of peace.

"Good," I whispered.

Chapter Six

"For the record, I vote that this is the worst idea in the history of bad ideas," Miller grumbled, raising his hand to knock on the door and then dropping it and shoving me into his place. "You do it."

"Some man you are," I grumbled back, trying to remind my body, my heart, and my brain that this wasn't real, that we weren't really in a relationship, that if he was on my team, he would be the crappiest teammate ever because when I was at my most vulnerable he abandoned me.

Mix that in with all of the hurtful things he said to Jax while he thought I was in the bathroom, and I was just done with trying to figure out whatever was between us. Ready to toss in the towel and stop with the farce. But then I'd seen the concern in Miller's eyes, heard the concern in his voice, and knew that my brother, the guy on the other end, needed me to keep up with it.

And while it was completely asinine. I was doing my part in keeping his mind on what he could control—by allowing it to be me.

And even though it physically hurt to let anyone control me, it was different when it was done out of love—and not fear.

I shivered.

"You gonna do it or what?" Miller's gruff whisper hit my right ear, making my right leg shake, and my entire body light on fire with awareness.

"Yup." I nodded then knocked again. "I just, I mean we were friends in college, I've seen her a handful of times over happy hour, all I know is she's single, super pretty, smart, and oh, who am I kidding, I barely know her, but he needs a date, otherwise his entire focus is going to be on you and me, and he's going to be able to tell that I—"

Miller stiffened behind me. His hands ran down my arms, causing an involuntary shiver to run through my body. "He'll notice that."

"Can't fake that." I jerked away from him. "It's lust, it's not like I spent my summer screwing every guy available like some people."

"I don't screw guys."

"Whatever," I hissed. "You know what I mean!"

"I'm sorry."

I was so stunned he said the words that my jaw dropped, just as the door jerked open. Harley was wearing low-cut boyfriend jeans, black combat-style boots, an off-the-shoulder white shirt, and a hat that said, "Emotionally Unavailable."

Miller whistled.

She was drop-dead gorgeous with fiery red hair and electric-blue eyes, barely wore any makeup except mascara and lip gloss, and would make any insecure girl want to throw herself off a cliff.

She was also one of the most independent people I knew.

Which was the reason I had called her in the first place.

And begged her to come when I hadn't hung out with her in weeks not because I didn't enjoy her company, but because I'd been overseas and she was an athletic-gear model who traveled the world and did yoga on sandy beaches—she really didn't look the part. In fact, she looked more like the type of girl who'd be the lead singer of a rock band.

"What?" She shrugged. "You guys ready to do this?"

Miller held out his hand. "I'm Quinton—"

"Yeah, I know who you are, I own a TV, and I also saw a really racy picture of you guys on the news." She winked. "I think it's safe to say even my grandma knows who you are, and she's blind in her right eye. Let me grab my coat."

"Great." Miller exhaled. "That's not weird at all." He turned his gaze to me. "You're absolutely sure your brother didn't send you any warning texts that he was going to kill me?"

"Not one." I frowned. "It's all so disappointing, if you ask me, I mean what relationship doesn't need a little spice?"

"A little spice is a sex shop. Jax's version of spice is a machete." Miller shook his head. "Big difference between those spices, Waffle Girl."

"Waffle Girl?" Harley reappeared, coat in hand.

"Ignore Chicken, he's upset his cock didn't get out of the henhouse this morning." I patted Miller on the shoulder. He sent me a seething glare. I winked.

"I have a bad feeling about this," Miller said aloud.

"Chin up." I gripped his hand. "At least his focus won't be on killing you. And you say I'm heartless."

We glossed over his apology, which had only been minutes ago.

I wasn't sure whether to be thankful or disappointed.

Because for one second, he actually sounded like he meant it.

Better that I ignore any sort of apologies on his behalf—Quinton Miller as a man whore and annoying friend/pretend boyfriend was easy to handle. Quinton Miller as a man who was sorry, a man who looked at you like he meant it, like he wanted to prove it . . .

Well, no woman would be able to deny that.

And I was weaker than most.

After all, I'd already slept with him twice in one night, with full knowledge that he'd most likely freak.

I just didn't think the freak-out would include him packing my bags for me.

I cringed.

"You okay?" Harley asked.

"Never better," I lied.

We all walked to the car in silence.

Miller drove even though I begged for the keys.

And I tutored Harley in all the ways she was going to win Jax over and distract him from all the stress in his life.

I just hoped it worked.

My phone vibrated.

Mom: Dad wants to see you on Monday. He should feel better by then.

Finally. I exhaled a breath of relief.

Me: I'm there.

Mom: He's excited, just . . . be prepared.

For what? I wanted to ask. *For him to look sick?* I didn't give a damn if he looked like a skeleton, he was my hero, and every hero needed a sidekick.

I didn't realize the car had stopped until I heard a door slam.

When I looked up, Harley was already walking toward the restaurant.

And Miller was staring directly at me, his blue eyes searching mine for answers I knew I wasn't ready to give.

Why I was sad.

Why it hit home so much.

Why Jax was so overprotective.

Miller was perceptive, so I had to bank on the fact that his look was one of genuine concern and nothing more.

"What?" I reached for my seat belt.

He pressed his hand over mine, holding my hand there. "Something's wrong."

Not a question. A statement.

"You mean other than my dad having cancer?" I snapped, then hung my head.

"Kins—"

"I'm hungry and you're trapping me in the hot car." I gulped, the forced smile hurting almost as much as the lump in my throat.

"Kins—"

"No." I licked my lips. "You know, before Vegas, we were friends, right?"

"Right." His eyes didn't leave mine. "I'm pretty sure you forced the friendship but whatever."

I knew he was teasing, but my armor wasn't up.

So, instead of laughter, I felt more tears well in my eyes, threatening to spill onto my cheeks.

"Shit, Kins." He unbuckled my seat belt and pressed his hands on either side of my face. "I was joking."

I tried to fight his grip but he held tighter.

It felt so good.

Too good to be held, to breathe him in and think about nothing except the way he made me feel safe in his arms, when I was so terrified of everything crumbling down around me.

"Friends," I whispered. "Maybe when nobody's watching we can just do that . . . and forget about the in-between."

"The in-between being the two times I've seen you naked and given you multiple orgasms while you screamed my name and bit my shoulder with your teeth—that in-between."

My face heated. "Please."

His chest heaved; he sucked in his bottom lip, then released it, and my body responded with alarming need to do the same thing—only with his lip, not mine, to make sure it tasted as good as I remembered.

Maybe I needed some form of sick reassurance that despite the chaos around me—Miller's taste was still the same.

A safe place.

That wasn't really safe at all.

"Please," I said it again. I swore I'd never be the victim again when it came to a guy—and yet with Miller I'd let myself be the kicked puppy, the girl he shoved away, the one he took—and discarded so easily.

Maybe Anderson was right.

He'd said I was lucky to have a guy like him, that I was useless, trash, a stupid cheerleader.

No.

I shoved the thought out of my mind.

And that reason right there was why I couldn't do this, not with Miller. I could pretend for cameras, pretend for my brother so he thought I was safe from Anderson's clutches, but being with Miller in private—no matter how much I craved it, how easy it would be.

Would kill me.

It would kill any piece of myself I still had left.

The strong pieces that Jax gave back to me were constantly at battle with the weak ones Anderson had tried to infuse into my psyche. I refused to let him win.

"Kins." Miller's forehead touched mine. "I never meant to hurt you."

"Pardon?" Awesome. Perfect. What every girl wants to hear. "You never meant to hurt me when you came over to my house, packed my bags, and didn't as much as look at me while you dropped me off at the freaking airport? You may as well have kicked me out of the country with a pat on the ass, Miller! And I'm not that girl! I don't sleep around, so don't sit here all high and mighty in your expensive-ass car, with your heart on your sleeve, and tell me a bullshit line that every single girl in this world hears on a daily basis, when the same guy who screwed them into oblivion the night before suddenly decides he doesn't want anything but a piece of ass. If that's what you want—you're more than welcome to find it elsewhere. Friends. Take it or leave it. And even now I feel like I'm being too generous. We're doing this so my brother doesn't lose his mind over my dad, and over the possibility that . . ." I stopped talking. I had to.

"That he might not recover?" Miller finished like he was questioning me.

"Just"—I jerked away from him—"play your part, and I'll play mine, we'll shake hands when this is all over, and if you kiss me again, ever, without my permission I'll tell Jax all the other places you kissed without his permission and we'll see where that leaves you . . . and the team."

"And when I tell him you begged for those kisses, what about that?" He leaned in until his mouth was an inch from mine.

"That leaves you without two friends and a championship."

He pulled away so fast I thought his head was going to smack against the driver's side window. "Friends it is."

He held out his hand.

His eyes met mine, a spark of electricity flared between us, so real, so heavy with meaning, that I gripped his hand. I needed his word. I needed to know he wouldn't touch me, kiss me, tempt me, make me believe that he was willing to offer what he wasn't even in possession of since losing Emerson to Sanchez.

When our fingers touched, I jumped.

He bit back a curse and dropped my hand so fast it hit the console.

"This isn't going to work." His smile was sad. "Is it?"

"Hell yes, it will." I offered an encouraging smile. "You just need to be aggressive, B-E A-G-G-R-E-S-S-I-V-E about our friendship and not crossing any lines that have been put there for a purpose."

"For the record, Kins, I can do that cheer by heart, and I mean everything, the moves, the clapping. I'm kind of a cheerleading pro."

"We'll see."

"Why were you really crying . . . *friend?*" He emphasized the word loudly.

"I'm sad . . . because my dad could be dying . . . *friend*."

"Then . . ." He sighed. "I guess all that's left to do is this . . . friend . . ." He got out of the car, walked around the front, opened my door, pulled me to my feet, and wrapped his muscular arms around me. "Hug time."

"Every hour?"

"I wish it was every half hour," he complained.

And I laughed.

Hard.

So hard that tears started running down my cheeks. "You got my *Trolls* reference."

"Come on, Flat-ass—you know how I feel about my animated movies."

"Hey! I thought that nickname was gone!"

"Eh, I missed it."

I swatted him on the chest and pulled away. "We should probably get in there before Harley decides my brother needs a smile on his face and ducks under the table to give him a reason to."

"She wouldn't . . ." He frowned. "Would she?"

"I may have encouraged all sexual advances. You were the one who said he needed to get laid!"

"Not during dinner!" Miller grabbed my hand and ran.

I laughed the entire way.

Like I would ever encourage Harley to do something like that—like any girl would ever need encouragement when it came to Jax.

For a guy who kept it in his pants, according to the female population he was walking, talking sex.

Yeah, tonight was going to be interesting.

Chapter Seven

On the outside, I was calm.

On the inside, I was a mess.

Because I was being faced with another choice, one I was being forced to make.

Date her. Don't touch her.

Protect her. Don't touch her.

Spend time with her.

Fall for her.

Lust for her.

Want her.

Do. Not. Touch. Her.

I suddenly needed the first preseason game and practices like I needed my next breath of air. The distraction, the pain, the stress would be welcome after spending the last twenty-four hours with a girl I couldn't have—story of my life—and didn't deserve. It was the first time since Emerson I felt it.

That deep—pull.

The connection that you feel without using words.

And I wasn't just confused, but angry as fuck that the one girl who was hands-off was the only one who had managed to pull it out of me.

Months ago, I'd slept with her and told her it was just once.

I'd lied to her.

I'd lied to myself.

So I did it again that same night to prove that I had control of the situation, and then I sent her packing to prove that I didn't need her—or anyone.

And when she left, all I felt was panic, and a surging anger that she could remove herself from me so easily when I still felt her skin on my skin—when I tasted her in my dreams.

Shit, I was going to die before this was over with.

"Did we miss anything?" I pulled out my own chair since Kins had already seated herself. The restaurant was incredibly loud for a high-end burger joint. It was dark enough that I knew we wouldn't be recognized, at least not by our faces. Our sizes, however, often gave us away.

Because what else did a few guys who were over six foot five do with their lives other than play football?

Sanchez gave me a look that said not to bring up the subject, while Em made a cutting motion across her neck.

"Explain to me again, what a quarterback does, other than throw a stupid ball?" Harley directed the question to Jax.

"Oh shit," I said under my breath then elbowed Kins in the ribs.

She glanced at me and mouthed, *"What?"*

"I take it you're not a football fan?" I reached for a fry, thank God they'd already ordered something, I was starving.

Harley grinned over at me. "Oh, I love football. I just don't like offensive players."

I choked on my fry while Sanchez murmured a curse under his breath.

"And in saying that, you do realize"—Jax's jaw did that scary-as-shit ticking motion—"that every guy at this table is offense?"

55

Harley looked around and shrugged. "Look, I'm sure what you guys do is very hard, but the defense is more aggressive to me. Sorry. Plus they're bigger." She eyed Jax's arms and gave him a sheepish smile.

"There will be blood," Sanchez said under his breath while Emerson kicked me under the table. What, like I knew how to make things better?

"Funny, how you'd insult something you know shit about," Jax said in a way-too-calm voice. "I guess that would kind of be like me showing up at your job and telling you that you were doing it wrong. What is it you said you did?"

"Athletic gear. I model it. I also teach yoga around the world . . ." She leaned in, until I thought Jax was going to chicken out and back up, but he shocked me when he met her halfway, his face completely void of emotion. "You gonna show up at my job and bend over?"

Emerson covered her face with her hands. Sanchez let out a low whistle, and I couldn't peel my eyes from the train wreck.

Jax didn't move a muscle, instead he tilted his head and finally smirked. "You know, it's kind of funny . . ."

"What?" Harley's eyes narrowed.

"How much you don't know about football, life, men—or probably even your own occupation. Hey, Sanchez—"

Sanchez cursed. "What?"

"How many hours a week do you do yoga?"

I bit down on my lip to keep from laughing.

I knew he only went to yoga because Emerson made him go, because she was convinced it would help keep him from getting injured again. The guy was afraid to go by himself, so he forced both me and Jax to go with him.

It took us one week of getting our asses kicked to beg the coach to hire someone full-time to work with the trainer and the team.

We'd been doing yoga twice a week for the past six months.

And Jax, well, he'd taken to it like a pro.

He was the perfectionist of the three of us.

"Ah." Sanchez reached for a fry. "I'd say no more than three to four hours a week, nothing crazy."

Harley jerked back. "You?"

"Us." Jax grinned, reached for a fry, and shoved it in her open mouth. "So maybe think before speaking next time, or just sit there and look pretty, it might gain you more fans."

She chomped down on the fry.

And Jax waved over our waiter. "You guys ready to order?"

"That went well," I whispered to Kins.

She pressed her fingers against her temples and whispered back, "Maybe I should have told her to start with the sex and end with the talking."

"There's always next time." I winked.

"Don't feel bad"—I patted Kins on the leg—"at least he was so pissed at us for inviting her that he completely dropped all his anger about the kiss."

Kinsey groaned and slammed her fist against the couch cushion. After dinner, Jax had told her she had the apartment, he was going to their parents' and he'd see her there in the morning.

It was his way of saying he needed space.

I'd dropped her off and then followed her in because she refused to go any farther unless she had backup—apparently she was scared of the dark. I went into every fucking room and turned on each light to make sure someone wasn't waiting to take her to a foreign country and sell her as a sex slave.

I'd finished the last room ten minutes ago.

Ten minutes ago, I should have left.

Instead, I sat.

Damn it, why was I torturing myself?

"He fled his own apartment, Miller. I'd say he's pretty pissed. Is it so much to ask for him to focus on his own life for a minute? To have fun?"

"There has to be a story there." I pulled the remote from her hand and changed the channel. What was with her and that *Ballers* show? It was offensive, and while completely realistic, just a reminder of how the world viewed us, or maybe how the entire league viewed themselves.

She tucked her feet up under her butt, which was now covered by the gray sweats she'd changed into while I'd been playing private security detail. "He's just . . . he functions better when he can compartmentalize things. When he can't, when areas of his life blur, he gets frustrated. He's hypersensitive about dating the wrong girl . . . almost as sensitive as he is about finding the right one and not being enough, I think." She frowned. "Our parents . . . they have a pretty awesome relationship. Honestly," she said, shrugging one shoulder, "it's a lot to live up to—and a pretty big dream to follow when you're not only the leader of America's team, but their perfect captain, the golden boy, the one who doesn't mess up, who rarely drinks, who visits hospitals on his days off and wants world peace." She giggled. "Okay, so maybe he got drunk last year when you guys won, and he's never said anything about world peace, but you get what I mean, right? You guys have this huge magnifying glass on your lives—I think sometimes, because of that, he's afraid to live it."

Guilt flashed across her face before she added, "But, he made a promise he'd try—a couple of years ago—so he should at least follow through on his promise to date."

"And stop locking you in closets before big dances like prom."

"Yeah, well, now I have my big bad boyfriend to fight him for me." She winked and jerked the remote from my hand and flipped it back to *Ballers*. "So, no monsters?"

"Only the ones I told to hide out and wait until you were asleep to make themselves known. Hope it's cool that I told them they could help themselves to some soda." I grinned down at her. God, she was pretty, with her makeup-free face, shiny dark hair, and full kissable lips.

I adjusted myself without thinking.

Only to find her watching me.

Hell.

I blew out an exasperated breath, knowing I couldn't really stand yet, not if I didn't want her to know—hell, she already knew, it was painfully obvious where my thoughts were headed.

"Thanks, friend." She said it again to remind me, maybe to remind us.

I nodded. "Anytime."

"You know . . . since we're friends, you can stay a bit longer if you want. It doesn't have to mean anything, just that you're willing to take guard duty very seriously."

"Nah." I shook my head. "That's probably not a good idea."

"I know," she whispered. "Honest moment?"

"Honest moment," I repeated.

"I could never live by myself, I get too freaked out."

"And since Jax is gone . . ."

"How about if we pretend to be roommates with absolutely no sexual past who decide to have a slumber party where no touching takes place?" she pleaded. "I'm sorry, I swear I didn't plan this. I just, now that I'm faced with you leaving, I'm thinking about all of my escape plans and weapons."

"Give me one escape plan, one weapon example, and I'll stay." I crossed my arms.

"You'll make fun of me."

"Probably."

She growled, "Fine, so my first escape plan"—she leaped off the couch and ran to the door—"say someone breaks the door down. I'm all the way down the hall, so there's this weird hiding spot near the hall closet." She ran down toward the hall closet, I chased after her.

Kinsey bent over and pulled the screen off one of the vents, then tossed me a flashlight she'd hidden in there along with a prepaid TracFone. "Hold these."

"Why the hell do you need a flashlight?"

"Intruders always turn off the power first."

"Shit, I need to talk to Jax about letting you watch TV at night."

"HLN is my jam," she teased and winked.

"Never say that sentence again." I pointed the flashlight at her. "Where to?"

"Here." She crawled across the floor. "Hurry, get down."

I fell to my knees, and they cracked against the hard wood floor. "This is crazy. You know that, right?"

"*Shhh.*" She kicked my shoulder with her foot. "This is survival."

I grinned; she was cute. Psychotic, but cute.

"Here it is." She finally made it to a small bookcase, and next to it, a nook, a cupboard that couldn't hold half of my body. "I put a lock on it from the inside."

"You?" I pointed the flashlight at her. "Put a lock on? By yourself?"

"So I like Home Depot! What of it?"

"You're hearing yourself, right? This entire conversation? Crawling across the floor? Why all the fear?"

Her face fell. And then she stood. The moment was lost. "You're right, we should—"

"Friend." I spoke the word so close I nearly touched her lips, then brought her back down to the floor. "Let's try the truth, just this once. You talk, I'll listen.

"Sometimes the truth is scarier than the lie, Miller."

"Sometimes it is, Kins."

"How about we leave it at this . . . It's important to use every minute of the life you're given, and I'm a lot like my brother in that, when faced with what I can control, I want to control it. I want to know that if someone breaks down that door, I did everything in my power to save myself." Her eyes shut closed as she whispered, "Because life isn't full of people who are willing to save you—sometimes, all you have is you."

My heart stuttered. I felt its cadence sputter to a stop as I cupped her face with my hands. "That's the fucking saddest thing I've ever heard, Kins."

"The truth can be sad too . . ." she admitted.

And maybe I had no right.

But I promised myself. In that moment, that if it ever came down to me or her—it would be me. Because girls like Kinsey, ones who blindly trusted, who saw the best in everyone, who made it their job to find happiness, they were the ones who deserved a savior, someone to fight for them, so that in the end, if it came down to it, they'd die knowing that it wasn't because they were alone.

The sound of the door opening had me leaping to my feet.

She made a startled noise and then pulled me into a bedroom, shut off the lights, tugged me into a walk-in closet, and pressed a hand over my mouth.

"Kins?" Jax's voice definitely had my heart kick-starting again.

"Shit," I hissed. "If he finds me in here."

"We'll tell him we were playing hide-and-seek!" Kins elbowed me.

"With my dick?" I hissed back at her. "Because you know that's exactly what he's going to assume!"

"Kins?" he called again.

"Shit, your phone," I whispered in her ear. "Where is it?"

"Pocket."

I quickly shoved my hands in both of her pockets, and then groaned when I slid it in the back pocket, cupping her ass in the process. She gave a little yelp. I squeezed, unable to fucking help myself.

Because that woman's ass.

"Miller, focus," she whispered, holding her hand out.

I gave her the phone, but kept my hand in place.

And told myself it was because any sort of movement could make noise, even though we were talking.

She turned her phone on silent.

And I was suddenly thanking God that I'd left mine in the car.

My keys, however . . .

"Your keys." She started patting me down like I was getting searched at the airport. And even though I knew my keys were on the kitchen counter, I let her. "I can't find them."

"Look harder." I smirked down at her busy hands as they moved slower this time, over my body and then stopped when they reached the front. "Sorry?"

"You liar!" She smacked my chest. "You don't have them, do you?"

"I forgot." My smile was firmly in place while my dick was ready to launch an all-out war against my jeans and break free.

I caught her hand before she slapped me, then the other until both of her wrists were pinned above her head.

Footsteps sounded.

I slowly backed her up against the far wall of the closet, behind a few winter coats, and pressed my body against hers.

Kinsey's eyes didn't leave mine.

Our bodies fit perfectly.

I already knew that though.

I'd been inside hers and I was still pissed off over the loss of her heat, of those legs wrapped around me.

Of the tight way she held on.

"Stop that," she whispered.

"I'm not doing anything."

"You're . . ." She looked down. "You are."

"I can't control everything, not with you, Kins, sorry."

The footsteps got louder.

The door to her bedroom opened.

A light flicked on.

The closet light was still off.

Her worried expression wasn't helpful. Then again, neither was the fact that if he found us, he'd assume the worst, because we were blatantly hiding from him together.

Tears welled in her eyes.

And suddenly it occurred to me. This was more than fake dating.

More than her dad's sickness.

More than Anderson.

I just didn't know how the dots were connected and why it was so important that I protect her.

"Look at me." I licked my lips. "Just focus on me."

She nodded her head and didn't blink.

Minutes later, the sound of the front door closing echoed through the apartment.

I exhaled.

My body on fire.

Ready.

Kinsey stood up on her tiptoes and kissed me on the cheek. "Thank you for that."

"The pat down? Anytime." I tried joking when all I wanted to do was strip her naked and slam her against that same wall, enter her with all the enthusiasm that had been building up between us, and sink between her legs, live there for a few years in bliss, and repeat the process.

"You know what I mean." She held my hand and led me out of the closet.

And later that night, when she fell asleep on the couch, she was still holding my hand.

She might as well have been holding my fucking heart.

Chapter Eight

Jax

I woke up with a pounding headache.

Harley.

What the hell kind of name is Harley anyway? For a girl? I made a mental note to add her to the list of girls I would never speak to again. All she did was insult not only me but my occupation the entire damn dinner. It bothered me that I was still thinking about her, just like it bothered me that the minute she walked in the restaurant I had done a double take and nearly tripped over my own feet before sitting at the table.

Her eyes were an electric blue that cut straight through me like a knife, and it was for that very reason that I made myself stare right back. I was rarely challenged in any area of my life, football included, so for her to look at me like I didn't matter? Like my job didn't matter? Like I was just another dumb football player? Pissed me the hell off, mainly because it made me realize how highly I must think of myself—of what I did.

Humble pie tasted like shit.

My phone buzzed, and I wiped my face and grabbed another blanket from the couch and flipped on the TV. I was still at my parents'; thankfully I'd grabbed some clothes from the apartment last night, the empty apartment that Kinsey was missing from.

Not the first time, probably not the last.

Besides I knew she was safe. She'd been with Miller.

My phone buzzed again.

With a grunt, I looked at the screen.

I didn't recognize the number. And only a few key people in my life even knew it to begin with.

I swiped and looked at the text.

Unknown: I just wanted to formally apologize for sticking my foot in my ass last night. I watched the championship game last night on ESPN Classic. Apparently the football gods were angry and wanted to prove me wrong. You were good. Would you believe me if I told you it was physically painful to type that?

The hell?

Unknown: PS—your ass still looks fat in those pants though.

I barked out a laugh.

And reread the texts.

The girl had balls of steel.

I found myself smiling down at my phone like I'd just been given an Olympic medal for perfect passing, and started to type.

Me: I'm surprised you were even able to type that apology—or was it more of a statement?—without dying. Must have been just about as painful as the realization that my ass doesn't look as good as I thought it did in black.

There, that sounded good.

And I was still staring at my phone.

"Jax?" Mom called out. I was downstairs in the family room, making the couch my home because of last night and Mom's text that Dad wanted to talk to me. I made Kins think I was pissed at her—I just didn't want her to know the details, the gory ones, the ones that would keep her up at night. Dads, big brothers, men, that was our job. It was how I was raised. I took the role my dad gave me very seriously. We were built to take on the burdens. I'd grown up that way, and I sure as hell wasn't going to let my dad down now by making it hard for Kinsey to sleep at night because she was so worried about him. It wouldn't make things better or easier for her. If anything, she could get sick again. So I gave my parents strict instructions that shockingly enough they'd listened to.

I get details.

Kins gets the happy.

The end.

"What's up?" For some reason I hid my phone, as if I was a teen looking at porn, then mentally scolded myself. I was thirty-two, not thirteen.

She finally made it down the rest of the way and into the room. Her silvery-brown hair was piled on the top of her head in a short ponytail, and she was wearing her ever-present Victoria's Secret sweatshirt and yoga pants.

With a frown, she scrunched up her nose at the TV. Hell, I wasn't even sure what was on.

I heard moaning.

Oh, good. HBO. Good one, Jax.

"I don't get you and your sister's obsession with this show." She sighed and shook her head.

"Don't let Kins hear you say that. *Ballers* is her jam." I made fake air quotes as my mom grinned and chucked a pillow at my face. "Hey!"

"I like it when you stay here."

"Me too." I looked around. "Reminds me what life would have been like had Dad not forced me off my ass and outside. I'd probably still be right here in this spot, living in your basement and asking you to do my laundry."

"Not likely." Smiling, she winked. "I would have killed you before then."

"Love you too, Mom."

"We need to talk."

Yup, feeling thirteen alright.

My phone buzzed twice.

Had she texted back?

Why did I care?

Why was I literally losing focus that fast over a stupid text that might or might not even be on my screen?

"You look stressed." Mom patted my hand.

"Not at all." Lie. I lived in a constant state of stress, sleep, stress, sleep, repeat.

Her lips rubbed together and then she said the words I'd been dreading for the last few months. "Honey, I think it's time for us to call hospice."

I sucked in a breath and stared down at her clenched hands. A tissue was wadded up between her fingers, her wedding ring glistening back at me.

Unfair.

It wasn't right.

He'd played college ball.

Still ran marathons.

My dad was healthy.

Hospice?

"We need to tell Kins, honey." Mom's voice broke. "It isn't fair to her. I told her to come visit Friday, I keep sending her the happy texts that you wanted, but honey, he's not getting better, he's not—" Her voice ended in a sob. "Honey, he's not going to."

"You don't know that," I said with a whisper. "The doctors said—"

"He doesn't want to do chemo anymore. He . . ." She shuddered. "He wants to live, honey, but not this way, with constant sickness, the numb feeling, tiredness, pain."

The chemo had been killing him, slowly eating him from the inside out. I put on my strong face and pushed down the anger, the sadness, every feeling that would betray my voice, the way I stood, the way I talked.

"I understand." I nodded and pulled my mom in for a tight hug, hating the fact that I wasn't shaking because I was sad. I was shaking because he was losing the battle, and there wasn't a fucking thing I could do in this universe to help him win it.

She pulled away and wiped under her eyes. "Well, no more sadness. Tell me how dinner went last night."

I groaned at her subject change. She was always good at redirection, she'd say things like "Oh honey, I'm so proud of you for winning that game, did you know that Lola's granddaughter just got a job near town? Isn't she pretty?"

"Wow." I chuckled. "Nice, Mom, real nice."

"The dinner?"

"You." I let out a small laugh. "If you must know, the girl that Kins set me up with . . ." Mom's eyes lit up like a Christmas tree. "Yeah, by the look on your face you're already planning my wedding and getting ready to hand me condoms with holes in them."

"I would never give my son condoms." She put her hand over her heart.

"Mom! You gave me condoms last year!"

"You aren't married yet! I need grandbabies!" she yelled. "I was trying to be encouraging. Dr. Phil says that—"

I plugged my ears.

She jerked my hands away. "So? It went well then?"

"She insulted me."

Mom didn't seem fazed at all.

"And my friends."

Not even a flinch.

"And basically told me that I had no muscle whatsoever."

Mom tilted her head. "Well, you are quite lean."

"You don't even know her and you're taking her side! This is why I don't bring girls home! You'd have us married before she walked back out the door!"

"What's so wrong with marriage?"

"Who's getting married?" came my dad's raspy voice.

"Oh, Ben, isn't it wonderful?" Mom yelled.

Dad was at the top of the stairway grinning from ear to ear.

"Go back to bed!" I ordered him.

"I want a sandwich!" he yelled.

"At least he has his appetite back." I gave my mom a hopeful look.

She stood. "This isn't over yet. Why don't you bring your young lady to family dinner this Friday? When Kins comes?"

"We don't do Family Dinner Fridays anymore," I said in a deadpan voice. "We stopped those when Kins moved out."

"Good news, Ben!" Mom yelled but was grinning at me the whole time, "We're doing Family Dinner Fridays again!"

"Hooray!" I clearly got my sarcasm and all-around demeanor from my dad.

I did a lame fist pump and then shook my head slowly at my mom. "Not happening."

"Happening." She poked me in the chest so hard I was afraid her nail was going to impale itself on my skin. "Now be a good boy, and call that girl." Her expression changed from happy to sad in an instant. "You know, it would make your dad feel good to see you settled down."

"You're using a sick man to manipulate me. That has to be against the rules somewhere."

She shrugged. "I'm a mom, I make the rules. Bring her. Make your dad happy. How hard could it be?"

Hard.

Hell.

Dad poked his head around the corner. "Where we at on that sandwich?"

"More good news!" Mom started walking toward the stairs. "Our son is bringing home a girl!"

"Huh, and all this time I thought he was gay."

"Love you too, Dad." I flipped him the bird while my mom's back was turned and received one in return as she glanced back at me to give me a thumbs-up.

I almost felt sorry for the poor girl that would have to sit at our dinner table. If you didn't grow up with the crazy, it was a bit hard to get used to.

I grinned, just thinking about how Harley would handle my parents.

Probably perfectly fine.

She could insult every damn thing to their faces, and they'd still be so excited a breathing female walked through the doors that they'd welcome her into the family with open arms. Just what I didn't need.

And yet, when I grabbed my phone and saw another two texts from her, I couldn't help but imagine what it would be like.

I quickly put her name in and added the number she'd been texting me from, then read the script.

Harley: Hate to break it to you but with pants that tight, even Grandma could see that ass.

Harley: She says hi by the way, big fan.
Jax: At least someone in the family likes me, maybe I'll take her out instead of you.
Harley: Correction. It was a setup. You didn't even know I was going to be there, so that's not a real date, QB. Besides, I'm vegan.
I rolled my eyes.
Jax: Shocker.
Harley: I was kidding . . . I like meat.

I nearly choked on my tongue, because my imagination definitely went there, and tried to think of a response.

Harley: All meat.
Jax: I literally have no appropriate response to that text.
Harley: You're a guy.
Jax: Not apologizing.
Harley: Wasn't asking.
Jax: Go out with me?

The minute I sent the text I wanted to crack open my phone and find a way to take it back.
What the hell was I doing?
She texted back immediately.

Harley: Why? Didn't get enough of my charm last night?
Jax: If that was you being charming . . . and honestly, I don't know. The only thing you have going for you is you have a nice ass, unlike myself.

Was I really having to convince a girl to go out with me?

Harley: Aw, a compliment. Okay, QB, I'll go out with you on one condition.
Jax: What's that?
Harley: You have to bring a signed football for Grandma, she's literally trying to wrestle the phone away from me right now and asked if you were into older women.

I shuddered.

Jax: Tell her if I was—she'd be the first woman on my list.
Harley: She said she either had a stroke or a . . . never mind, I'm not finishing that sentence.
Jax: Things just got weird.
Harley: I live with her. You have no idea.

I glanced at the stairs and chuckled.

Jax: I think I actually do . . . oh, and our first date is you meeting the parents. Suck on that, yoga girl.
Harley: I'm like the parent whisperer—watch me work, QB.

I would have texted her all day had my phone not rung. Had Miller not been up my ass about getting in a workout.

I hung up as quickly as possible and shot off a text to Harley. Like she wasn't some strange blind date from last night—like she was a girl I could actually see myself dating.

Damn it, Kins.

Karma was kissing my ass.

Jax: Gotta go build some muscle since someone said I wasn't big enough. FYI, some of us make up for our lack of muscle in other areas, just saying.

Harley: Go get em, QB. PS, I'm well aware of that fact. Your uniforms are freakishly tight. Either football turns you on or you're packing. I saw front and back. Grandpa pressed pause. We're very dedicated . . . fans.

I laughed.
Hard.
Then stopped.
Because I suddenly realized it had been a long time since a laugh that real had passed my lips.

Chapter Nine

KINSEY

I woke up clinging to Miller like a second skin. The guy slept like the dead, which gave me the perfect opportunity to crawl away. The minute I made a decision to move, his arm shot out and tugged me against him, I was the small spoon to his big spoon. Why did his spoon have to be so warm?

I tried to fight it.

Not very hard.

But it's the effort that counts, right?

We'd slept another hour in each other's arms, and when my phone went off for the third time with Emerson's name on the screen, the moment was shattered.

I grabbed my phone, he grabbed his.

No words were exchanged, but I still felt the heat from his body and wanted nothing more than to shut out the world, to forget about all the promises of friendship and just ask him to hold me. Sometimes that's all a girl needs, a good holding, a hug, a touch.

I quickly called Emerson back. Apparently, she and Sanchez were going down to the practice stadium to work out.

"I'll make protein shakes, if you want to get ready really quick." Miller stood and started making himself at home in the kitchen.

And I had it.

Those horrible visions of what life would be like if everything was exactly like what it seemed.

Miller in the kitchen, shirtless, rummaging around the cupboards after having the best sleep of his life in my arms.

And me, getting ready, putting my toothbrush next to his and asking him if he can stop at the store for tampons.

Get a grip, Kins!

"Uh . . ." I scratched my head, did a circle, and put the blanket back on the couch. "Yeah, sure."

"We can all work out, I'll call Jax." Miller wasn't looking at me.

Rude!

I crossed my arms and then briefly remembered getting hot in the middle of the night, and taking off my . . . bra.

Braless.

Hello, headlights.

"Trying to be a gentleman here, Kins, but when you cross your arms it just makes it worse for me. Maybe you gained weight in your tits too, because I do not remember them looking that damn edible." He leaned his massive body against the counter and finally looked at me. His slow perusal was enough to make my entire body shake with need. "Yeah, you need to put on some clothes . . . friend."

"Says the shirtless football player." I arched my eyebrows.

He took two steps toward me. "Don't make me carry you."

"That desperate to get some clothes on me?"

"So I don't rip them off you? Yeah, pretty much." One more step and a heave, and I was getting carried like a sack of potatoes all the way down the hall and into my bedroom. I was too stunned to fight back. He set me on my feet, turned around, and walked away.

"Thanks for the ride!" I called after him.

Miller poked his head around the corner scaring the crap out of me. "That wasn't a ride and you know it, Kins. You're familiar with the kind of rides I give, and when this whole friendship thing goes to hell and you actually ask me to kiss you—to touch you—you're going to need to buckle up, sweetheart, because it's going to be rough."

"Funny, I remember smooth."

"Poking the bear, friend."

I was breathing way too hard for a girl who was standing still. "Maybe I like to poke."

He groaned and banged his head against the side of the wall before walking off and yelling, "You have ten minutes."

I scowled and managed to take a much-needed inhalation of oxygen before I quickly changed into my workout clothes. A wave of dizziness washed over me, just brief enough to force me to grab ahold of the door before grabbing my practice bag.

And with that dizziness—fear.

It was debilitating.

You're being ridiculous. You're healthy. You're fine.

I closed my eyes and shut out the world, then focused on the one thing that wasn't a reminder of my past—of what my dad was going through—of what he was battling.

Miller.

My eyes snapped open.

Why did I see him?

Funny, since Jax was the one who taught me how to meditate, to take control of my thoughts before they took control of me. And it was always Jax's voice that brought me to that place of peace, where nothing could touch me, where I simply lived.

I gulped.

Instead, it was Miller's raspy voice, his full lips, that beckoning smile, that forced my fear to dissipate.

"Kins!" Miller barked. "You ready?"

"Yeah." I placed a hand on my chest and gave my head a shake. "Sure, coming."

He grumbled something about Jax having the patience of a saint with me, and by the time I joined him in the kitchen, he'd somehow already changed and made two protein shakes. He tossed me a bottle full of some green-looking crap that made me gag before I even smelled it.

With a grin, he grabbed his keys. "Don't knock it until you try it."

"What is this?" I shook the bottle and cringed, the green sludge didn't even move! I'd need a spoon! "Poison?"

"Kins." Miller opened the door for me. "Do you really think I'd poison you before tasting you again? Not so smart on my part. Then you'd probably haunt me whenever I was trying to get laid and completely ruin every single future orgasm."

I swept past him. "So basically I don't need to watch my back until after you've had a little snack?"

"Eh." He grabbed my bag out of my hand and pressed the elevator button. "I'd say more like a feast."

My ears burned. "Sorry, friend, restaurant's closed." I clenched my legs to prove it, and noticed Miller give me a once-over, his lips quirked like he knew what he was doing to me.

"We'll see."

"What happened to last night? Our conversation about being friends?"

"Selective memory loss." He ushered me into the elevator; his large hand took up half my back, at least it felt like it.

I shrugged away from his touch and plastered myself against the far wall. "Well, good thing I still remember the conversation."

A grunt was his only answer.

Another wave of dizziness hit me.

I gripped the railing.

And suddenly Miller was in front of me, his hands on my face, his eyes crazed. "What the hell was that?"

I straightened. "Huh? What?"

He wasn't buying it, his lips pressed into a firm line. "You know exactly what I'm talking about. You stumbled like you were going to pass out."

I faked a smile I didn't feel and shrugged. "I'm tired, I shared a couch with a behemoth last night and nearly got suffocated."

"Bullshit." He pressed his hands on either side of my body, pinning me against the wall. "You slept fine, want to know how I know?"

Probably not. I gulped. And shook my head.

"Tough shit." The elevator stopped. He didn't budge. "I know you, Kins. I know your skin, I know your smell, I'm acutely aware of every movement you make, even in your sleep, I saw you take off your bra, I felt you press that tight ass against me when you thought I was asleep—I know you. And this, this isn't you . . . so I'm going to ask again. What's up?"

I was too stunned to answer.

Thankfully, the doors opened and people started piling in.

"This isn't over," he murmured, grabbing my hand and leading us out of the elevator into the apartment lobby.

I was saved by the curious stares of people around us, and when we made it into the adjacent parking garage, I knew it was only a matter of time before he found out.

Not because I was going to say anything.

But because he knew me.

He saw everything.

And if I kept getting dizzy like that, he was either going to beat it out of Jax, or just force me to go to the doctor.

Not that it mattered.

I was healthy.

Totally fine.

My dad, on the other hand . . .

It was Thursday. I could see him tomorrow.

I clung to that promise like dear life.

Everything was going to be okay, I just needed to force myself to believe that.

Chapter Ten

MILLER

"He's literally been on his phone for the past half hour." Sanchez nodded his head in Jax's direction. "Dude, I know this sounds insane, but I think . . . I think Jax's texting."

"It's definitely something of Armageddon proportions," I agreed, finishing my set and leaping off the bench so that Sanchez could start his. "He stopped midlift."

"Jax," Sanchez grunted as he heaved the bar from the rack, "doesn't stop for shit, you've seen the way he works out. Like he's being chased by fucking flesh-eating zombies."

"Two more." I had my hands under the bar just in case. "We should probably steal his phone."

"It's like we share a brain when we bro lift, man, because I was just trying to figure out a way to crack his code."

"Birthday."

Sanchez finished lifting and grabbed a towel. "Shit, man, this is Jax. Do you really think he'd still keep that as his password? He's not lazy like us." We both glanced behind us to where Jax was standing a good ten feet away.

Jax set his phone down and then cracked a smile.

"Did he—" Sanchez smacked me with a towel. "Did he smile? At his phone? Did you see that?"

I couldn't believe my own eyes. Jax Romonov was texting a chick, and by the looks of his face, a smoking hot one.

"Jax!" I called him over. "You're up."

"Oh." He coughed into his hand, dropped his phone onto his gear lying on the ground, and slowly made his way over. "Sorry, I was just . . . um. Texting."

"Who?" Sanchez's mouth widened into a smirk.

Jax scowled and lay down on the bench while I spotted him. "How about none of your damn business?"

He lifted the bar off the bench and started pumping out his reps. When he got to the last one, Sanchez came over, grabbed the bar, and slowly pressed it down until it almost connected with Jax's chest.

Jax groaned in an effort to shove it back up.

"The hell, man!" he roared, arms shaking. "You trying to kill me?"

"Depends." Sanchez grinned. "Who you texting?"

"This is two-twenty, you jackass!" Jax hissed, his face turning red.

Sanchez whistled. "Wow, man, I wasn't aware. That's really heavy. Isn't that heavy, Miller?"

I coughed out a laugh. "Sure is."

"Just tell us who you're texting and I'll lift the bar off."

"This is, this is . . ." Jax kicked his legs out, flailed, gave up, and glared. "I'm telling the defense to take you both out by any means necessary next week."

Sanchez yawned.

I sighed. "Who is it?"

"What are you guys doing?" Kinsey screamed, running over to the weight section with Emerson on her heels. "Stop it! You could kill him! That's at least two-twenty-five. You know his max is only fifty over that!"

"He's fine." Sanchez pushed down harder. "Plus Miller's hands are right underneath it, the bar isn't going anywhere until he confesses who he was texting."

"What the fuck is this? Middle school?" Jax rolled his eyes.

"Texting?" Kins's eyes lit up, and in seconds she was by my side. "You're texting?"

"I text all the time!" Jax roared.

The guy was getting pretty worked up over a few text messages. I would bet my entire contract that he was texting a girl. I just wanted to know who.

Emerson grinned from her spot behind Kinsey. "Maybe we should just grab his phone and see?"

"Give it here." Kins held out her hand.

"Kins," Jax's voice pleaded. "Don't you dare."

"You locked me in a closet during prom," Kinsey said as Emerson slapped the phone in her hand. "I'll dare any damn time I want."

"I can't believe this shit," Jax mumbled.

"Seriously?" I eyed Kins. "Do you know everyone's password?"

"It's her gift." Emerson sighed. "She cracked mine in seconds, I don't know how she does it."

"Annoying as hell!" Jax roared, fighting against Sanchez, who was still laughing his ass off.

Kins quickly hit the pass code and then gasped out, "No way!"

"What!" we all exclaimed, nearly forgetting about a struggling Jax, before he yelped.

Sanchez pulled the bar off him and set it in the rack, and then ran over to Kins. We huddled around like kids with nothing better to do than gossip while Jax swore like a sailor on the bench, alternating between yelling at us and throwing a towel against the floor.

"Harley." Kins quickly hid the phone. "Wow, brother, I didn't think you had it in you. I mean I gave her your number because she said she wanted to apologize, but this . . ." Her grin was bright, hopeful. God, she was beautiful when she smiled.

I put my feelings on lockdown.

It was one thing to lust after her, to want her. It was quite another thing to want more—to think more was possible after all the shit I'd been through last year. I was too fucked up to be anything except her friend, even though for the last twelve hours my actions and my words had been completely opposite of the promise I'd made.

I'd promised because her face damn near broke my heart.

But after last night, her confessions, the couch.

I was back to square one.

Wanting her naked and underneath me.

More than once.

More.

Just, wanting more.

Damn it.

"Guys!" Kins locked the phone and tossed it to a pissed-off Jax. "By this projection, I imagine Jax is going to get laid."

Sanchez started a slow clap while Jax's face flamed bright red.

Emerson and I exchanged a high five while Kins did a little shimmy, her ass pointed in my direction long enough for my mouth to go completely dry.

Em elbowed me in the ribs. "You gonna make it?"

"Shut up."

She held her hands up in mock innocence and winked.

It was my turn to blush.

"It's okay, you know," she whispered while Sanchez and Kins continued their relentless teasing of Jax, including planning his outfit for their date tomorrow night.

I played dumb. "What is?"

"Liking her."

"Wow, we really have reverted back to middle school, haven't we?"

Em giggled. "Um, we nearly got a teacher fired in middle school."

"God, Mrs. Perkins was the absolute worst!"

"Remember when she told us we were going to end up in prison?"

I wrapped my arm around her shoulders and gave her a side hug. "Who the hell says that to eleven-year-olds? You cried for two days and told me you wouldn't survive in a place that didn't let you express yourself creatively."

She groaned, tucking her head against my chest. Man, I'd missed Em so much, but it was different, holding her was different, like a piece of my life had returned, but not in the same way. We didn't fit like we used to, we belonged together, just not in the way I'd always envisioned.

"Admit it, I was a nerd that you took under your wing because I was the only girl in school who brought extra fruit snacks."

"The Power Ranger kind. Sometimes I still crave the blue ones."

"You sick man."

"They're two for five dollars at the grocery store on the corner right now. I can maybe supply you with a few if you do me a solid."

She peered up at me with those pretty brown eyes. "I'm not stealing the Bucks mascot."

"That was high school, and you totally kicked ass in that YouTube video when they caught you in the men's restroom with your foot in the toilet. Horrible hiding spot but who am I to judge?"

"Shut it." She shoved me. "What's this favor?"

"Find out why she's been getting dizzy."

Em frowned. "She being Kins?"

"Yeah." I gulped, my eyes finding Kins like she was the only person in the room. "She got dizzy like she was going to pass out. Thankfully I'd already made her a shake with extra electrolytes and shit, I just . . . something seems off."

"And you know her well enough to tell that." Emerson said it like a statement, and then pressed her hand against my forearm. "I'll find out, but have you thought of asking her?"

"She'd lie . . . besides, we're just, you know, taking things slow with this whole relationship, almost like friends but more . . ."

Em choked out a laugh. "Suurre. So no naked time yet?"

I slapped a hand over her mouth. "Say that around Jax, and you know he'll find a reason to have me killed."

She pulled my hand away. "Fine, I'll ask."

Jax's phone went off.

We all turned our attention to him, grinning.

"You gonna answer that?" Sanchez crossed his bulky arms over his chest. "Or just let it go to voice mail?"

Jax flipped us all off and answered the phone as he jogged out of the room.

"This just in," Sanchez announced. "I'm inviting myself to family dinner tomorrow night. No way am I missing the shit hitting the fan. Hell, this might be better than football, our little Jax growing up and getting naked with chicks."

Kins winked at me then joined Emerson at the free weights while Sanchez and I finished our sets.

I tried to focus on preseason warm-ups.

On the fact that practice started next week.

But my eyes, treacherous bastards, kept finding Kins and locking gazes with her through the mirror.

I was in deep.

Chapter Eleven

I felt better after working out with the gang, and once I finished the rest of the green gunk, which oddly tasted sweeter than I'd expected, I'd forgotten all about the dizziness and was suddenly über focused on Bucks practice.

As one of the team captains, it was my job to make sure that all the girls were doing their assigned conditioning and encourage those who were struggling. Last year that had been Emerson. She was a talented cheerleader, but I knew it would be hard for her since she didn't fit the mold of a typical professional cheerleader.

She had a killer ass, gorgeous curves, and boobs that girls would murder her over—my theory still stood that Sanchez was hypnotized by her rack then fell in love with her heart. Both her rack and her heart were amazing, and I was just glad that they'd found each other and it was the perfect fit.

I rummaged through my bag in search of the schedule for practice. I wanted to double-check the start times and make sure that everything was in place.

"Hey." Em jogged into the locker room. "You want to go over some stuff before practice?"

"Yup." I quickly looked up from the sheets and sighed, finally feeling like myself. "I just need to get this all organized first." I scrunched up my nose.

Em tilted her head. "You'd tell me if you were pushing yourself too hard, right?"

I dropped the paper. "Huh?"

Em rolled her eyes. "I'm not trying to be nosy—"

I arched my eyebrows.

"Okay, that's a lie, I totally am. But I just want to make sure you're doing okay with everything . . . your dad . . . Miller . . ."

"I'm good." I wanted to talk to her, to tell her my doubts and insecurities, but it felt weird. She was my best friend, but she'd also been Miller's whole world for years. The entire situation was confusing and because I'd kept my past secret, the last thing I wanted was to break the news to her and have it get leaked by some eavesdropper with nothing better to do with their lives. "I promise."

She eyed me and then nodded slowly. "Fine, you know where to find me when you need me."

"Yo!" The door to the weight room swung open. "Em, I thought you were going to wash my back?"

I snorted and rolled my eyes while Em just shook her head and grinned.

"Coming."

"Yeah, you will," Sanchez yelled back.

"Control him." I laughed.

"Impossible." She gave me a side hug and jogged off. I followed as far as the main hallway that met in between both locker rooms and paused, letting my thoughts take over.

At least by myself, I could focus on practice and anything else that could and would distract me from Miller's addictive mouth.

"Didn't expect to see you here." The sound of Anderson's nasal voice sent chills down my arms.

"Oh?" I refused to look at him. Didn't want him to see my irritation— or the fear behind the calm mask I tried to portray. "Well, I do work for the Bucks organization as a cheerleader, so I don't know why that would be so shocking."

"No, I meant in the gym, working out." His voice was cool, detached. "You don't seem to be as fit as the last time I saw you. I just assumed you'd stopped trying."

Stopped. Trying.

It was weird how memories could be forgotten and then suddenly a noise or a smell—that damn cologne he always wore—brought them all back to the surface like they'd been attached to little buoys just waiting to bounce back up. The hurtful words were just as harsh now as they were a few years ago.

I clenched the paper in my hands and suddenly wished for badass ninja skills so I could slice my schedule across his throat and call it a freak paperwork accident, one that involved blood and dismemberment.

"What?" He moved closer until I could see his Nike sneakers and track pants. "I wasn't trying to be rude, you know. I like to be completely honest with my friends."

"We aren't friends," I snapped, shoving the paper back into its folder and the folder back into my bag. "We were never friends."

His cool eyes locked on mine. "Is that what you think? After dating me for a full year? That we were never friends?" His smile was sad, it was manipulative; I wanted to strangle him and his boy-next-door façade. "Maybe I remember things differently, you were happy, we were happy . . ." I flinched when he moved his hand to my face, his cold fingers pressed against my cheek. I was frozen in place. Paralyzed with fear. "We could have it again . . . the amazing sex . . ." My stomach rolled. "The closeness . . ." He grinned. "We were good for each other, we were great together, and then you had to go and tell your brother bullshit about me being controlling."

I swallowed slowly and whispered, "Because you were."

"I was helping you." It was like he truly believed what he was saying. His smile fell, his face full of sadness.

God, he was a master manipulator.

"No, you hurt me."

"I would never hurt you."

"You did." It was all I was capable of saying. I needed to get out, to get away from him, from the crestfallen look on his face and the guilt that he threw at me that made me feel like somehow, everything was my fault, including his controlling attitude.

"Anderson." Miller barked out his name like a curse. "Coach just came in, wants to go over next week's schedule with you."

Anderson didn't move.

Miller clenched his teeth together then said it louder. "Now."

Anderson dropped his hand and gave me a wink before slowly sauntering past Miller like he owned the place.

I don't know how Miller got to my side before my knees gave out, but suddenly I was in his lap, my head pressed against his chest, his heart hammering in my ear like it was seconds away from thumping through the skin and slapping me across the face for my stupidity.

"You okay?" His chin resting on my head, I could feel the vibration of the words sink into my body.

I nodded, the weight of his head moving with me.

"Waffle, it's wrong to lie to your Chicken, you know that, right? That's like . . . peanut butter cussing out jelly, just plain wrong."

I snorted out a laugh, and then found myself wrapping my arms around his bare torso and for the first time realizing he was basically half-naked.

"You're in a towel." My hands froze behind his neck.

His lips found my right ear. "Do you want me to be in a towel? Because I can be out of it in seconds."

"You *would* proposition me to get my mind off things."

"Things being that dickhead?"

I nodded again. His breath was hot on my neck, I wanted to curl into him, beg him to wrap his arms around me and protect me from the bad—Miller always felt so good.

What was it about him that felt that way?

He was genuine.

Loyal.

But definitely not safe. Not safe by a long shot.

No, the way he felt was very different from the reality of what he was—a dangerous man, one I was stupidly falling for more and more even though I'd been twice burned by him.

And yet, my stupid heart kept going. Maybe things have changed? Maybe he's different? Maybe he wants more?

Quinton Miller?

No, he'd experienced love once.

I highly doubted he would take the risk again.

Especially on me.

"You're sighing an awful lot for a girl who just realized only a towel's separating her and her favorite object."

"So now you're an object?"

He pulled his head back. "Only parts of me, how's that?"

"Jax would kill you if he saw you right now."

"Jax can kiss my ass." Miller growled low in his throat, his forehead touching mine just as his lips descended.

"Whoa!" Sanchez walked in then walked right back out.

I jerked away from Miller and cursed my own weakness.

"Give me one reason not to go remove Anderson's head from his body." Miller completely ignored the fact that Sanchez had just walked in on me in his lap. "One reason or I'm going after him, with or without this towel."

"First of all, your nakedness would probably do the trick in scaring him away—"

"Because I have a big dick?"

I covered my heated face with my hands. "Yeah, because his is so small."

"Hah!" Miller burst out laughing then pulled one of my hands away and gave me a high five. "Up top, Flat-ass, that's the kind of sass you need to show him next time he gives you shit."

I shivered, which was enough for Miller to lose his smile and give me one of those penetrating stares that had all my girly parts cheering for all the wrong reasons.

"Kins, promise me, just stay away, and if he corners you again, you give him attitude, you walk away, got it?"

I nodded a few times. "Got it, bossy pants."

"Or I will show him my penis," he promised with a wink.

Jax chose a really poor time to walk in on us.

I was fully clothed sitting on a half-naked Miller, who was holding me close enough to be kissing me, and he'd just said he was going to bust out his penis.

"Nobody is showing ANYBODY his penis!" Jax roared, shoving a finger in Miller's direction.

"Not to me." I rolled my eyes and feigned ickiness as I leaped off Miller's lap only to nearly face-plant on the ground. He had that much of an effect on me, oh joy.

"Kins, you feeling okay?" Jax was at my side in an instant, the same worried expression on his face that I'd seen him wear and try to hide over the past few years whenever I as much as sneezed or had anything above a ninety-eight-point-five-degree temperature.

I jerked away from him, my eyes finding Miller's narrowed ones. I refused to let him know that part of me, the part that would make it even more difficult for him to fall for me.

What was I even saying?

That I wanted that now?

No.

Stay strong.

Resolute.

He only wants sex.

Wow, suddenly I felt so much like Emerson last year with Sanchez, stuck with a guy who only wanted one thing from me when all I wanted was more.

Of everything.

If there was one thing I'd learned from Anderson—and my past—it was that I deserved more.

And I was going to fight to have it.

No more weakness.

No more—

The towel fell.

It freaking fell.

To the ground.

Miller was quick in picking it up.

I slowed down time—or maybe time just slowed down time for my benefit. He was . . .

"Cover yourself, man!" Jax shot him a seething glare then brought his attention back to me, but not before I caught Miller's wink.

Bastard did it on purpose!

Yeah, he was going to pay for that later.

After I relived the moment at least a few dozen times and then stored it in the furthest recesses of my mind labeled: Miller Naked. Which just so happened to be right next to: Best Orgasms of My Life, which was directly in front of: Miller's Kisses.

Miller held up his hands in defeat and walked back toward the men's locker room, most likely to get changed.

"Kins," Jax groaned. "Look at me."

I met his eyes.

Damn it, I hated the concern there.

"I know Mom texted you about family dinner. She literally did it right in front of me after Dad flipped me off, of course."

I giggled. "And by those texts it looks like you're bringing Harley."

Jax's left eye twitched, he quickly looked down at the floor. "I was basically forced by Mom."

"Yes, I can see how that would happen. She's what? Five foot two? A hundred and fifteen pounds dripping wet? Poor guy, what did she do? Sit on you? Poke your chest with her finger and threaten to drop saliva onto your forehead?"

"Very funny." He smirked, his eyes still not meeting mine. "She, uh, used coercion, let's just say she's very good at heaping on piles of guilt and making you say thank you in response."

"Like someone else I know."

"Um . . ." He took a step forward, looked behind him, then braced his hands on my shoulder. "You're not . . . God, I can't believe I'm even asking this, I mean it's you . . ." Insert awkward chuckle. "There's nothing going on between you and Miller, right? You know, beyond the whole fake dating so that asshole Anderson stays away?"

I smiled brightly. It was a liar's smile. I knew it. I just hoped that he wouldn't know it—then again, it was Jax, he could read me like a book. "You asked us to date, so that's what we're doing. Nothing more."

There, that sounded good.

"So you're just . . . friends."

"He's the chicken to my waffle, brother, no worries."

"I could go for some waffles." He patted the flat six-pack behind his tight white T-shirt. He could probably eat a barn and still look like he belonged on the cover of *Men's Fitness* for the third time.

"You and food." I shoved his chest.

"I love food."

"Junk food," I taunted.

He slapped a hand over my mouth. "Tell a soul and I'm locking you up again. Hard time."

I bit his hand, he jerked away with a yelp. "Mr. I-only-eat-salads-in-front-of-everyone-else-but-in-private-I-have-a-stash-of-candy-in-every-single-nook-in-the-apartment! Even in your nightstand! Forget condoms! You've got jelly beans!"

"Kins, I swear, if you tell anyone—"

"Skittles." I crossed my arms. "But only the red kind."

"That's it." Jax lunged for me, tossed me over his shoulder with one hand, then grabbed both of our bags and started marching outside. "Time to go home before you spill more trade secrets."

"Oooh!" I laughed. "Like how you only have pineapple on your pizza the day before the game and will literally send said pizza back if you don't have exactly thirty-eight pieces of fruit on it?"

He pinched my leg.

"Hey!"

"Whoa!" Miller was just coming out of the locker room, fully clothed, dang it. "She giving you trouble, man?"

"When is she not giving me trouble?"

"Good thing we now share that burden," Miller called, winking at me before following us out.

"Right?" Jax joked.

But the joke was on him, because the entire time Miller followed us, all he did was stare right down my shirt with a promising smirk on his face.

I was screwed.

Chapter Twelve

Family dinner.

Something I hadn't done since my mom was alive.

The thought of actually sitting through an entire meal with Kinsey's parents had me ready to run in the opposite direction.

It hit too close.

Before my dad discovered the love of his life—alcohol—he'd had another. My mom.

And although they didn't have the perfect marriage, they always managed to keep Sundays for dinner together.

It was always the same. Pot roast with carrots, and a few potatoes thrown in. Sometimes there was dessert and almost always, we'd finish our meal in the living room while watching *Sunday Night Football*.

Tradition.

The word burned.

Made my chest feel like it was expanding too fast, as if I couldn't stop myself from imploding from the inside out.

But Kinsey had asked.

And then added, like I wasn't already dealing with enough emotional shit, that it would make her dad happy to see her with someone.

Great.

If only he knew that I'd hurt her, not once but twice.

That I'd probably been the reason she was so angry when she got back from Europe.

That I was only capable of doing it again.

And that despite all of it—I still wanted to, wanted her—maybe because when I was with her, she did make me want more.

And if that wasn't terrifying, I wasn't sure what was.

I'd lost Em.

I'd lost my mom. The only two women in my life I'd ever loved had both been ripped away from me by different circumstances. I wasn't sure I could survive it a third time.

I wasn't sure I wanted to even try.

And girls like Kins, bright lights of bouncing sunshine that knew how to break and enter, but were still afraid of the dark, they deserved a hero.

Not an emotionally fucked-up football player who would rather sleep his way through other women than actually commit his heart and risk losing it all again.

It was stupid.

I was stupid.

The only explanation I had was even stupider.

I think . . . no. I knew.

My heart wasn't whole.

So how was it fair of me to even attempt to give something that wasn't even functioning properly to a girl who had the biggest heart I'd ever seen?

It wasn't fair.

It didn't make her any less desirable and it sure as hell didn't make the flame of lust die out.

Not by a long shot.

The sound of dinner plates being passed around brought me back to the present. My current hell.

The Dinner.

"So, Harley." Paula, Kinsey's mom, passed her the salad. "What do you do, sweetie?"

"Yoga," Jax interjected gruffly. "And she models . . . what was it? Children's wear?"

Harley grabbed her fork and poked Jax in the hand, hard, before going, "Whoops, I thought it was my chicken."

Jax rubbed his hand.

"And, it's actually athletic wear, which your son should know since he claims to be an athlete, but that's yet to be proven this season, isn't it . . . honey?"

Sanchez reached across the table and handed Jax the carving knife with a solid nod of encouragement.

"Now, boys." Paula laughed. "I think the girl has a point. You've got a tough year ahead of you."

"How nice"—Jax sounded like he was choking on the words—"of the model to point that out to us." He grabbed the knife and started cutting through the chicken so hard a piece flew onto my plate and then Kinsey's.

"Careful, sweetie!" Paula instructed, "It's a soft bird."

"I know something else that's soft," Harley said in a low voice.

Emerson choked on her wine while Sanchez reached for the bottle and filled up Jax's empty water glass with wine, giving him another nod of encouragement.

Once the food was passed around, I had assumed there would be peace.

Chewing.

Small talk.

A bit of coffee.

I'd go home, bang my head against the wall, take a cold shower, and attempt not to dream about Kinsey naked.

All in all, exactly what I'd been doing for the past few months while she was away in Europe.

But fate wasn't that kind.

"So, Miller," Ben piped up, knife in his left hand pointed in my direction like he was getting ready to throw it. "You sleeping with my daughter?"

Wine spewed out of Jax's mouth directly into Sanchez's face.

Emerson handed him a napkin but not before laughing into it first and wiping away a few tears.

Sanchez cursed and wiped off the red wine then tossed the napkin in Jax's face.

"Daddy . . ." Kins just had to speak. Right now. With a knife pointed at my heart. "That's a silly question, we just started dating!"

"Uh-huh." The knife didn't budge. "And your mama and I were virgins on our wedding night. You do realize that Jax was either a preemie or born out of wedlock?"

Sanchez gave a fake gasp while Harley shrugged and said, "Huh, I'd say preemie. Doesn't that affect muscle development?"

Jax groaned into his wine and kept drinking while Harley gave a little yelp like she'd just been pinched.

"Hah-hah." Shit, was it hot in there? I tugged at the collar of my shirt and gulped against a dry-as-hell throat. "Sir, with all due respect, I would never—" Lies, all lies, I saw her boobs! It was literally on the tip of my tongue to confess, I was usually better under this kind of pressure, I was a tight end, for shit's sake! "I wouldn't disrespect her in that . . . way."

He lowered the knife.

I exhaled.

He raised it again.

My dick twitched with absolute guilty horror.

"So you're saying . . . that the kiss you two shared—what was that, Paula, two days past?"

"Sounds about right." She nodded excitedly. "Dear, your tongue was quite . . . visible."

"Very visible," he agreed. Hell, I thought the man had cancer? Why did he look seconds away from castrating me? "You're saying that's as far as you've gone with my little girl."

"Sir, yes sir." I was suddenly in the military. Ready to die for king and country—or just protect all the lower extremities from the current terrorist with the knife.

"Huh." He dropped the knife. "Well, what the hell's wrong with you? Don't you think she's pretty?"

Jax growled, shoving a piece of meat into his mouth, leveling me with a glare that would make most men piss themselves.

"Beautiful," I said, staring down at my plate. "One of the prettiest girls I've ever seen."

Small fingers grazed my thigh and then a hand followed—I knew it was Kinsey, I gripped her hand like a lifeline.

"So, she's the prettiest thing you've ever seen and yet . . . you've kept it in your pants?"

"For fear of this one chopping it off." I pointed at Jax. "Sure, yeah, pretty much."

Kinsey snorted a laugh next to me.

"Well, if there's anything I've learned . . ." He started cutting his meat again. "It's that this life is so damn short—hell, don't be that guy, son. The one that lets the pretty girl get away. Had I done that with Paula I wouldn't be stuck with this jackass over here." He pointed at Jax. "Or my little princess."

"I'm a princess!" Kinsey laughed in Jax's direction while he grinned back at her. Apparently, this was normal for their family.

"Okay, sir . . ." I exhaled. Had I just agreed to have sex with Kinsey? Did her dad just . . . ask me to? What the hell kind of family was this?

"Thank you," Kinsey said under her breath. "He's very passionate about . . . love."

Her eyes fell.

And with that, the guilt over the whole situation came surging back. Because I was withholding everything from her—because of my own fear, my own selfishness.

"You do know how to perform?" Oh good, more questions from Ben . . . the guy needed his own sitcom.

Kinsey's hand moved to graze the front of my jeans.

I nearly leaped out of my chair.

"Miller?" Sanchez piped up. "Trust me, if you would have heard the noises coming out of his apartment this summer, you really wouldn't be needing to ask that question."

Kinsey jerked her hand away.

While my dick wept with the loss of her fingers.

Fuck.

I lowered my head.

Two girls. I'd slept with two meaningless girls while she was gone. I hadn't planned to tell her—it wasn't like we'd been dating.

But I knew it would matter.

To her, it would matter.

Because, like she said yesterday, she wasn't that girl, the one you sleep with and send packing the next day. I bet that the last guy she was with was Anderson, the asshole who still had a crazy mental and emotional hold on her.

I'd gone and had meaningless sex with two girls who saw nothing but cash in my pockets and a body that could give them a good time, and I was just as guilty because I used them to forget about Kinsey.

Silence fell over the table.

Emerson shook her head slowly at me.

Great, now Em was disappointed too.

Like she wasn't marrying the guy that last year told her he wanted to screw her for fun.

And look how that turned out!

"Mom." Kinsey's voice shook. "I'm just going to check on the pie, okay?"

"I'll come with you." I moved to stand.

"No." Jax gave his head one shake. "I'll go."

I tried for a smile.

I failed.

And wondered if I had lost Kinsey.

And then wondered, had I really had her in the first place?

Chapter Thirteen

KINSEY

I was over him.

Over it.

Until Jax forced the big dummy back into my life without giving me a choice in the matter. Maybe if we both had kept our distance, it wouldn't hurt this bad. If he hadn't apologized.

If he hadn't searched every room in my house for an intruder, if he hadn't promised he was going to kiss me again once I gave up on the friendship ruse and asked. If he wasn't such a big giant flirt with his crystal-blue eyes and mocha skin.

If he didn't tell me with his eyes and actions that all he wanted to do was protect me from the world.

But Miller did all of those things.

Two days. It took him two freaking days to get under my skin again like a disease, to make me believe that maybe, just maybe, I could trust him, trust the words he said.

"Hey there." Jax's voice was calm, rational, exactly what I needed. "Want help with the pie?"

"No." I jerked it out of the oven and sat it on the granite counter, tossed the oven mitts onto the floor and started cutting really uneven pieces, getting sugar and crumbs all over my hands before Jax grabbed me from behind, placed his hands on mine, and whispered, "Stop."

I did.

I closed my eyes.

I breathed him in.

The constant in my life.

The two men I trusted more than anything, my brother, my dad.

And yet again, it had just been proven, maybe that's all I'd ever have, and I wasn't okay with it—I wanted to be. Maybe someday I could be. Not now.

"He's young and stupid," Jax said in a low voice. "When you're in the league, and you have that much money, fame." He sighed. "You forget how many girls propositioned me before I got my legendary ice man reputation. I had one girl literally strip in front of me, spread her legs, and ask me for at least one minute of my time so she'd die happy."

I shivered. "You're kidding?"

"That happened all the time, Kins. I'm not saying go back in there and give him a high five for thinking with his dick—especially since this is one of the many reasons I don't want any player near you. All I'm saying is, when you're single, there's temptation. Miller's one of the good ones, and he just had a rough year last year, with everything that went on with Em and Sanchez."

And there it was.

It would always go back to Miller's past.

His past with Em.

And now, it felt like I would never really be a part of his future.

"You're right." I didn't feel better. I didn't get it. I never would. But I didn't want my brother to know why it hurt me so deeply—why when I was on that plane to Europe and the first-class flight attendant had to give me more tissues, I thought my heart was going to explode.

While Miller was having naked time with some nameless face who probably didn't even know his favorite color.

Pink. It was pink.

Don't ask.

"I just . . . it's been a stressful night, you know?" I turned in Jax's arms and gave him a bear hug. "Thanks for being the best big brother ever."

His face fell while his arms squeezed around me like a tight band. "I'm not."

"You are."

"No, Kins." He pushed me away. He'd never done that before. Pushed. "I'm really not."

I'd never seen that look on his face—it reminded me of guilt, of the kind that you didn't get out from underneath, the kind that followed you until it killed you. The kind that I used to suffocate in when Anderson made me feel bad about myself, my body. "Jax?"

"I knew."

"Knew?"

"About Dad," he whispered. "Before I sent you to Europe. I knew."

The world fell around me, first in tiny shattering pieces, and then all at once, the ground gave way, and I was on the floor, on my knees, staring up at the one man who had sworn he'd never let me down—who had said he'd always be my rock.

"Wh-what?"

"Kins." His eyes filled with tears. "I'm sorry, so fucking sorry, I didn't want you to get sick again, you know what stress can do to you, and at the time it wasn't so bad. The chemo worked on the first round, and—"

"Shut up, just shut up!" I screamed, tears running down my face. "I could have had months with him, MONTHS, and you sent me away!"

"I thought—"

"You thought?" I yelled, pounding my fist into the wood surface. "You thought what? That you'd just do what you do to everyone? Pull an Anderson on me and control the entire freaking situation? YOU THOUGHT?"

Mom and Dad suddenly ran into the room, Mom's face pale, Dad's even paler.

I closed my eyes.

Suddenly frail arms were around me. "We didn't want you to hurt." Daddy.

Both of them.

Betrayed by both of my parents and Jax.

I sank into myself, wanting to crawl into the floor and cry, scream, and repeat the process. "You had no right."

"I know, honey." Dad kissed my head. "We misjudged how fast the cancer was moving, we just . . . we had no idea. We wanted to protect you—"

"It wasn't your call to make," I said in a low voice, one I didn't recognize, one that dripped with such sadness and betrayal I felt like a foreigner in my own body. "I need . . . I need to go."

"Honey." Dad squeezed me tighter. "Don't go, not like this."

"You all knew." I ignored him, and chose to eye my mom, brother, and finally my dad. "All of you? And you still chose this for me? When your time has been literally cut to what? A year?"

Dad glanced away.

I swallowed. "How long, Dad?"

"Six months, honey. Maybe less. I've stopped treatments."

"And you were going to keep that from me too?"

"Tonight," Mom interceded, "we were going to tell you tonight."

"Some family dinner," I mumbled. With a sigh, I kissed my dad on the cheek. "I love you, but I need to go. I'll be back tomorrow to check on you, I just . . . need space right now. I don't want to leave angry, but . . . I'm so angry." My voice shook.

Jax gave me a nervous glance before helping me to my feet. I jerked my hands away from him and glared. "I'm moving out."

"What?" he roared. "Over this? Over me protecting you?"

"That's all you do! You're an overbearing pain in my ass! How about you focus on living your own life, instead of trying to keep me from living mine!"

I charged out of the room, grabbed my purse, and ran outside.

It wasn't until I made it to the curb that I realized Miller had given me a ride.

Two seconds later, his familiar scent wrapped around me. "Where to?"

"Jax's apartment. I'm grabbing some stuff."

"And going where?"

"I don't know yet. A hotel. I'm still pissed at you. I don't even know why I'm talking to you."

"Me neither," he whispered. "I'm just glad you are, even if it's louder than you normally talk."

"That's because I'm trying not to scream at you."

"It shows."

I would not smile.

"I'm driving." I snatched the keys out of his hand.

He let me.

Chapter Fourteen

MILLER

Every single person at dinner heard the yelling. Even Harley had sobered, her expression pale while Jax yelled at Kins, while she yelled right back.

I'd known them a little over a year. Not once had I ever seen them fight—it used to bother me, the type of relationship they had as brother and sister was scary close. I wasn't stupid. There was something else there between them. Something that I and everyone else in their lives didn't get, some bond that was unbreakable.

Part of me was afraid to ask.

Afraid of the answer.

Afraid of what it would make me feel.

I was still pissed at Sanchez, but the more I thought about it, the less my anger felt directed at him and more inward, like I was the dick that decided to have a few meaningless one-night stands because I was too chickenshit to admit my feelings for Kinsey were fueled by more than alcohol and lust.

"Kins." It was useless trying to calm the woman down. In the ten minutes since we'd been at her apartment she'd grabbed two duffel bags and shoved so many clothes into them that she couldn't zip them up. A pair of flip-flops went flying by my head, followed by a heel that narrowly missed my right ear. "Did you want me to carry these?"

"Or stab yourself with them," she said in a sweet voice. "Just try not to get any blood on the cloth part of the shoe, those cost a fortune. Jax bought them for me last year. On second thought, light them on fire, I don't care." Her grin wobbled like she was going to burst into tears and then thought better of it.

She heaved another bag into the living room then marched over to the fridge and jerked it open—was she humming?

With a smile she pulled the cap off the milk then chugged the jug, her throat moving slowly as she tilted her head back farther to get all the liquid. Some missed her mouth, dribbling down the sides and into her shirt. Fuck, I couldn't look away.

"Does a body good, hmm?" I joked.

She slammed the empty jug against the counter and turned her piercing gaze to mine. "His biggest pet peeve is when I finish the milk."

I crossed my arms, needing something to do so I wouldn't reach for her and end up with broken fingers. "That would be any athlete's pet peeve, especially one who likes his protein shakes every morning."

She wiped her mouth with her sleeve, and I felt my body shake with a savage desire to lick the rest of the milk away from those swollen lips, or at least lick my way down her body to see if any liquid found its way down her curves.

I took a slow, even breath, knowing already that my body was betraying me by swaying toward her, my lips parted.

"Don't." Her nostrils flared. A finger was pointed in my direction. "Right now I'm more pissed at him than you—count yourself lucky, Miller."

Kins's mouth suddenly broke out into a smile, and with a wicked grin she grabbed a bar stool, crawled up on it, and opened the cupboards above the stove.

"Catch!" She threw a giant box of fruit snacks at my face so I had no option but to put my hands out since I missed the memo about bringing my football helmet. Another box of fruit snacks followed, the kind you get at Costco that could feed an entire lunchroom full of first graders, and then two five-pound bags of M&M's were careening toward me.

She hopped off the bar stool and wiped her hands on her black leggings. "I suddenly feel so much better."

I snorted and lifted one of the bags of candy in the air. "Because you got your stash of sugar?"

"Nope." She winked then whispered, "Because I've got his."

I frowned. "Jax? But he eats salad." The guy was notorious for being the only one on the team that ate like a rabbit whenever we went out to dinner, no chance in hell would any sort of white processed sugar pass through his trap. The last time a guy brought a Snickers to practice he'd swiped it.

Son of a bitch. Had he eaten it?

"Jax is a liar from the pit of hell, he's got a sweet tooth the size of his stupid egotistical head—which, FYI, is ginormous, the asshole."

I was stuck in a position where I felt like I needed to take sides and either burn his jersey in the sink and dance around it while giving Kins a talk about women empowerment, or defend him and whatever the hell he did to piss her off.

Kins licked her lips as tears filled her eyes for the second time that night.

"Shit." I grabbed her before she could lunge away from me, and the minute her body came into contact with mine, I was hit with such longing I wanted to smack my head against the granite counter. She was sad. I was hugging her. And suddenly I felt better than I had all day?

It made no sense.

"I hate him." She sniffled.

"No you don't." I spoke against her hair, which smelled like coconut and lavender. I gave it another whiff, barely suppressing the groan building in the back of my throat.

Kins glanced up at me with teasing eyes. "Did you just sniff my hair?"

"Would it be creepy as hell if I did?"

Her nose scrunched. "Only because it seems like you did it twice."

"Maybe I just wanted to make sure."

An eyebrow arched. "Make sure that your nose works?"

"Nah." I tilted her chin up. "Maybe I just want to make sure that I don't ever forget what you smell like, you know, just in case I piss you off even more in the near future, which let's be honest, the odds aren't in my favor. I want to remember the way you smell when I'm alone, in my cold, depressing bed, and you're off drinking all of Jax's milk and stealing random strangers' pass codes and house keys."

Her smile fucking broke my heart, the corners of her lips were met with tearstained cheeks. "You make me sound like a psychopath."

"If the blood-caked stiletto fits . . ."

She punched me in the shoulder. "I was upset, alright?"

"And you hitting me means you're happy?"

"I'm getting there. I just . . . I need time to process."

"I have ears."

"Yup, two of them, I've noticed. You gonna tell me you have a penis next, then whip it out to prove it?"

"Hah!" I barked out a laugh and released her. "Is that your cute way of asking me to show you again? Already miss it, huh?"

"Can't miss what you never had, Miller. And I don't really remember having it, you know, all that drunken sex, fuzzy thoughts . . ." Her voice trailed off.

"Bullshit." I gripped her by the elbow and pulled her flush against my body where she could very well damn feel every single inch of me against her. "I'm calling your bluff."

"Call it all you want. That doesn't change the fact that nobody's seeing anybody's penis, even if it is . . ." She licked her lips and glanced down, making the damn thing feel the need to meet her halfway. "Impressive." She made air quotes.

I'd never wanted to strip so badly in my entire life.

"Impressive." I repeated the word, rolled it around my tongue, nope, not the word I was looking for, I rejected it immediately. "I think you can do better than *impressive*."

At least the tears were gone, the reminder that they'd been there in the first place was in her streaked makeup and flashing brown eyes.

It was a moment I would never forget.

The heat from her body pulsed against mine in perfect rhythm, like my heart was straining to match the cadence of hers—it was more than just the feel of her in my arms, or the way she looked up at me with trust I didn't deserve or earn—it was every single piece of the puzzle fitting, pulsing, tempting.

Kiss her.

Kiss her.

I needed to kiss her.

To suck the sorrow away from that mouth, to press my lips against those tears, to make it all go away.

To make her forget.

Or maybe, to make us both remember.

Why it was so good in the first place.

Why I was still so afraid of what it felt like to have her beneath me, to slide into her while she watched with rapt attention.

Kins bit down on her bottom lip and slowly shook her head. "I should find a hotel, or something."

"Or something." I barricaded her against the counter, my body still firmly pressed against hers. "I think I know a place that has an opening."

Her head tilted, those lips parted enough to suck in whatever air she needed to probably yell at me to stop micromanaging her life like her brother. Instead, she closed her mouth and looked down before saying, "Does this place have HBO?"

"Maybe."

"Does this place allow equal remote control benefits?"

"Of course . . . I'm not a monster." One heartbeat, two, I could feel my pulse skyrocketing the longer she was touching me. "You may even get fed."

"Wow. How fancy." She smiled up through tear-filled eyes. "It almost sounds too good to be true."

"Yeah, well, nothing's ever free."

"I figured."

"But you might enjoy the payment."

She rolled her eyes. "I'm not sleeping with you, Miller."

Her cheeks were bright red, her eyes clear, lips pressed together like she was trying not to think about the last time we kissed.

"Did I say anything about sex?"

"No, but—"

"One kiss," I finished for her.

"One kiss?" Her eyes narrowed. "And then I can crash in your spare bedroom?"

"One kiss," I repeated. "Harmless."

We both knew it was a lie.

There was nothing harmless about the way we touched, just like there was nothing harmless about the way she tasted, the addicting flavor of her could be my downfall, and even though I knew that, I still lit the match and waved it around like it wasn't going to burn the hell out of my hand.

"Okay." She closed her eyes. "Go ahead."

Her face was void of emotion, perfect, still. "That's not what I meant."

One eye opened then two. "You said one kiss?"

"Right, but you have to kiss me."

"Miller!" An edge of irritation tinged her voice. "It's the same thing."

"If it was the same thing you wouldn't be arguing with me, would you? But, hey." I pulled away just enough to put a few inches of space between our bodies. "If you'd rather rent a hotel room, with what I'm assuming is your brother's money, then . . ." It was a low blow. One that reminded her that as much as she hated her brother in that instant, he was the reason she was able to live and breathe cheerleading like it was her life.

Because she got paid absolute shit.

It was a gamble.

Using her pride against her.

But I was a desperate man.

Desperate for her kiss, her touch, and maybe just desperate to prove to her and to me, that something between us could be good.

Even if it meant it couldn't be forever.

"Fine." She bunched the front of my shirt with her right hand, and stood up on her tiptoes. I let her pull me down to her level while her head descended. I wanted to meet her halfway.

But meeting her halfway would ruin the point.

So I nailed my giant feet to the floor and waited for the first brush of her lips.

In a hypnotic, heart-twisting movement, her mouth fused against mine, her lips slowed.

One step.

Two.

Her legs tangled with mine, her hips bumping against my thighs as I drew a powerful breath in through her lungs, through her mouth, making it mine. Claiming the air, the space between our bodies.

Heat radiated between us as she slowly slid her hand up my chest and wrapped it around my neck, her other hand joining her as she hung on to my body. I lifted her by the ass and set her on the countertop, never once pulling away from her lips, but drawing each kiss from her mouth like a drug, just one more hit, and then another.

Words that were said between us incinerated—going up in smoke as our kiss intensified, as the need tripled. I kissed down the slender column of her throat, taking my time to taste her before claiming her lips again.

Her tongue explored my mouth, slowly, tenderly before she pulled back and gripped my biceps, digging her fingers into my skin just hard enough to make me stop my assault of her mouth.

"One kiss," she repeated, her voice hoarse.

"That *was* one kiss," I corrected.

"How do you figure?"

I tucked her hair behind her ears, she gave a little shudder. "Because my mouth never left you once."

And even though I wanted to pull her into my arms again, kiss the hell out of her, and get her naked.

I didn't.

I took a step back, and then another before turning around and grabbing her duffel bags. "We should get going."

"Right." She slid off the counter, pressed a hand to her flushed face, and then did a full circle before picking up the last bag and the pair of flip-flops she'd thrown at my face. "Thanks, for this . . ."

"This is what friends do."

I don't know why I said it.

Why I drew that damn line in the sand again.

Maybe it was self-preservation.

Or just my mind protecting every remaining piece of my heart.

Because for those few brief minutes, I could have sworn, she wasn't just kissing me, she was sucking the hurt away, the pain, and forcing me to forget all the reasons I helped send her out of the country in the first place.

And all the reasons that I'd do it again.

Because I was still selfish.

And when you're selfish, you focus on the only thing you can think of that can blind you to others' pain.

Your own.

Chapter Fifteen

Two weeks.

That's how long I'd lived with Quinton Miller.

And in the entire time we've lived together it had turned into a terrifyingly normal thing to not only see him in nothing but a towel at least ninety-nine percent of the time, but get flashes of naked ass when he forgot—right, forgot—to do laundry.

In the mornings, he drank milk shirtless, I know because I almost always ran into those muscles every morning in the kitchen.

He made his coffee strong enough that I was worried that one day I'd wake up with chest hair.

And he bought a special mug for mine.

It was pink.

It had a K on it.

In short, Quinton Miller was slowly killing me.

He made protein shakes like a boss, always kept fruit snacks in storage just in case the zombie apocalypse happened and there was a shortage, his words not mine, and he was the perfect gentleman.

I'm talking perfect.

One night after a double practice, I'd come home to him not only drawing me a bubble bath but asking if I'd like champagne to go with it.

It wasn't until day fifteen that I snapped, completely lost it and nearly rammed my fist through his perfect face, because how the hell dare he! It wasn't his job to make me happy, or cook me eggs, or make sure that I had my own ceramic coffee cup! We weren't really dating and all he was doing was making me wish we were, which was really unfair since he was like an emotional terrorist who bombed your heart only to tell you that you'd have to leave the country to find a hospital big enough to fix it!

By the time I got home that night, I was fuming, fuming! He'd left a note in my bag to have a good day.

Right. It said *Have a good day*.

That's it.

I was still irritated that I was upset over something so small, something so nice, something that for some damn reason brought tears to my eyes at least four times during practice.

Jax had given me a wide berth the past few weeks, and knowing that I was this pissed was probably killing him as much as it was me.

And then there were the phone calls and visits with the parents, where I pretended to be brave, then cried myself to sleep after.

"Miller!" I slammed the note on the kitchen counter of his immaculate penthouse apartment.

He was nowhere to be seen.

"QUINTON MILLER, YOU GET YOUR ASS IN HERE NOW!" I was full-on squeezing my hands into little fists and getting ready to start throwing dishware all over the kitchen when he rounded the corner.

In a freaking towel.

Again.

"That's it!" I charged toward him. "This is the last straw!" I tugged the towel free, not really thinking about anything other than how irritated I was that he was basically naked again. I had the towel in one hand and the note scrunched up in my other hand.

And Quinton Miller, sexiest tight end God ever created, was looming over me with a confident grin and little water droplets sliding off his abs onto the floor by his feet. "Kins, you okay?"

"Y-yes." Look away, just look away. "I mean no, no." God bless football, and God bless the V, it was so deep I wanted to reach out and touch the valley between his lower abs until my hands grazed his ever impressive—

"Kins?"

"Hmm?" I jerked to attention. "Yes?"

"You were yelling."

"I was."

His eyebrows shot up. "And you stole my towel. I'm kind of at an impasse here, little Waffle, did you just want to see me naked, or what? Because I've got a date in a few."

"A date?" Deflated, I let the word hang in the air like a complete idiot. "Of course you do."

Jealousy slammed into me. Heart weak, I felt like I needed to sit down. Why was I upset again? Oh, right, because he was making me like him more than I already did, he was being nice, and now? Now the rug was getting pulled out from underneath me. Of freaking course. A date.

"You can join me if you want." He grinned that stupid grin that had elderly women everywhere grabbing their chests and either fainting or going to the ER for heart attack symptoms.

Damn it. "No, um, I wouldn't want to intrude."

"It's not really that kind of date, Kins."

"Oh." I shifted on my feet, and then handed him his towel, all done in jerky movements like I was the one in the wrong when he was the one running around treating me like the best friend he'd never had. I gulped, "I should probably change."

What was I saying?

Was I actually thinking of going with him?

Seriously?

"Great." The guy pissed me off further by patting my head like I was a child, and then he mussed my hair. "Just wear what you normally wear, jeans, leggings, nothing too sexy."

My eyes narrowed into tiny slits.

"What?" He looked genuinely confused as to why that last statement had me ready to rip his eyeballs out. "You do want to go, right? We have to be there in fifteen minutes. Come on, you've been moping for two weeks. It's time to get out, Kins, live your life, and stop being sad."

"I'm not sad," I argued like a child, even going as far as to cross my arms.

"You're right," he whispered. "You're angry. Which is almost worse. Because at least when you're sad you can mourn. Sadness you can battle. But anger? Anger we just justify until we're miserable as hell. The last time I saw you smile was in your brother's kitchen, you're losing weight, and you forgot to shower yesterday."

"I did not!" Embarrassed, I wanted to crawl under the couch and let it suffocate me to death. "I've been busy with practice!"

"You're working out too much." His fingers grazed my chin. "You've been crying yourself to sleep, and we're out of ibuprofen. How many headaches have you had?"

I jerked away from him. The psycho actually counted the ibuprofen tablets? Who the hell was I living with? "You're not my brother."

"You're right." He flinched as if I'd just smacked him, and then a smile brightened his features. "I'm your pretend boyfriend, so you may as well go out with me. Hell, I'm even willing to face the wrath of Jax in order to get that smile back on your face."

"You forget, I've been living with you. I'm immune to your charms." I was such a liar, but it was all I had, he clearly saw all the little things I'd been trying to hide. The headaches, the exhaustion, the dark circles under my eyes. It was bad enough that Jax was suspicious, but Miller wasn't even supposed to know me that well.

"Clock's ticking, Waffle, go change."

I looked down at my athletic shorts and Nike shoes. "What's wrong with what I'm wearing?"

"I can see you're going to be difficult." He tossed me over his shoulder, carrying me into the guest bedroom and depositing me on the mattress. I bounced up, my head nearly connecting with his chin while he rummaged through one of my bags. Soon a pair of jeans was sailing by my head, followed by one of my favorite tops, how did he even know that? Was it a coincidence? He found a pair of Gucci boots and added them to the pile of crap getting thrown in my direction. He paused and then walked over to the dresser where I kept my jewelry. His massive hand grabbed something and then he was walking over to me.

With a sigh, he grabbed my hand and pressed a pair of diamond studs into the palm. The studs my dad had given me when I graduated college. The same ones I hadn't worn for two weeks, out of fear, irrational anger, sadness.

"You have two minutes."

He shut the door behind him.

And rather than give him attitude or argue, I stood on wobbly feet, and changed.

Chapter Sixteen

MILLER

She was killing me.

It wasn't a swift death either.

Kins represented everything I swore to myself I'd never repeat. Like becoming friends with a girl who I could potentially fall for, and somehow, after that first night, when I heard her cry herself to sleep, I'd gone and lost my damn mind.

It wasn't that I just cared.

If it was that simple, I'd just give her a shoulder to cry on when she asked.

No, it was worse.

Somehow, every little quirk about her had my body on high alert; the first time I'd taken a shower after her I'd nearly banged my head through the wall. Lavender and coconut nearly choked me to death, and every day since that first fateful shower, my shower time more than doubled, for obvious reasons, just thinking about her had me ready to excuse myself from the room.

I could take her yelling.

I could take her crying herself to sleep.

What I couldn't take? The emptiness on her face. Kinsey was a strong woman, who'd suddenly lost something, I just didn't know what. Why was she so haunted?

All I knew is that Jax kept her father's sickness from her until it was too late. He took time from her.

Time.

Fuck.

I knew the feeling all too well.

It was all we had.

I never had more time with my mom.

And it still traumatized me that she was ripped away before I could have one last meal with her, one last smile.

I shivered.

"So." Kins's perfume was going to be the death of me. I swerved the car by accident and nearly hit a pedestrian while I tried to shift my weight to my left leg, all in the vain effort of shielding her from the fact that I was so turned on I had double vision. The friction from the tight jeans I was wearing really did me no favors, damn jeans. "Where we going?"

"On a date." I smiled at her discomfort.

"Right, but you said you were getting ready for a date."

"I was."

"So who are we meeting?"

"You'll see." I turned the car into the hospital parking lot and parked. "Just try to have a good attitude, and don't yell."

"Don't yell?" She frowned harder. "Why the hell are we at a hospital?"

"Hey, wanna grab the jerseys from the trunk?" I ignored her on purpose. "I need to send a quick text."

She grumbled something about making her do all the work, and grabbed the box from the back of the car.

I took it from her once I sent a text to Jax and urged her forward. "Hurry, we're late."

"Late for what?"

"I told you already."

"No, all you keep saying is *date*," she hissed at me before the hospital doors slid open. The lobby was decorated in our team colors and a few of the hospital staff had their cameras out.

One of the nurses waved me over. "Everyone is on the second-level lobby. Just take the elevator up and take a right." She smiled warmly at me and then at Kins. "You look familiar."

Kins straightened and held out her hand. "I'm one of the Bucks cheerleaders."

"Your girlfriend?" the nurse asked with a nice smile.

"Yup," I said before Kins could ruin everything and scowl, technically it was one of our first official outings, and now that the preseason was in full swing, it just meant she was going to have to suck it up and play nice so Jax could focus on all the other shit he had running through his head, including the fact that Harley's grandmother had somehow snatched his number and wouldn't stop texting him selfies.

"Come on." I nodded toward the elevators.

"Have fun!" the nurse called after us.

Kins gave me a confused look. "Seriously, what's going on?"

"Can you press the second floor?"

The elevator doors closed. We waited in silence while music trickled on, and when the doors opened, it was to complete and utter madness.

"Bellevue Bucks First Annual Homecoming Dance Party!" The banner was in black and white and a few teammates were dancing around with high school students, most of them in fancy dresses and tuxes.

And all of them with some sort of terminal illness that was slowly killing them or making it impossible to attend their own homecoming. It had been Jax's idea, and the rest of us had run with it.

I knew something was wrong the minute Kins stepped off the elevator. Her movements were jerky, her hands shaky, her skin pale.

"Kins?" I dropped the box onto the floor and pulled her into my arms. "What's wrong?"

She raised a shaky hand to her tear-filled eyes. "Did you organize this?"

"No, that would be me." Jax's voice filled the air.

She stiffened, and then suddenly threw her arms around her brother like she hadn't seen him in years. "Thank you."

"I figured it was the only way to make it up to you."

She cried against his chest.

And I stood there dumbfounded. Sure, it was Jax's idea, but I was the one that brought Kinsey in the first place. He'd been convinced she wouldn't come on her own.

"I can't believe it." She sniffled. "Thank you, Jax, just . . . thank you."

She turned around and hugged me just as tightly as she'd just hugged him, then kissed my cheek. "I know you think I'm crazy, but this is everything to me, thanks for forcing me out of the house and . . ." Her voice lowered. "I'm sorry for yelling. And about the towel, and for using your toothbrush."

I glared. "My toothbrush? What is it with you and breaking rules?"

"What is it with you and having them?" she argued. "Plus, I couldn't find mine that first night."

Jax was watching us closely, waiting for a reason to hit me, no doubt. I leaned forward and whispered, "It's okay, at least I got you in my mouth, right?"

Kins made a choking sound before coughing and then giving her head a shake.

"Hmm, I may dream about that tonight."

"Jax is watching."

"I don't give a fuck," I growled, suddenly realizing that I didn't. I pulled her into my arms and kissed her, kissed her like I owned her, kissed her like it was real, kissed her because I was so damn happy to see her smile that I felt light-headed. I deepened the kiss to the hoots and hollers of my teammates and wasn't pulled away from her like I expected, instead, I stopped and stepped back.

Jax's jaw pulsed.

His nostrils flared.

But he couldn't do shit.

Because I was doing exactly what he'd asked.

Dating his sister, right?

I gave him a wave.

He flipped me off.

Meanwhile, Anderson watched us from the other side of the room, his smile crude, his body language pissed.

I was making a lot of friends that day.

"Why does this mean so much to you?" I asked her once we started unpacking the jerseys from the box on the floor. "I mean I think it's killer, but why does it matter to you?"

Her hands froze on the jerseys then started to shake again. "Let's not talk about the past right now, are you okay with that?"

"Since my past is probably more fucked up than yours, absolutely."

"I wouldn't wager that," she whispered before folding another shirt across the box and handing me a pen.

"Are you trying to make me curious on purpose?"

"Maybe." She shrugged. "Thanks for taking me, by the way."

"Kins." I couldn't stop myself, although I tried. The kiss was making me lose my mind and say shit that would end up biting me in the ass, but I literally couldn't stop the next few words from falling from my mouth. "Let me kiss you again."

"No."

"Let me take you to dinner."

She smirked.

"No."

"Let me get you naked."

"No."

"I'll wear you down one day."

"And send me packing the next?" She arched her eyebrows.

"Biggest mistake of my life," I said honestly. "One dinner."

She gulped. Not meeting my eyes.

"One harmless dinner."

"It's not just one dinner."

"No, probably not."

"You're not harmless."

"Definitely not."

"You're not safe."

A smile spread across my face. "If you wanted safe, you should have fake dated one of the rookies still scared shitless of your brother."

"Hah." She shook her head sadly. "I'm not worth it, Miller. Find some other girl for a one-night stand."

"I didn't say I wanted a one-night stand."

"Wow, changing your spots?"

I gripped her hand; she tried to jerk it away. "What if I want two? Maybe three? What if I want four?"

"Then I'd say you're greedy."

"When it comes to you?" I growled, pulling her to her feet. "Yes."

Everyone was dancing around us but it felt like we were alone. Jax had since walked to the other side of the room. I backed Kinsey up against one of the walls, a potted plant guarded us, but not by much.

"I'll just keep asking."

"I'm not ready to move back in with my brother," she huffed. "And if we complicate things, and it goes bad, which it will, what happens then?"

"So take a risk."

"You're asking me to trust you?"

"No." I shook my head bitterly. "In every area of your life, your safety, your happiness, your health—you can trust me. Just don't give me your heart, not when I'm not even sure I still have mine."

She snorted. "So it's going to be about just sex."

"Distraction from your dad, distraction from Jax, let's call it a mutual distraction between really good friends . . . the best of friends." I kissed her temple then snaked my hand around her rib cage, lightly tickling her skin with my fingers as I raised her shirt, my knuckles grazing her belly button as I went higher and higher until I cupped her breast. She sucked in a breath, and I moved my hand back down her stomach until I came into contact with the front of her jeans.

"What are you doing?" she hissed.

"Nothing," I whispered against her ear, kissing the hollow of her neck while my hand cupped her and then lifted her hips onto my leg, bracing it against the wall. I moved just enough for her to buck against my leg, and press her hands on my chest. "Nothing at all. You get to decide what happens."

She huffed out a curse and pressed down on my leg again. "You're a very bad friend."

"I'm the best damn friend in this room." I kept peppering light kisses against her mouth. "Come on, Waffle, time for the syrup."

"Bad." She rode me slow, she rode my leg hard, I imagined pulsing inside her, the walls of her body squeezing me into a slow painful death. "This is . . . so inappropriate."

"You drive a man to want a hell of a lot of inappropriate, Kins. You've been driving me fucking crazy for two weeks. And since it's all about your terms, I'm giving you the keys—you know you like to drive—so give yourself a ride, sweetheart . . . take it."

I gripped her hips and guided her just enough so she could get a rhythm, then slowly scooted us into the shadow behind the plant and the chair to my right. We were hidden, but not enough that we couldn't get caught.

"I need . . ." She let out a little moan and punched me in the chest, and then gave her head a shake and started mauling me with her mouth.

I grabbed her hips, slamming her tight little body against mine, and she climbed all over me, her body meeting my thrusts like we were two horny teenagers skipping class.

It felt so good, I was seconds away from getting her naked against the wall. She slowed her movements, arching against my leg, then pressed her palm to my dick; the touch set me off so hard that I drew blood against my bottom lip.

"I can't decide," she whispered, "what I like more." She moved harder, I was so close and I had all of my clothes on. The hell? "If I like riding more—" One last thrust against my thigh. "Or—" Her hand rubbed against me, up and down, I went blind in both eyes, nearly saw my soul leave my body, and begged her not to stop. "Or—" She slid her hand in my jeans. Dead. I was dead. "Driving?" One last squeeze.

I exploded.

Welcomed insanity with open arms.

Crushed my mouth to hers.

And made a decision.

One that I had no business making.

"You're mine," I growled against her mouth, my teeth nipping her bottom lip. "Say it."

"Yes."

Chapter Seventeen

Jax

I felt lost without my other half.

Food didn't taste good.

My apartment was lonely as shit.

Harley still texted me.

But I was a shit human being, because after that night, I'd sent her a text saying I wasn't sure things were going to work out between us.

Since then I'd been the happy recipient of her grandmother's selfies. I was pretty confident that she purposefully gave her horny grandmother my number in an effort to get even for kicking her to the curb after sleeping with her. Oh, right, left out that part.

Completely and totally, used her in a way that made me cringe, and why? Because I'd been pissed.

And felt so out of control that when she'd suggested we get out of there, I'd driven straight to my empty apartment, opened a bottle of Jack, and set down shot glasses.

We were four shots in when the stripping started. It only went downhill from there.

(Then)

"You wear Superman underwear," I said dumbly while she did a little twirl in her plain black sports bra and comic-book underwear. Her socks had tiny four-leaf clovers on them. She had a tattoo on the right side of her leg in the shape of a tree. I wanted to lick it to see if it tasted as good as it looked.

"Go ahead," she taunted.

"Fuck, did I say that out loud?" I groaned, covering my face with my hands. "I don't drink. Ever. Especially not days before practice."

"Eh." She tipped her shot glass back, even her throat was pretty as it worked that Jack down, damn. "It seems to me that you need to let loose a little, especially after all that yelling, so go ahead, lick the tattoo, I won't judge you. And I won't tell Grandma."

I snorted out a laugh. "You normally tell your grandma about all your sexual encounters?"

"Why, Jax Romonov . . . is this turning sexual? Oh, hell!" She covered her face with her hands, laughter rolling off her. "Are you blushing?"

I stiffened. "Are you making fun of me?"

"You still blush." She sauntered over to me, kissed my left cheek then my right, and then sucked on my chin with her lips before pulling back. "Mmmm, blush tastes good on a quarterback . . . you a virgin too?"

"No." Two women. I'd had sex with two women. The first one broke my heart. The second broke my trust. "And there's nothing wrong with deciding not to sleep my way through my football career."

"Absolutely not." She twirled in front of me, her red hair whipping around her creamy skin, getting caught in her bra and around her shoulders. She was like this brazen little elf, a vixen, she was torture. "But, it couldn't hurt to live, maybe just tonight."

"With you," I finished for her. "You think Grandma would approve?"

"I think she would have already stripped." Harley laughed then lifted her leg to the counter. "I got this tattoo when my parents died. Grandma took me in right away. I can't find it in my heart to leave her. She's . . .

everything." The tattoo was an intricate tree design, haunting, I'd never seen anything so beautiful.

I gripped her calf, ran my hand up her skin, and then bent over, sliding my tongue up the trunk of the tree, kissing beneath her knee before gripping her ass and lifting her into the air, helping her wrap her legs around my waist as I slanted my mouth against hers. She gripped my hair with her hands like she was holding on for dear life, and when I broke off the kiss she was blushing.

I grinned. "Harley, are you . . . are you blushing? Girls still blush? What? Are you . . ." I whispered roughly against her mouth, my stubble rubbing her perfect skin, "a virgin?"

"With you?" She pressed her breasts against my chest. "Yeah, kinda feels like it . . . remember, I look tough on the outside, I'm all soft on the inside."

"Holy fuck, you're an M&M!" I laughed so hard I had tears in my eyes. Then I kissed her again, this time tasting her mouth, memorizing her. "Those are my favorite."

"Oh?" Breathless, she clung to me harder. "What's your favorite flavored color?"

"Where have you been all my life?" I whispered hoarsely. "You're the only person who gets that the colors mean flavors."

She shrugged. "Can't help stupid people."

"Yesterday . . ." I walked her down the hall. "Yesterday, if you would have asked me that question I would have said brown."

"And now?" She slid down my body, then tugged my hand as we walked into the master bedroom. "Now what's your answer?"

I picked up a piece of her hair, twirled it around my fingers, then jerked her against me. "Red. I'd say red."

"Good answer." She licked my bottom lip. "Good answers get rewards."

I let out a groan as I tugged her bra off and tossed it in the corner. Soon my pants were gone, the Superman underwear went flying toward the dresser, and I had the most beautiful woman I'd ever seen beneath me panting my name like a prayer.

"I don't do this," I confessed.

"Good." She gulped as fear crept into her face. "Neither do I. I mean, I live with my grandma."

"Let's leave her out of the bedroom, ya?" I chuckled, nuzzling her neck, licking all the places I could find, hungry for the ones that I couldn't. "God, you taste good."

"Remind me next time to soak in candy-flavored body wash."

I groaned. "Stop teasing me."

"Okay." She shrugged, and kissed me so hard I forgot why I was sad. Why I was angry.

I forgot about self-control.

I forgot about my image.

I forgot about my dad.

I forgot about Kinsey.

I forgot a condom.

I shook the memory away and sent Harley another text, another apology for being an asshole.

And got a middle-finger emoji back.

It wasn't the sex that had done it.

It was the fact that when I woke up, I panicked, I told her it was fun, and I literally left her alone in my apartment to go work out. Oh, I pointed out where the towels were and told her she could hang out, but I also managed to let her know just how busy I'd be that day.

I was a complete dick.

A terrified, chickenshit dick.

"Hey." Sanchez smacked me on the shoulder. "You seen Miller?"

"No." I scowled. "Though if he kisses my sister like that again in public, I'm removing his head from his body."

Sanchez moved his hand. "No offense, but Miller's a good guy. So he gets to see her naked, it's not like you're perfect." He smirked as if waiting for me to deny it. "Right?"

I glared. "What the hell do you know that I don't?"

"Oh, you mean about . . . a certain girl named Harley?"

"Out with it," I snapped.

"Nah, I think I'm going to hold on to it a bit longer, but I do have one question . . ."

"I don't even want to know." I fought the urge to groan into my hands.

"When you did that thing with your mouth." Yeah, I was going to physically injure him. "And you know, the tongue move, you get so deep—"

"I'm out." I walked away backward and went in search of Kinsey. We had shit to talk about, and now that she was finally speaking to me, I had a lot to say.

Chapter Eighteen

KINSEY

I avoided my brother like salt before a big game.

And this time it wasn't because I was pissed.

It was because his best friend, the one that I was starting to really favor, had given me an orgasm behind a potted plant with nothing but his thigh and a heck of a lot of enthusiasm on my part.

I was a hussy.

And yet, every time I tried to find the guilt, it wasn't there. Trust me, I searched for it. In my brain I was on my hands and knees looking underneath every object, opening every folder that said *whore* or *slut*, and nothing.

Maybe it was because he didn't walk away this time.

He righted my hair.

He kissed my bruised lips.

And then slowly, lowered my feet to the floor, but not before placing an open kiss against my neck and whispering, "Remember whose you are."

"Yours?" I'd responded.

"You're also yours, Kins." He'd winked, grabbed my hand, and led me toward the punch and said I should cool off.

Right, like Kool-Aid was going to really help me not melt into my clothes and fling them in his face while I beg for round two.

My treacherous body shivered at the actual thought.

What was I doing?

This wasn't me.

It wasn't.

He made me want to be bad.

And after Anderson, I'd sworn to myself that when I was with another guy it would be on my terms, it would be because he loved me, because he cared. Yeah, and look how that turned out! I'd jumped into bed with the next football player on the roster and gotten burned.

Sanchez literally popped up out of nowhere, making me spill my juice all over the floor. I barely missed my black Gucci boots. "You need to fix your face."

"Gee, thanks, Sanchez, nice to see you too," I said in a singsong yet annoyed voice as people danced around us.

He gave my elbow a little tug and then suddenly the most arrogant wide receiver I'd ever met in my entire life was handing me a napkin and pointing to my mouth. "Seriously, Kins, I'm not trying to be a dick, but you have Miller all over you."

"Huh?"

"Lip gloss . . . a guy notices these things. Hell, it's on your nose, Kins. What did the guy do to you?"

Heat flooded my cheeks.

"Shit, guess that's my answer." He shook with laughter. "Girl, you have lip junk in your ear, your *ear*!" He howled louder, slapping my shoulder with one of his bear-paw hands. "Oh, this is great. You're so lucky I found you before Jax. He's been looking for you for the past hour."

"I've been walking around like this for an hour?" I screeched.

"Maybe Miller wanted to make his mark, and since peeing on you isn't really all that attractive, he decided to spread your lip gloss into every crevice." Sanchez's eyes narrowed. "Never mind, I don't want to know."

"You don't." I wiped my ear and turned to him. "Okay, how do I look now?"

His eyebrows shot up.

"That bad?"

"That bad? Or if you're Miller, just that good. I wouldn't worry about it too much though, I mean Jax is encouraging this, right?" His eyes narrowed.

I coughed. "Of course. His idea."

"And there it is." He crossed his arms. "Why would it be his idea, Kins?"

"Uhhhh." I started backing away and nearly collided with another male body.

I knew it was Anderson by the spicy cologne. It still made me gag when I smelled it. I stumbled toward Sanchez and clung to him like he was my only lifeline. Thankfully, since Em had tamed him a bit, rather than shoving me into the punch bowl like the jackass he typically was, he put a protective arm around my shoulder.

Anderson looked confused. "A bit possessive of your girl's best friend, Sanchez."

"A bit stupid for football, eh, Anderson?"

I bit my lip to keep from laughing.

The guy literally had no fans.

I just hoped to God that once practice was in full swing, he'd show his true colors to the coaching staff and get kicked to the curb. He was out for money, recognition. He was out for himself, which was sad, because he did have raw talent, he just wanted himself more than the team.

"Everything okay?" Miller's voice interrupted Anderson and Sanchez's tense stare down.

Sanchez turned to Miller. "Yeah, just telling Anderson how great it is for him to make it down to the hospital for such a killer cause, right, Anderson?"

"Whatever." Anderson marched off, clearly pissed. I exhaled a sigh of relief while Sanchez released me into Miller's arms.

"Jax's idea . . ." Sanchez put a finger to his mouth and then grinned. "Hmm, I think I understand." With that, he walked off and left me in Miller's embrace.

"Do you think he knows?" I whispered.

"Does it matter?" He turned me around in his arms. "In the grand scheme of things, who the hell cares what anyone thinks?"

I nodded and then it was like I was brought back to an hour ago when his mouth was sucking the life out of mine, when his hands roamed my body like he owned me, when I gripped him like a lifeline.

"Stop," Miller hissed. "I really don't have as much self-control as you think I do. Living with you for the past two weeks has been absolute torture, and you're making it worse when you look at me like you want me to—" He cut himself off and swore. "Look at me like that when we're home."

"Home," I repeated.

He nodded, just as Jax made his way over, his face pale. "I, uh, you guys good here? I need to be somewhere."

I frowned and then panic set in. "Is it Dad? Is he okay?"

He sighed. "Yeah, it's not Dad, I swear I won't ever do that to you again, okay? It's just . . . don't worry." His easy smile was back. "Everything's fine. I just forgot I needed to be somewhere, and I feel bad leaving since I'm one of the main organizers."

"We got you." Miller held out his fist. "No worries, man."

"Thanks." His shoulders sagged with relief. "Kins, we need to talk but . . ." He swallowed and looked at his phone. "Look, I'll call you or stop by, what hotel are you at? Mom and Dad never told me."

Miller looked down at me with a smirk. "Yeah, Kins, what hotel was it?" He snapped his fingers. "Shit, it's slipping my mind."

I cursed him and kicked him in the nuts, all in my head, of course, before I grinned at my brother and stuttered out, "Kimpton Hotel, the one downtown on the pier."

"The Alexis." Miller added, "I remember now, sorry, too many hits to the head."

I itched to stomp on his foot.

"Cool." Jax nodded. "I'll try to stop by tonight, alright?"

"Awesome." I waved him off.

Once he was out of eyesight I smacked Miller in the chest. "What the hell was that?"

"You didn't tell him!" he said at the exact same time.

"You notice all the small things and yet don't see all the reasons why I wouldn't randomly text my brother and say, oh, by the way, I'm shacking up with one of your best friends!"

"Funny, because I thought shacking up included sex." Miller grinned that stupid sexy grin that had me fighting between scratching his eyes out and climbing him like a tree and squeezing my legs around his thighs and—

Miller growled, "Damn it, I told you, not in public." He swore and ran a hand over his buzzed hair.

"Sorry!" I held up my hands. "And I thought you'd be happy I didn't tell him! You're alive! You're welcome!"

He sent me a glare. "Fine. Let's help with cleanup and then we'll go get a room."

"We?" I repeated. "What's this *we* business?"

"Teammates." He pointed between the two of us. "Friends. Remember?"

I crossed my arms. "Most of my friends don't seduce me behind potted plants."

"That's why I'm your best friend." His eyes crinkled, as a cocky side smile gave me plenty of things to fantasize about for the next ten years of my life. "And I'm not letting you check into a hotel by yourself."

"You're not letting me?"

He groaned. "You know what I mean."

"No," I seethed. "I don't! You don't get to take Jax's place as the overprotective crazy person who doesn't let me have an opinion about everything because he's so damn afraid that I'm going to—" I gulped.

Miller froze.

"Hey, can I have your autograph?" A small boy on crutches limped over to Miller. He had no hair on his head and one of the biggest smiles I'd ever seen in my entire life.

Miller smiled down at him. "Wow, man, that's some cast, you must have been playing super hard, yeah?"

The kid nodded. "My mama says it's because my bones are sick. I played football all last year but got injured lots so I had to come stay at the hospital." He crooked his finger. "I'm not supposed to be at the party but one of the nurses said she thought it would be okay."

Miller smiled brightly and pointed a few feet behind him. "Is that her right there?"

The boy turned around and then nodded back at Miller. "Yes sir, she told me so, but she had to bring me down here because I'm little."

"Little!" Miller gasped in shock. "No, I don't see a little boy in front of me"—he leaned in—"I see a man."

"You do?" The boy's eyes widened. "Well, I have been walking lots lately with my crutches."

He showed both crutches to Miller and hobbled on his good leg.

"Impressive." Miller examined both crutches like they were the most precious thing he'd ever seen. "I bet you can go real fast on those things."

"So fast." The boy giggled.

"What's your name?" Miller asked.

"Marcus, but my friends call me Marco."

"Wow, that's a pretty cool name."

Marco shrugged and blushed.

"Why don't we have my girlfriend, Kinsey, go over and grab you a jersey while I sign these crutches?"

"Whoa!" Marco nodded eagerly. "That would be boss, Mr. Miller!"

My eyes welled with tears as I quickly ran over to the box of jerseys, grabbed one, as well as a football, and ran back over to them.

Marco was whispering something in Miller's ear by the time I returned, and for some reason the look on Miller's face nearly broke my heart.

"Marco, I'm going to tell you something really important, and I want you to remember it for a long time, okay?"

With rapt attention, Marco waited.

"Sometimes, in life, you fall down, you get hit, sometimes you have hard days, days that make you want to quit . . . sometimes your body makes you think it's time to quit." He gulped. "But never forget about your heart." He tapped Marco's chest lightly with his finger. "The heart is strong. The heart can convince the body of anything. It can convince your mind of anything. Your heart allows you to be whatever you want to be, you just have to trust it."

"I do, Mr. Miller, I trust my heart."

"And what does your heart say?"

"Well, when I get hooked up to machines it makes a beeping sound."

"Whoa!" Miller pressed a hand to Marco's chest. "Does it thump, thump, thump, like this?"

"Yes!" Marco giggled. "Just like that! What do you think that means?"

"It means you've got the strength of a lion." Miller grinned. "That's your heart telling the rest of your body that it's okay, that's the way the heart tells you that it's fighting. That thump, thump is the heart's war cry. Don't you want to be a warrior, Marco?"

He nodded. "I want to be like you."

My heart squeezed, I had to look away so they wouldn't see my tears.

"Nah, Marco, don't be like me . . . be better. Think you can do that?"

"I can try!"

The nurse walked over. "We should head back up, Marco. You've been on that leg a while now."

She mouthed a *"thank you"* to Miller, and tears filled her eyes as Marco launched himself into Miller's arms and wrapped his scrawny arms around his neck.

When they were a safe distance away, I gripped Miller's hand and whispered, "What did he ask you?"

Miller's voice was hoarse when he replied. "He asked me if he was going to die."

Chapter Nineteen

MILLER

The kid's face reminded me of mine when I lost my mom. His eyes—they were so sad, and for him to ask a complete stranger, one he looked up to, if he was going to make it? God, it almost killed me.

It brought back memories of not wanting to live—of wanting to go to sleep and never wake up so I could be with my mom. But then I'd go to practice and remember all the games she went to and all the times she supported me—and I went on. Because of her. Because football wasn't just a distraction anymore, no, it had turned into this need—because when I played I was closer to her. My mom's death taught me that the future was never certain.

To see a little boy with that same look.

At his age.

Damn, the kid needed hope, just like I'd needed football.

Pain slashed through me.

Raw.

Pain.

The emptiness of losing my mom.

And then Emerson.

The pain of losing our child that I hadn't even known existed.

Physical pain I could deal with, but emotional pain? Sometimes I wasn't sure I was equipped to handle it, I sure as hell didn't handle it well. All I had to do was take one look at Kinsey and it was obvious that I wasn't a fan of putting myself in any position to feel anything like loving and losing again.

And yet.

I was currently checking us both into a hotel.

Separate rooms.

That had an adjoining door, because for some reason the idea of her being by herself at any point while she went through her father's illness made me sick to my stomach.

"Home sweet home!" I tossed one of my bags onto the bed and walked into the adjoining room, where Kinsey was busy tossing her stuff all over the room so it looked like she'd been staying there for more than ten minutes.

"How does it look?" She crossed her arms and examined her handi-work. Shoes were piled in the corner, clothes hung off one of the chairs, and a bra was strategically placed on the TV. Nice.

"It looks like a tornado swept through and decided to strip your clothes just so I could see you naked one more time before your brother ruins my life." I shrugged. "So yeah, pretty good."

She sighed. *"Good."*

"The bra's a nice touch." I picked it up and closed my eyes, then purposefully moaned a few times before she snatched it out of my hands and swatted me with it.

"This isn't playtime! I have to focus. You know, that whole keeping-you-alive thing."

"We're adults," I pointed out. "Do you really think he'd be pissed enough to kill me? Honestly?"

She froze, dropped the bra on the bed, and hung her head, her dark hair spilling over one shoulder while she visibly trembled. "Yeah. I do. You're a football player."

"So he'd be more pissed about me being a football player? That makes no sense. Kins, you're old enough to make your own decisions."

She lifted that one shoulder, as more hair spilled back. "Yeah, I know that. He even knows that. He just . . . he doesn't want to see me hurt."

"Do you think I'd hurt you?" It was out before I could stop it.

She turned around, her eyes sad. "You already did."

"And you think I'm dumb enough to repeat the mistake?"

"It has nothing to do with brain cells, Miller, otherwise you would have already been out of the running." She winked. "It has everything to do with your ability to move past whatever you need to move past. You're the one that said you aren't even sure you have possession of your own heart, that's not really the kind of risk most girls want to take. I mean you're basically telling me that you're unable to commit, and sorry to break it to you, but most girls want commitment."

I nodded, unhappy with the direction of the conversation, and desperately needing to do something about it, like kiss all the doubt from her mouth and get her naked.

We would be good together.

More than good.

I was at war with myself, wanting to prove to her how good it could be while simultaneously telling myself that it could be bad, there were too many uncontrollable factors.

"Damn it, Kins." I groaned, tired of my own thought process. "What if I want to try?"

"What if *try* isn't good enough?" she fired back.

A knock sounded on the door. I froze. She froze.

I ran to the adjoining door for my room. Locked. Shit. I'd forgotten my key.

"Kins!" Jax's voice sounded. "It's me, do you have someone in there?"

"No!" Kins yelled, "I, uh, it's um . . . TV is so loud, hold on!"

She shoved me into the bathroom and then hissed, "Get in the shower."

"You've got to be kidding me," I muttered. "Kins, this is ridiculous."

"Get in!" Tears welled in her eyes. "Please?"

Tears were my downfall, especially when they came from a girl so strong, a girl who rarely let people see the tender side of her. I'd known her over a year and every day she impressed me with her strength. "Can't believe I'm hiding in the bathroom from your brother," I muttered, stepping in the tub and pulling the curtain across to shield myself. "If he comes in here for any reason other than taking a piss, I'm out!"

"Fine!" The door slammed after her as she ran out of the bathroom and said a bit too loudly, "Jax!"

"Why are you yelling my name?" He sounded amused. "I mean, the yelling I expected, but you seem genuinely excited to chat."

"Well, I am." She giggled.

Ah, hell, we were screwed. The worst liar in the history of liars was trying to bullshit a guy who read body language for a living. Great.

"You sure you're okay?" Jax asked, concern laced in his voice. "Are you taking all your medication and getting enough sleep?"

Medication? The hell? What kind of medication was she taking? And why, after two weeks of basically living with her, had I not clued in on it? Angry, I clenched the curtain with my fingers, ready to jerk it off the damn rail.

"I'm not stupid," she said in a harsh voice. "Okay, speak."

"I'm sorry," he blurted.

My eyebrows shot up—color me impressed, two apologies in one day. I released the curtain and hunkered down in the tub. I tried to get comfortable, but my body was so massive that I had to hug my knees to even fit, let alone sit in the small space without accidently hanging myself by the same curtain I'd just been mutilating.

"I know you are." Her voice was sad. "I know you've been stressed. I just . . ." Another sigh. Damn it, I needed to get closer. "You can't fix everything. You can't save everyone."

He was quiet.

"Jax, you know that, right? You aren't Captain America."

"But that's just it. I've always been able to fix things. I've always been your hero, just like Dad, and I failed. I honestly thought getting you away from everything would help, that if you got sick you'd never forgive me."

Sick?

Like the flu? A prickling sensation pinged the back of my neck as I waited for more information.

I kept listening. Even though something told me I shouldn't.

"Let's focus on Dad. On us. Not the past."

The same damn thing she'd said to me.

What the hell was so horrible about her past? Other than Anderson?

"Just like that?" He didn't sound convinced. Hell, I wasn't convinced. Push her, man! Make her talk! Open up! You're an NFL quarterback, for shit's sake! Man up!

"Jax . . ."

"Right." His voice softened, and maybe it was my imagination, but he sounded terrified. "I know we both have practice tomorrow so I'll be around if Anderson gives you shit . . ." He sighed. "I noticed things are going great with Miller. Too great, if you ask me. Mind telling me why he keeps kissing you?"

"Because I'm irresistible."

I smirked at her teasing tone. Damn right she was.

I barely held my laugh in when he cursed. God, just thinking about her writhing against me had me ready to turn on the cold water and let it hit me for a good ten minutes.

"You swore you'd never date a football player after Anderson." Interesting. "You love football, hate the players." Well, damn. "Anderson tried to break your spirit, Kins. I know Miller is different, but remember, this whole fake-dating scenario is to keep you safe. This isn't . . . it's not real, Kins."

Cock-blocking son of a bitch.

"I know." Her voice was small. I hated that defeated tone. "I know that, okay?"

"Miller's a good guy." That was better. "But he's young." The hell? I was of legal drinking age and had been forced to grow up more than pricks twice my age! "He's still not over Em."

I was going to kill him.

With my bare hands.

"Oh." Her answer as she cleared her throat.

I was so tempted to launch myself out of that tub that my fingers went numb clenching the ceramic.

"They had a history, you know that."

"I know."

God, he was just making it worse.

"He's a good actor."

Maybe I'd just run him over with my car instead? The idea had merit. Bare hands, I needed hands to catch balls.

"Look, it's best you know. The only reason I chose him is because I know that he won't touch you when he's still torn up over the past, and maybe he thinks he's fine, but I truly don't think he's had closure in that relationship. And to bring you into the middle of it would be pretty shitty. So yeah, I trust him not to hurt you, because I don't think he's enough of an asshole to do something like sleep with you and then bail."

She sucked in a breath.

Blood roared in my ears.

Pounded through my veins.

I squeezed my eyes shut and muttered a curse while a deafening silence spread out for what felt like an eternity.

"You're right," she whispered in a small voice. "I don't know what I was thinking . . . I just . . . got caught up." No! I was so damn tempted to run out of the bathroom, to explain everything to her, to him, to ask for her forgiveness even when I didn't deserve it.

"You're beautiful," Jax said with a hint of agony in his voice. "Look, when the season's in full swing and we know what kind of battle we'll have with Anderson playing—we should maybe . . . I don't know, find you a guy worth dating."

I was that guy, damn it.

Me.

Not some faceless dick who wanted to taste what was mine. A primitive growl rose from my throat.

"Sure." Kinsey actually agreed? The hell! "Miller and I will just lay low until then."

"It's for the best," Jax said in a hollow voice. "Especially if you're developing feelings for him, Kins. That won't end well."

I was going to murder the son of a bitch with my bare hands. He didn't know shit about me. He just thought he did. Micromanaging pain in my ass!

Even if he was right.

No.

I shoved the thought away.

I was completely over Em.

We'd had closure. The only reason she was still in my life was because we'd been best friends—still were, to an extent. But now that she had Sanchez, I'd done the only thing that made sense. I'd bowed out in order to give them time.

How the hell did that make me the bad guy?

"You look pale," Kinsey pointed out. "Everything okay, Jax?"

"You mean other than the fact that Dad's dying, Anderson's a pain in my ass, and Miller had his tongue down your throat earlier? Nope, can't think of a thing!"

"Well, when you put it that way . . ." She sighed. They both fell silent again. I strained to hear anything—even just her breathing would have been nice. Instead, nothing.

"Love you, sis." Jax sighed. "You sure you don't want to come back to the apartment?"

"Soon." Like hell she was. "I have the room for a few more . . . days."

"Love you."

The door closed.

I kept sitting in the bathtub, thinking, wondering . . . when the curtain was jerked back I didn't need to ask what Kinsey was thinking, it was written all over her face.

Hurt.

Sadness.

Anger.

"No." It was the first word I was able to blurt.

She frowned, releasing the curtain and crossing her arms. "No? No, what?"

"You're not going on some sick blind date with a sociopath."

"Who says only sociopaths are attracted to me?"

I sneered.

She held up her hands. "Whatever, I'm tired."

"Kins, hold up." I nearly broke the towel rack in an effort to get out of the tub. By the time my massive body was freed, she was already out of the bathroom and back in the bedroom, turning on the TV and hugging a pillow on the bed.

With a sigh, I made my way over to her and sat.

She scooted over.

I followed.

With a huff she glared. "What do you want?"

"You," I whispered. "Just you."

She gulped, and looked down at the remote control, her fingers pale against the black and gray buttons. "No."

"Yes."

"No." A smile formed across her lips. "Just friends."

"Okay."

Her head jerked to attention.

I cupped her face with my hands and whispered across her lips, "Just friends it is."

The remote dropped from her hand onto the mattress and then she was straddling me, her small body writhing against mine like she'd been waiting years to taste my flavor on her tongue.

"I'm not sharing you," I murmured down her neck. "Not now, not ever. Tell him no."

She grinned, deepening the kiss. "You getting possessive?"

"Yes," I growled, my blood heating to a painful degree. "I am, tell Jax no."

"Or what?"

I spanked her on the ass with my right hand, a lingering sting slammed into my fingertips. "Sorry, I slipped."

Her eyes narrowed. "Slipped, my ass."

"It's a nice ass." I smacked it again.

She squealed and then tried to pin me to the bed. Amused, I gripped her hands in mine while she struggled for a good five minutes and then sagged against me.

"You tire yourself out, Kins?"

"You're huge."

"I know."

She slugged my shoulder. "Stop taking everything sexually."

I ground my hips against her. "Then stop encouraging me."

Kins's eyes dropped to my mouth. "Tell me something that's true . . ."

"I hate hippos."

"Something I can't google." She crossed her arms.

My eyes searched hers, they were always doing that, like they were trying to find reasons for my reaction to her. Because I had beautiful women surrounding me on a daily basis, but for some reason, this one, this off-limits little firecracker—had me. And I was powerless to stop my descent into hell, the fires licked my face, and still, I leaned forward, I stole kisses with the knowledge that it wouldn't end well. How could it? When I didn't know what the hell I was doing? How could it, when her brother would hate me forever?

"I can't take it back."

"Take what back?" She linked her fingers in mine, our palms pressed together while I drew another languid kiss from her mouth.

"Vegas," I whispered. "I'm not sorry. I won't take it back. I'd do it again, and again, and again. I can't decide if that makes me selfish or just very addicted to something that I know will end up being very hard to quit."

"My turn," Kinsey announced. She lowered her mouth to my ear and whispered, "I don't want you to quit me."

"I should."

"I know."

"More truth . . ." I hugged her close to me. "I don't want to hurt you."

"Then don't."

"You make it sound easy," I whispered with a ragged breath. My heart squeezed. God, I would do anything for her. It was terrifying. "Like breathing."

"Miller, that's how it should be. Have you ever thought that maybe the person making it hard—is you?"

I gulped and then licked my lips. "I want to change my first answer."

She frowned. "About the hippos?"

"I hate hippos, but my greatest fear is losing someone I care about, someone I love—having them one day and losing them the next. And it seems to be a thing with me, losing what's most important—and being the only one left behind."

There, I'd said it.

I'd never admitted that out loud.

I wasn't sure I wanted the words floating between us. In fact, I was pretty damn sure I wanted to pull them all back, suck them into my mouth, and hold my breath until I turned blue.

Kinsey locked eyes with me, and then very slowly, peeled off her T-shirt and tossed it to the side of the bed.

My breath hitched, I wasn't able to move, and it hurt like hell to breathe. "What are you doing?"

"Helping you conquer your fear," she whispered gruffly before taking my mouth in hers, tangling her hands in my shirt and jerking it off my head.

"It may take more than once." I flipped her onto her back.

She grinned up at me. "Good."

Chapter Twenty

I was breathtakingly aware of the way he kissed me, with a mix of urgency and tenderness, as if he was afraid that I was going to pull away, when five minutes into Jax's conversation with me I knew things were going to end this way.

It wasn't good-bye.

Not really.

It was a risk.

A risk that I wanted to take, because I liked him, because I was falling for the man that I saw beneath all of the football bullshit. He was more than he let people see, and sometimes it's easier to recognize hurt in other people when it reminds you of yourself.

I never told him about my ghosts.

My scars.

And I had to wonder, if he knew about them—would he be more willing to take a chance on what we could have—or would he push me away? Because the possibility was there, not in the scary way it had been before, but my health issues still lingered, and knowing Miller, the truth would be scarier than the lie I kept telling by way of omission.

I was his.

But for how long?

Until he found out about my past?

Until Jax found out about us?

Life is full of selfish choices.

Quinton Miller was mine.

And just like he said he wouldn't regret Vegas, I couldn't bring myself to regret kissing him, urging him on, begging for his friendship, his trust, his body, knowing full well that if he peeled back the layers of my soul he'd most likely tell me that it wasn't worth the risk.

That the odds weren't in my favor.

That he refused to hurt again.

I absorbed the feel of his rough hands as they roamed over my body, the taste of his plump lips as he moved his wicked mouth down my neck like his only goal was to taste every part of me in the most erotic way possible.

He closed his hands over my breasts then slid down the bra strap on my right shoulder, and his mouth kissed the expanse of skin. He did the same on the other side then locked eyes with me. He looked drunk, crazed.

"Tell me to stop." His gravelly voice sent chills down my spine. "Otherwise, I won't."

I gulped.

He didn't move.

I pulled my bra off all the way and tossed it to the side.

"Fuck." His eyes rolled to the back of his head and then he pressed a kiss between my breasts, resting his head against my chest for several heartbeats before pulling away and finding my mouth again.

His powerful body was enough to give me chills as his agile fingers dug into my hair, giving it a forceful tug before rough kisses nipped at my mouth, bruising me, marking me as his.

A hitch caught in my throat as he pressed a finger to my lips then dragged that same finger down the crevice between my breasts. He rested his palm against my belly button and grinned wolfishly up at me before tucking his hand into the back of my leggings and slowly tugging them down to my feet.

They joined my bra on the floor.

He braced my hips with his hands then slowly crawled up me, his face menacing, beautiful, full of promises, full of pleasure.

I gulped. I was out of my league with Quinton Miller.

A frisson of tension swept through my body as I gave him a come-hither grin.

He bit down on his lower lip, sucking it so hard it lost all color. "I can't stop staring."

"Then don't."

"You have goose bumps." He pointed to my arms and then pressed a kiss to my ribs. "I'm going to dream of this ass." He squeezed the skin with his fingers and then pressed an open-mouthed kiss to my stomach before biting down on my underwear and slowly peeling it down, his breath hot on my skin, making more goose bumps erupt all over my thighs.

I was completely bare to him.

Shivering.

And he was grinning like a wolf who'd just discovered an entire nest full of innocent little birds.

Hell, I was the bird.

I was Tweety Bird.

Did that make him a pussycat?

He licked his way down my thigh, making a trail of kisses that burned each time he breathed across my fevered skin.

"You're going slow." I gripped his shoulders with my hands. "Why?"

He stopped and blinked down at me. "Maybe because last time I didn't get to see all of you. Maybe because right now I know you're powerless to stop this thing that's happening between us, almost as powerless as I am to stop staring. Maybe . . ." He pressed a rough kiss to the arch of my foot before massaging it with his fingers, digging into the sore muscles like he had a master's degree in massage therapy. "Maybe I just want to savor you."

Tears filled my eyes. "You say things like that, and I may just get attached to you, Quinton Miller."

"That's kind of the point, Kinsey Romonov."

He'd never said my full name before.

Fear built up in my chest like a vise, squeezing it until I couldn't breathe. The secrets of my past were going to tumble forward . . . not today, nope, not today.

Today. I was just a girl.

With a guy.

A very sexy guy.

Who somehow knew every pressure point in my body, and knew how to manipulate every single angle so that I felt him everywhere. I felt him in the air, I felt him in the tension swirling between our heated bodies.

"Take off your jeans," I whispered.

"No."

A wisp of disappointment threatened to deflate my mood. "No?"

"No." He grinned. "I get naked, and this is all over before it even starts . . . Tell you what . . . you owe me two and then I'll take off my jeans."

"Two?" What? Dollars? Hugs? High fives?

He threw his head back and laughed. "Sometimes I wish you'd just say what you're thinking, I can feel your brain overloading."

"Two . . . what?"

"Guess."

"Kisses?"

"Hmmm." He drew two kisses from my mouth. "Tastes good, sounds good, but no, actually I was thinking something else, Kins."

"Two . . ." I swallowed slowly. "Hugs?"

A rumble started in his chest before he burst out laughing. "Tell me you're not serious."

I couldn't think. Not with him hovering over me, touching me. Being naked wasn't exactly on the agenda for the day.

His clever, masterful hands rested on my hips then slowly started inching toward my core. "Two."

"Two." I gulped.

He grinned.

"Two." I needed to stop repeating myself. An unbidden tightness built between my legs, the need to cross them, to run away, to lock myself in the bathroom.

"Orgasms." He shrugged. "I need two, Kins, and then just because I'm feeling generous, I'll give you one more . . . if you can take it."

"Ah, so you're a confident jackass in the bedroom?" I tried teasing away my fear.

He kissed my lips so hard that I gasped in his air, struggling to keep my grasp on reality. This was real, but was he? Was what was happening between us more than that? I hoped to God it was.

Because nobody ever talks about it.

The after.

The buildup toward sex is everything.

The act—relentless in its selfish pursuit of getting you to think about nothing but pleasure.

But the after?

The seconds that turn into minutes, that turn into hours.

What about the after?

Would he walk away?

Or stay?

"Stop thinking." He cupped me with one of his hands. "All you need to worry about is feeling."

"But—"

I arched in order to accept him.

And squeezed my eyes shut.

My thighs clenched around his hands; he used one to spread them open and worked me into such a frenzy that I thought I was going to lose my mind as my body sank against the cool sheets—on fire, I just needed release, to be free, to—excitement built within me as Miller's mouth met my ear, his tongue wet, his chuckle warm.

"Ready?"

"Huh?" Dizzy, I opened my eyes.

He didn't prepare me.

Maybe that was part of his plan.

A sensation I can only describe as perfection hit me so hard that I almost smacked my head against his, his fingers toyed, stretched, played like I was a football play he'd memorized with ease.

"That's one."

My brain refused to focus. One? One, what comes after one?

Me.

Two.

Wait.

I circled my hands around his neck as his brazen hands worked me into a fevered lunatic. I think I scratched him, agile fingers built more tension, and then I bit into his shoulder. He swore, and I started hyperventilating.

My cry of release wasn't pretty.

It was almost painful.

The sensation was so strong that I was disoriented, and then jeans went flying.

Number two almost killed me.

Three would be my end.

"Need to be inside you," he begged.

I nodded, not trusting my voice.

I reached for him, he reached for me, holding his body over mine while his lips bruised, ached, claimed.

He pulled back, watching my face.

And because I was worried, because he'd seen too much, I tried to close my eyes.

"Kins," he pleaded, "look at me."

He pressed my hands above my head and positioned himself.

I felt his throbbing heat.

My body yearned for it.

For him.

Tears filled my eyes. "Please."

"I haven't been with anyone, I've been tested, I've—"

I shut him up with a kiss, my lips parted in a rush as he slid into me only to withdraw and do it again, this time so hard the bed made a creaking nose. The table next to the bed shuddered, a lamp fell.

We lost our minds.

With frenzied kisses I met him thrust for thrust. "I need you."

"Not as much as I need you." He swore, his tongue swept into my mouth, dipping, swirling, as he picked up his rhythm, he rose over me one last time as a sea of pleasure exploded between us. He teased my lips apart with another kiss and took me over the edge. His body spasmed, mine was numb with pleasure.

He collapsed next to me.

We both stared up at the white ceiling in comfortable silence.

I ran my hand over his chiseled chest. "I think Jax's interview is on ESPN tonight."

Miller kissed my forehead. "You wanna watch it?"

I nodded, thankful that he was just as comfortable with me as I was with him.

Miller flipped on the TV.

The sound of the news filled the tense silence.

"Stay tuned for sports next! Take a look at interviews from some of our favorite players, including Quinton Miller who, rumor has it, is dating quarterback Jax Romonov's sister! We also have a special report about her early days with the Romonov family and the adoption that almost didn't happen!"

I froze.

Miller froze.

I closed my eyes.

Afraid to open them and see judgment or at least the anger that I knew would be there when Miller discovered that I wasn't biologically related to the very guy who was obsessed with protecting me from everything big and bad in the world. It was going to be like Anderson all over again. I clenched my eyes tighter as memories washed over me.

"Does he fuck you too?" Anderson pulled my hair, dragging me against the wall, then punishing me with another bruising kiss. "I saw the way he looked at you yesterday, checking out your ass." He smacked my butt. "Worse yet, I think you like it!"

I shook my head no. Ever since Anderson learned Jax and I weren't related by blood, he acted suspicious of our relationship.

He gripped my neck and squeezed. "If he touches you, I'll kill him."

"My brother," I rasped, "he's my brother."

Anderson's eyes softened. "Oh, baby, don't cry. I'm sorry, I just . . ." He released me then pulled me into his arms. "I just get so jealous . . . you're so beautiful and most guys aren't good guys like me, they won't protect you like I will . . ."

He released my hand.

It fell lifeless to my side.

The bed dipped.

I exhaled as the sound of the shower running filled the tense air.

I lay there.

And seconds later was getting picked up and carried to the bathroom. A muscle flexed in Miller's jaw, but he didn't say anything.

He washed my back.

He kissed my neck.

He pinned me against the wall and took me again.

And when he was through, when it was hard to breathe through the water streaming down both of our bodies, Miller whispered in a calm voice, "Time for more truth . . . *friend*."

He left me.

In the shower.

The water turned cold and I wondered how long I could hide out before he came and got me again.

So with a shiver, I turned off the water, grabbed a towel, and went to meet the one guy who after tonight, I was pretty sure was going to be pissed.

Chapter Twenty-One

I was pissed.

Livid.

Beyond ready to break something with my bare hands. And I had practice in exactly six hours.

Which meant, either we talked or we slept.

How the hell did the media get ahold of that sort of information? Especially since it clearly wasn't something either of them felt the need to tell me?

Kinsey came back into the room, her face unsure as she slowly crawled onto the bed, the towel still wrapped around her small body. "I don't know how the hell they found out, but because Anderson's been a real prick lately, I imagine he's behind it. My adoption was just another thing that made him jealous of Jax. It was the tipping point between us, he could never handle the relationship Jax and I had—have." Her eyes filled with tears. "But, Miller, I'm still his sister, in every way that matters."

"That's what you lead with?" I tried and failed to keep the edge out of my voice, but something about the situation was pissing me off, and I had no clue why.

"What?" Kinsey pulled the towel tighter like she was trying to protect herself from me, like I was about to hurt her. "What do you want me to say? That I'm sorry I didn't tell you? When would you have liked me to give you my life story, Miller? Hmm? Was it before you slept with me the first time? Or after? How about in between naked times? Or no!" She snapped her fingers. "Wait, I got it, at the airport, right? When you gave me your cell number . . ." She made a face. "Oh, that's right, you didn't. Or how about all of those times you emailed? No, that wouldn't work either, well, maybe right when I got back from Europe. Yup, that works perfect, except this happened." She gestured between us. "And I'm sorry that I've been a bit distracted lately but, come on!" Tears spilled onto her cheeks. "When is there a good time to tell someone you care about that the two people in her life who should have loved her the most chose drugs over her? Hmm? Or that the minute they got out of prison for selling drugs, the only reason they reached out to me was because they'd discovered that the family who'd adopted me had a son in the NFL? By then I was old enough to know that the only thing they would ever want from me or from my family would be money."

Chills racked my body. "What?"

"Jax is my brother," she said defensively. "He's always been my brother, ever since I was eleven he's been my brother . . . but before then . . . he was just . . . my next-door neighbor. The kid whose house I slept at when my parents were on benders. His dad—I mean, my dad, my mom—they're my real parents, they're the ones who gave me Christmas presents when I didn't even have a candy cane in my house, they're the ones who remembered my birthday, they made sure I had new winter boots, that I had a jacket for school, Mom would even take me for ice cream after the first day of school and ask how it went, they've always been my parents." She crossed her arms, as a few tears slid down her cheeks. "I just, I didn't want to bring up everything, not with . . ."

"Your dad's illness," I finished for her, rubbing my hands over my face. "And all this Anderson shit . . ."

"I think he still hates Jax because of it and blames Jax for our relationship ending when really it was because he was an abusive controlling psychopath. But, for a while he made me feel . . . good and then it was like I was trapped in my old house just waiting for someone to rescue me." She blinked back tears. "He was always accusing Jax of looking at me like he wanted me."

"Kins." God, I was a dick. "Tell me you know I'm not like that, that I would never lay a finger on you, or even think that there was something between you and your brother. Tell me you're not putting me in the same category as Anderson."

Her shoulders slumped. "I know you're not him, but you got so upset and—"

"Upset," I interrupted, "because I care about you, because I want to know you, I want everything, every damn piece of you. So when I learn that you're adopted from the news instead of you, yeah, I reacted, and I'm sorry, but know that I'd never treat you the way that jackass did."

She gulped.

"Besides, I was having one of those moments, the kind where an asshole takes control of my mouth and I let him."

She sniffled.

Shit.

"My dad was"—I coughed—"*is* an alcoholic. Once my mom died he just . . . wanted the bottle more, I think he just wanted the pain to go away, but when you love someone that much, I don't think it ever really does." I let out a rough exhale. "I don't even see him anymore, not for lack of trying, the guy asks for money, I give it, and sometimes he texts me an update on his life. We all have messed-up pasts, you know?"

Kinsey reached for my hand and squeezed.

I sighed. "We should go to bed."

"Yeah."

"Together."

"You actually claiming me, Miller?" she teased.

"Yeah, friend." I tugged her against me. "But lose the towel."

"I'm a lady."

"Yes," I said gruffly against her neck. "You're my lady."

She giggled. "That sounded so cheesy and yet, my stupid heart just flipped."

"Damn right it did." I pressed a kiss to her temple. "Because I'm Quinton Miller, that's why."

I got an elbow in the stomach. "Temper the arrogance."

"It's confidence."

"Oh?"

"Yeah." I turned around and flipped off the light then brought her body into mine, tucking her where she belonged, by my side. "For example, I'm confident I'm going to wake up at least once and sink between your thighs. I'm confident you'll let me."

Her breath hitched.

"I'm confident that tomorrow morning, when I press a kiss between your legs, I'll curse the fact that I have to go to practice, and you'll curse the fact that if you're late you'll have to do burpees." I turned her to face me. "I'm also confident that it's going to take a hell of a lot of hits to keep my focus on the game, instead of your face."

"Just my face."

"These too." I grabbed her boobs playfully then gripped her ass. "And this, let's not forget this."

She arched that perfect ass into my hand.

"Careful," I ground out, my fingers digging into her flesh. "I'll take it as another invitation."

"Funny, since I'm confident that you want to be invited in."

"Always." I laughed. "Except we really do need to sleep, day one is grueling."

She groaned and then wrapped her arms around my neck. "No more secrets."

I stilled. "Kins, we can't tell Jax."

"But—"

I kissed her doubts away. "Wait until after a few games, alright? Let him get used to seeing us together. Especially now that I know why he's so protective of you."

She frowned. "Because he's a big brother?"

"No, Kins." I sighed. "Because when you needed a hero the most, it sounds like he put on a fucking cape and rescued you like big brothers are supposed to . . . Because when you cried, when you were all alone, he was the one who dealt with the tears. Because when he closes his eyes at night, his only mission is to make sure those tears don't happen again. Take it easy on Superman, it can't be easy wearing a cape all the time."

"Or spandex," she added with a giggle.

I laughed. "Yeah, that too."

"I'm gonna go talk to Dad after practice tomorrow, wanna come?"

I flinched. I didn't mean to.

"Or not." She started to move away.

"No, that's not it." I locked my arms around her. "I just—don't you want some alone time with him?"

She ducked her head against my chest. "My dad knows everything about me. Let's . . . at least be honest with him about this."

She was asking me to tell her dying father that I had feelings for her. No pressure.

"Alright." I tried to breathe, but a pressure built up against my chest. "I'm not the best with death."

"Funny, you were amazing with that little boy today."

I sighed; she had no idea the toll it took on me emotionally not to burst into tears or just run away from it all—because even though my demons were different than hers, they still existed.

Loneliness still haunted.

Emptiness still lingered.

"Thanks, Kins." That was it. A thank-you, a silent message to stop talking and sleep so I could figure out all the shit in my head, starting with what the hell I was going to tell her dying father, when I wasn't even sure I knew what was going on.

Sleep didn't come for another hour at least.

And when it finally did.

I dreamed of my mother's face.

Her smile.

And the utter loss I'd felt when she was out of my life, when Emerson followed, and the numbness that took over the minute I realized the only person I could count on in this world was me.

Chapter Twenty-Two

MILLER

Jax released a string of curses at the offensive line. "Fucking swear to the football gods if you miss another block I'm going to kick your ass!" Jax kicked the grass, and basically threw a tantrum that rivaled those of some of the worst quarterbacks in the league.

"Give us a minute," I yelled at Jax.

Sanchez eyed me and told the guys to go grab water.

We both made our way over to him.

Sanchez held his helmet in his hand, his face was caked with sweat and dirt. The guy had caught every piece of shit Jax had thrown in his direction, nearly sacrificing his body in order to do so, and it was practice, not the big game.

"What?" Jax sneered at both of us.

Sanchez held up his hands. "Are you just that sexually repressed or did everyone just piss you off today?"

Jax stared down at the ground. "Sorry."

I ran my hand over my sweaty head. "Man, I know things are bad with your dad, I'm headed over there with Kins later to—"

"The fuck?" Jax glared in my direction, dropped his helmet, and grabbed me by the jersey. "You stay the hell away from her mouth!"

I jerked away from him. "You're the one who encouraged us being together!"

Sanchez grinned between the two of us. "Better than daytime TV. I'll just be over here watching, carry on!"

"I know what I said." Jax pinched the bridge of his nose. "I just, I didn't think . . ."

"What?" I roared. "That we'd actually become better friends? That she needed someone other than you to help her through this?"

His body gave a little flinch.

It was enough.

"Holy shit." Unbelievable! I threw my head back and laughed out, "You're jealous!"

Sanchez's eyes widened until I thought they were going to pop out of his head and roll toward Jax's feet. "Whoa! Time out! You're boning your sister?"

Jax groaned. "Could you just . . ." He shook his head. "Not be yourself for five minutes, Sanchez?"

Sanchez looked between the two of us. "Fill me in, then."

I looked to Jax, his lips were sealed.

Fine.

"It was on the news last night." At least that part was true. "Kinsey and Jax aren't biologically brother and sister. She's adopted."

"At eleven years old," Jax finished in a hollow voice. "She was supposed to come over for dinner, I found her in her house . . . she was bleeding, she'd tripped on some glass and there was blood everywhere, her parents were gone, needles littered the floor like trash." He swallowed, his Adam's apple slowly bobbed up and down like he was trying not to cry. "She said I looked like an angel."

Sanchez, for once, was quiet.

"She used to call me Captain America, lame, I know, but ever since that moment it's been me and her, my parents tried but couldn't have any other kids and it just seemed . . . meant to be, you know?"

"Are you?" Sanchez asked him point blank.

"Am I what?" Jax didn't look at me.

"Jealous? Are you jealous?"

Jax blew out a frustrated curse and kicked the ground, the rest of the team had already started to run back out onto the field. "I'm jealous as hell . . . because she looks at him the way she used to look at me, like he's her hero, and all I've done in the past few months is mess up, protect her, piss her off, protect her, piss her off—"

"Maybe," I interrupted, "it's time for you to just . . . let her live."

"Yeah." He licked his lips. "I used to be better at this shit."

"What? Being a decent human?" Sanchez just had to say.

"Nah, being a good brother, and then with my dad getting sick and . . ." His eyes were unfocused. "Everything else . . ." He shrugged. "I can't lose her too."

"You won't," I promised.

He didn't look like he believed me as he put his helmet back on and walked toward the huddle.

Sanchez elbowed me. "If we had our own reality show moment that would have been killer—just imagine, violin music, soft crying in the background—money shot." He sighed.

"Who *are* you?" I shoved him back.

He just laughed and said, "Grant Sanchez," like that made more sense than any answer.

"Hey!" He grabbed my arm. "Serious moment . . . do not, and I repeat, do not fuck with him right now." His eyes grew serious. "He has enough shit on his plate lately and if you . . . if you hurt her . . ." He rolled his eyes. "God, I feel like such a dick for even saying this, but if you hurt her, if he finds out about Vegas, if he as much as sniffs in your direction and finds out that you aren't just replacing him for now but planning on doing it in a more permanent way . . ." He shuddered. "I know you somewhat have his permission, whatever the hell that means, but it looks to me like he's still on the fence about you guys and that's without him knowing what went on between you two. If you hurt her, there won't be a far enough place for you to run where he won't chase you down and bury the body, and I'm too young to go to jail for you, man."

"Was that a pep talk?" I hissed.

"Yeah." He shot me a cocky grin. "How'd I do?"

"Shitty!" I was tempted to dislocate his jaw with the back of my helmet.

"Can't win 'em all." He shrugged and, with a wink, ran off to the huddle. I followed slowly behind him, guilt gnawing its way through my uniform the entire way.

I still smelled her when I breathed in.

I felt her on my fingertips.

Yeah, I was in no position to judge Jax.

Because when she looked at me like that, all I wanted was to be worthy of it. And almost every single time, it felt like I did nothing but fall short.

Chapter Twenty-Three

Jax

I was in a shit mood.

Brought on by an even shittier situation.

And unable to focus on anything except for the fact that I hadn't received a text from Harley since I basically fled my own apartment.

My throws were off in practice today.

My concentration was on a spitfire who tasted like bubblegum and had the sexiest husky laugh I'd ever heard.

I showered, grabbed my shit, and got in my car.

Rain pounded in rapid succession against the windshield, like it was just as angry, just as tormented as I felt. With a curse, I started the car and drove.

And somehow found myself at her apartment.

Dripping with rain.

In front of her door.

My feet took up at least half of the welcome mat, and there was a little sign that said "Blessings" hanging in the center of the door.

I hung my head and raised my hand, only to have the door swing open. A short elderly lady with bright white hair stared me down, her dark-brown eyes pensive, her lips pursed into a thin line.

I gulped.

"You." Her voice was hoarse, as though she'd smoked a pack a day for thirty years.

I licked my lips. "Is Harley—"

"Here." Harley's grandmother shoved a box into my hands. There were at least two jerseys inside, and a football.

"What's thi—"

"Black Sharpie's on the table. I'm going out for some air."

"O-kay." I drew out the word and walked past her in search for the mysterious black Sharpie. That had to be the oddest reception I'd ever had from a fan.

"I have grandkids." She sniffed, grabbed a light jacket and some keys, and then added, "Harley's on her way home."

The door slammed behind her.

"Well then." I sighed, rubbing my hands on my jeans before popping the cap off the Sharpie and getting started. I signed my name, my signature taking up at least half of the shoulder of each jersey, then made a mental note to get Harley's grandma more gear—especially when I noted the décor.

Bellevue Bucks wallpaper.

Harley hadn't been kidding about her grandmother being a fan.

A Bucks coffee cup was placed next to a crossword puzzle. The steam from hot coffee still billowed over the rim, like she'd been planning on settling in for a nice afternoon, but instead I'd knocked on her door and . . . what? She decided she needed a walk in the rain?

The sound of keys had me jumping to my feet in an effort to look like I actually belonged at Harley's dinner table. Shit, I never wanted to hide so badly in my entire life.

What the hell was I even doing there?

I just—I wanted to check on her, to apologize in person. To smell her? The hell! I was losing my damn mind.

The door swung open.

Harley placed her bag on the nearby chair and then looked up. Her mouth dropped open, and then she was walking toward me.

I braced myself for impact.

Waited for the slap.

Even closed my eyes.

But when nothing happened, I had no choice but to open them, to face the girl I'd slept with and abandoned. Who did that? Who slept with a girl they actually liked and then bailed the next day?

I did.

Jackass Jax did have a nice ring to it.

"You." She poked my chest with her finger. God, she was like a taller version of her grandma.

"Me," I answered.

"Why are you here?"

"Because you wouldn't talk to me."

"And that automatically means I want to see you? Invite you into my home? Make you soup?"

"There's soup?" My stomach growled on command. I was a sucker for homemade food, with all the traveling the team did. Not my fault.

"No." She crossed her arms. "I mean, well, there's always soup, it's our thing, don't ask."

My mouth watered.

I wasn't sure if it was because of her proximity, the way her wet hair clung to her cheeks, or the fact that I'd forgotten to eat after practice.

"I'm sorry." Could I sound any more robotic? And stupid? "For leaving you, for . . ." I ran my hands through my wet hair. "For just . . ." I rubbed my forehead. "For all of it."

"All of it?" she whispered.

"The bad parts." I took a step closer to her. Our bodies were touching, chest to chest. Breathing was taking more of an effort than it should. "Not the good ones."

"Who said there were good ones?" A challenging brow shot up from her forehead.

I smirked. "Really?"

"Really."

"You must have a shit memory, Harley."

"Or maybe it just wasn't that memorable."

I crushed my mouth to hers on instinct, wrapped my hands around her ass because I couldn't help myself, then hoisted her onto her grandmother's ancient dinner table and laid her down by the jerseys because I literally had no self-control when she was that close to me.

Harley's eyes closed as I kissed down her neck and ripped at her wet clothing, rubbing my hands everywhere I could, touching every sweet part of her before she shoved me away, before she told me that it was over, that I had fucked up.

"You're an asshole," she muttered against my mouth before biting down on my bottom lip so hard I winced in pain. "A giant asshole."

"I know."

"You left me alone." She kissed me harder then bit. Then the crazy woman grabbed the front of my pants and slid her hand inside, gripping me so tight my dick nearly went into a coma from blood loss. "Had sex with me and left me!"

"Shit." How the hell was I getting turned on by her psychotic touch? The woman was going to kill me! Make me sexless! And yet, I moved against her hand, my lips parted, I leaned into her. "I'm sorry, so damn sorry."

"And you're an asshole."

"The biggest asshole in the world," I agreed as her touch lightened, I jerked against her, and nearly went blind.

"Okay," she said softly.

I locked eyes with her. "Okay."

She released me, rubbed her hands together, and shrugged. "So you want some soup?"

What?

She threw me a grin over her shoulder. "Is that a no?"

I was having trouble stringing any sort of sentence together that didn't have to do with us getting naked on the kitchen table.

"Um . . ." I blew out a pent-up breath of frustration. "Sure, yeah, soup, soup sounds good."

Harley burst out laughing. "I was shitting you. You passed, by the way."

"How so?" I narrowed my eyes.

"Well, you were trying to be a gentleman when all you wanted to do was get naked in Grandma's living room. By the way, bad call, she has cameras."

I did a little circle.

"It's almost too easy." Harley kept laughing. "Come on."

She held out her hand.

I took it.

I shouldn't have.

She made me want things I had no business wanting.

All damn day I'd been thinking about her—not football, not my dad but her.

With a wink, she pulled me into a bedroom, shut the door behind her, then pulled her shirt over her head and tossed it onto the carpet. "Now that we're done talking . . ."

I didn't let her finish. I devoured her next few words, one hand tangled in her hair, the other working her jeans down her ass while she unbuttoned mine. Laughter bubbled up between us as we stumbled toward her bed.

I pulled her on top of me and sighed. "I missed you."

She stilled. "I missed you too."

It was all I needed to hear.

Before my mouth was on hers again.

Before I lost my sanity again.

"I'm on the pill." She moaned. "Just . . . thought, since last time and—"

"Yeah," I finished for her. "Not to totally ruin this moment, but is Grandma supposed to be arriving any time soon?"

"No, I don't think—"

The sound of a door opening stunned me into silence.

I was seconds from feeling Harley around me, inches from where I wanted to be.

"Harley girl?" Grandma called. "You in your room?"

She slammed a hand against my mouth. "Yeah, Grandma, just, um, playing a board game." She rolled her eyes as I licked her fingers.

She shivered while I tossed her onto her back, pinning her down with my body as I hesitated at her entrance.

"What game?"

I pressed into her and murmured, "Yeah, Harley, what game?"

Her eyes narrowed, "It's, uh, Chutes and, um, Ladders?"

"Am I the chute or the ladder?" I whispered.

A whimper escaped between her lips before Grandma called back, "Forgot my phone, you kids have fun."

Harley let out a frustrated groan.

"Better put a cover on that ladder, dear!"

Harley covered her face with her hands. "Thanks, Grandma."

"And when I say cover, I mean condom!"

"Got it, bye!"

I wasn't sure who was more horrified, me or Harley. But all it took was the slamming of the front door for the mood to go back to the way it was before the untimely interruption: desperate, needy.

"Huh." I grinned. "And here all this time I thought I was more of the chute."

She smacked me in the shoulder then pulled down on my neck, until our mouths met in another fiery kiss. "Your move first."

One long thrust and my world was suddenly righted again.

Chapter Twenty-Four

KINSEY

Sickness had a smell. I couldn't really describe it other than a mixture of medicine, sadness, and sterile equipment. The minute I'd walked into the house, I knew something was wrong.

All because of the smell.

It smelled like a hospital had been set up in my home. The patient, my father. And the fact that he was slowly deteriorating made me want to scream and then cry until my voice was hoarse.

Miller hadn't said a word the entire drive.

Which was fine with me, because the last thing I wanted to do was talk about my feelings—talking about the sadness only made it feel bigger and if it was bigger, it was harder to combat, at least in my mind.

Dad was sitting in the living room, hooked up to an IV.

"Hey." I winked and sat down on the couch. "Looking good."

"Liar." His eyes narrowed. "I've got this robot contraption piece of crap hydrating me, makes my arms feel cold."

I grabbed a blanket.

"Put that blanket on me like I'm a child and I'm going to tell your mother about the time you snuck out of your room and got drunk in the tree house."

I gasped. "You wouldn't."

"Paula!" The man might be sick, but he still had his lungs.

I winced.

Miller let out a chuckle.

My dad turned his eyes to Miller. "How long, son?"

"Uhhh," Miller gulped. "How long . . . what?"

Dad grinned and leaned back. "Oh, I see how it's going to be, I'll have to spell it out then. How long have you been sleeping with my daughter?"

To his credit, Miller didn't as much as flinch. "What makes you think I'm sleeping with her?"

Dad's eyes narrowed. "You look too happy for a man who's going without sex."

"A guy can't be happy?" Miller shrugged. "What if I'm just high on life?"

"Bullshit." Dad wiped at his nose. "You hurt her, I'll make it my personal afterlife goal to haunt your ass and send you into an early grave, you hear?"

Miller bit down on his lip and then grinned. "Yeah, well, if I hurt her, I may just give you permission to do that."

"Permission?"

Oh no. I was just getting ready to tell Dad to stand down when Mom came flurrying in with a tray full of coffee. "I have hot scones."

Miller had two in his mouth before I could warn him that they weren't going to taste like they smelled.

He swallowed, chugged his coffee, and glared at the offending pastries.

"My dad's on a sugar-free diet," I said. "It's supposed to help him live longer."

"Live longer my ass." Dad made a face at the scones. "If this was my last meal, I'd ask for a redo. Honey, why don't you hop back in that kitchen and make some chocolate chip cookies? The kind that go gooey in the middle."

I made a little noise in the back of my throat. That sounded amazing.

Mom put her hands on her hips. "But sugar—"

"I could go for some cookies," Miller said, coming to my dad's defense. "In fact, I can even help if you want?"

"Good man." Dad winked at Miller. "I knew I liked you."

Ah, how easily Dad switched sides when food was involved. If he wasn't careful, Miller was going to take over Jax's spot on the couch and be invited over for ESPN time. Yeah, my brother would probably murder his teammate before letting that happen.

Miller gave my shoulder a squeeze and followed my mom out of the room, leaving me, my dad, and the silence.

I looked away.

He grabbed my hand.

I squeezed back and fought the hot sting of tears.

"How's the squad this year? You whipping them into shape?" While I appreciated the subject change, and the fact that he wanted the focus to be on me, I wanted to talk about him.

"Good." I scooted closer to him then laid my head on his shoulder and let out the breath I'd been holding since walking in the front door.

Dad rubbed circles around my palm. He smelled like cologne and licorice, ten bucks said he probably had a few pieces of candy hidden in his pocket for emergency purposes. "You know"—Dad's voice was low, it rumbled through his body, tickling my ear with its vibration—"you used to sit here for hours with me when you were little. The damn TV never even had to be on. I think . . ." He swallowed. "Well, honey, I think you just wanted to be close to someone—anyone."

I squeezed my eyes closed as memories washed over me—of an empty stomach, the sound of fighting, violence too horrible for a little girl to witness on a daily basis. I used to watch Jax's TV programs by sitting on my windowsill and spying into his room, since I wasn't allowed to watch what I wanted. I hated it when it rained because the blinds were pulled. Then one day, even though it was raining, they kept the blinds open, and even though I was drenched, I sat there.

That was the same day Jax invited me over to play even though I was only five to his fifteen.

I was so desperate for any sort of attention that I jumped at the chance to spend time with anyone who would listen to me.

Luckily, it was Jax, basically the nicest, most gold-hearted male in the world, next to my dad, my adopted dad.

So when I came over that first day, I was surprised to see the table set for dinner, and I had a spot, they always made sure I had a spot.

I sniffled.

"You're the same now as you were then, honey," Dad murmured. "You need . . . to feel, to be touched, held." He kissed the top of my head. "And that's okay, you know. That's okay to want to be . . . treasured."

My dad and I didn't have conversations like this.

We had similar personalities in that we used sarcasm to shield our feelings, which meant only one thing, this was one of those talks, the ones you have with people you love before it's too late. I've never wanted to run so bad in my entire life.

"I know, Dad," I finally squeaked out.

"He good to you?"

I nodded and then answered, "Yes."

"He watches you, every movement. His hands aren't even at his side. He always seems like he's bracing for impact. I just don't know if he's waiting to run in the opposite direction, or into your arms."

"Hah!" I playfully pinched my dad's side. "Wish I knew."

"Men are stupid."

"Thanks, Dad." I burst out laughing through the tears collecting on my cheeks.

"Try not to hold it against him, honey."

Our laughter faded as my dad released my hand and pulled back so he could look at me. "You are my little girl."

I wanted to roll my eyes, to make light of the situation. Instead, I felt myself crumpling, my stomach heaved.

"You . . ."—Dad tilted my chin toward him—"are the best thing that's ever happened to this family. Through sickness, through health, come hell or high water, you are the glue. Your brother and mom are going to need you, you're going to need each other. And honey, it's okay to need to rely on someone else when you feel like you're about to break—that's life. Remember your promise back when you were in the hospital and we didn't know what was wrong?"

"To live," I whispered, "no matter what."

"So live." He shrugged and smiled. "Live well."

"What about you?"

Dad chuckled. "Oh honey, I'm the richest man in the world." His grin was infectious. "I have your mom, Jax, you, that old goldfish that died a few years back, what was his name?"

I rolled my eyes. "It was a beta named Todd, and you forgot to feed it."

"Right." He grinned. "Honey, a father never wants to outlive his kids. This"—he took a deep breath—"is the easy part. Living? That will always be the hardest thing you will ever do. It hurts like hell, it's full of bumps down every road, and you'll take wrong turns, but it's a blessing to have the chance to fail in the first place, am I right?"

I nodded again.

"Good talk." He winked. "Now, find out when those cookies will be done, and while you're at it, you swipe some dough on a medium-sized spoon and bring your dad a big glass of milk."

I rolled my eyes. "So basically I have to do your dirty work?"

He shrugged, grabbed the newspaper, and held it up so I couldn't see his face. "Well, I'm sick, come on, give a dying man his last wish!"

I stuck my tongue out at him. Unfair!

"Saw that." He sounded bored. "Remember, medium spoon with extra chocolate chips, don't let me down."

I grinned and walked into the kitchen in search for a serving spoon instead, only to find Miller holding my mom in his giant arms.

Her face was pressed against his chest.

And he looked pale, like he'd just seen a ghost.

"I'm so sorry!" Mom hiccupped. "I slipped and I haven't been sleeping and . . ."

Miller opened his mouth to speak and gave his head a little shake.

"Mom?" I called. "Why don't I finish the cookies? You go hang out with Dad on the couch, maybe lie down a bit?"

She nodded, wiping at her eyes, and left us in the kitchen.

"What happened?" I rushed over to Miller, who was braced against the countertop with both of his hands, his giant body still shaking like he was either going to punch something or pass out. "Miller?"

"Don't." He gritted his teeth. "I just need a minute."

I didn't listen, just touched his back, only to have him jerk away from me and run his hands through his hair.

Finally, he licked his lips and looked at me, his eyes haunted, cold. "I, uh, I have to go."

"Okay." My throat swelled. Sure, run, he was good at that, right? Or was it just pushing people away? Forcing them to be the ones that want to quit on him? "I guess I can have Jax come and grab me later."

"I'll call him." Miller gave me one last look and left.

The kitchen suddenly felt too small for the emotions I was feeling, the sadness of my conversation with my dad, the rejection from Miller when I needed touch.

I clenched my eyes shut.

All I'd wanted was a hug.

And for someone to tell me everything was going to be okay.

That came much later, when my brother found me huddled in my old bedroom, in the corner. It was the same corner I used to sit in when I first came to live with them. I was too afraid to want anything nice, because when you want nice things, when you like them, they can be taken away, right? My biological parents used to tell me that all the time—that nothing was free and if it was given freely it would most likely get taken away.

I'd been so afraid.

And I'd thought I was over it.

It was years ago.

So why? Why did Miller's haunted expression suddenly bring me back to that place? Where all I wanted was to be noticed, and instead—I was ignored? A part of me recognized that something was wrong with his expression, but my fragile heart could only concentrate on one thing—he ran.

Away from me.

Jax muttered a harsh curse then sat down next to me.

I put my head on his shoulder.

He grabbed my hand.

Silence.

And touch.

All I needed.

And yet, not enough.

Because I didn't want my brother—for the first time in my life, I wanted someone else, I wanted more.

I wanted Miller.

Chapter Twenty-Five

MILLER

Seconds after calling Jax, I drove my car around the block only to park across the street from her parents' home. I would be a shit stalker.

I didn't even turn off my headlights, just sat in the warm SUV while rain pelted angrily against the windshield. Even nature was mad at me, not that I blamed the rain, or anyone else but myself.

That was all me.

Running was all me.

And I wanted to stay, God, I'd wanted to plant my feet against the ground and tell Kinsey everything was going to be okay.

I would have been a liar.

And that's the part that got me.

It wasn't going to be okay.

At least not for a while.

It hit me so hard, sucking my breath away so violently that I had trouble breathing—thinking. Her mom tripped, she fell to the floor.

I grabbed her, and had a real, living, breathing flashback of finding my mom down in our kitchen.

And realization struck a very sensitive nerve in my body.

It gets better.

But it takes time.

And even now, I still had my weak moments. So to sit there and tell Kins everything was going to be just fine, that unicorns and rainbows were going to shit all over her face the minute the funeral was over, that the sun was going to shine again, that one day, she'd look back on this moment and not cry.

Well, it seemed to be like the most insensitive thing I could do— and I cared for her more than that.

The porch light turned on.

Jax walked out with his arm around Kinsey.

He saw me first.

His look of disgust wasn't misplaced. The bastard wanted to stab me with the nearest sharp object, and I wouldn't blame him if he did.

Kinsey sucked in a breath, rain dripped down her chin. I'd never seen anything so beautiful in my entire life.

My heart clenched, while she pulled her black hoodie tighter against her body. Jax looked between us. Indecision warred across his face.

And then, Kinsey whispered something in his ear.

I got out of the car and waited, hands shoved in pockets.

He walked through me, not even making an effort to walk around me, but literally right into me, causing my body to stumble back a few feet onto the wet grass.

He got into his car.

And took off.

Kinsey didn't move.

I was afraid to walk toward her.

Afraid of what the moment meant.

Because it was more than her dad.

More than my mom.

More than our pasts.

I was staring at my future.

And it scared the ever-loving hell out of me.

Her dark-brown hair looked inky black as it stuck to her smooth neck, the same neck I dreamed about kissing on a daily basis. With her fists clenched at her sides, she took two steps toward me; nostrils flaring, she sized me up. "Why?"

I licked my lips. "Why what?"

"Why did you leave?"

"You mean other than complete cowardice and all-around assholery?"

She didn't laugh.

I wasn't expecting her to.

"Because . . ." I gulped, taking a step in her direction. "The minute you walked into that kitchen, I didn't want to lie. The whole moment reminded me of when I lost my mom, that same sinking feeling, that same despair. And I didn't want to lie to you."

Her brow furrowed. "What do you mean? You've been lying?"

"Kins." I reached for her hands, she let me. They were cold and felt so frail in mine. "It won't be okay."

Her face fell.

"Look at me."

She shook her head.

"Fine." I took a deep breath. "It's not going to be okay. Not today, not tomorrow, not next week when you watch your dad suffer through good days only to have another bad day. And when—" My voice cracked. "When you go to his funeral, when you watch people talk about him in the past tense, when suddenly your world isn't as bright, when the ache in your chest deepens until a chasm of pain so severe you can't breathe becomes the only constant in your life, it won't be okay. I care about you, I do. More than I should. I want you. More than I should. But I can't lie to you, Kins. Humans aren't built for this kind of pain, this . . . brokenness." My voice caught. "I know what it's like to lose a parent, to lose someone you love so much you wonder if you'll ever be the same again, if you'll ever wake up and feel like your-self. I won't be that person. I refuse to be just like everyone else, giving you a pat on the hand and saying it's going to be fine. It's not fucking fine, Kins. He's dying. It won't ever be fine. But . . ." My damn voice wouldn't stop shaking. "One day—"

Her eyes finally met mine.

"One day the sun's going to be a little brighter, one day, it won't hurt to walk into that living room anymore. One day, you'll feel like smiling. And I just . . ." My world tilted. "I just wanted you to know that when that day happens, I'll be there, standing beside you, smiling right back."

She nodded her head as tears mixed with rain, making it impossible to tell if she was sobbing or just softly crying—both broke my heart. "Do you promise?"

"I swear." I pulled her into my arms. "No more running."

She hugged me so tight it was hard to breathe, and just when I thought she was going to pull back, she reached up on her tiptoes, offering me her mouth.

I stole a kiss I didn't deserve.

From the last girl I should be falling in love with.

The only one currently capable of breaking my already halfway-broken heart.

Wisdom dripped from her expression when she pulled back and cupped my face. "You're wrong."

"I am?"

She nodded. "Because right now . . ." Her hands slid down my chest. "I already feel better."

"Because of the freezing rain?" I tried teasing.

"No," she whispered. "Because of you." Her hand rested against my chest like she was trying to feel my heart. "Sometimes, all the heart needs to feel better is a reminder that somewhere else, other hearts are still beating despite being mishandled, broken, abused—sometimes, you just need to experience love in its purest form . . . even if that does sound like the most jackass thing to say."

I closed my eyes, resting my hand on hers, letting the rain fall on both of us while we touched.

And then Kinsey was pulling me toward my car.

I followed.

I'd follow her anywhere.

To hell with running away.

I wanted to run toward her.

She opened the door to the back seat and crawled in. I had no choice but to follow, I'd be an idiot to stay in the rain while she was in the warm car.

Kinsey jerked her wet hoodie over her head and threw it onto the leather seat. Her red lacy bra was the most distracting thing I'd ever seen in my entire life.

"Kins." My voice came out like a curse. "We're literally parked in front of your parents' house."

"Let's live a little," she pleaded.

And because I was done—done running from what this was, because I needed her just as much as she needed me, I pulled her into my lap and kissed the hell out of her.

I brushed the damp hair away from her face, my tongue skimmed her trembling lips as I slid the straps of her bra down her arms, my hands cupped her small shoulders for a minute while I caught my breath.

"What?" she whispered.

Her skin was so smooth, creamy—pale against my mocha hands.

"You're perfect." I ran my fingertips down her arms, drinking in the sight of her straddling me like this wet siren. With a chuckle, I pressed a kiss against her mouth and whispered, "I never stood a fucking chance, did I?"

"Never." Her laugh was soft while she worked my jeans until they were halfway hanging down my legs. There was nothing sexy or planned about the moment, and yet I was so hard for her I ached everywhere with this intense need to make her mine—to really make her mine, to make sure that she knew that this was what I wanted for my life, a girl with brown hair, mesmerizing eyes, and the ability to cut a man down without even using her words.

She shimmied out of her sweats, barely moving an inch as she did so. Our gazes locked.

"No more running." Her thumbs rubbed against my bottom lip, I drew each in my mouth, taking my time sucking her skin, tasting the rain with my tongue.

With a powerless sigh, I nodded. "I've got you."

I leaned my head against her, breathed her in, closed my eyes, and enjoyed the way she simply felt in my arms.

When I opened my eyes, she was still watching me as she slowly moved onto me and slid her body down mine.

I urged her on, gripping her hips with my hands as we both fell into the silent wildness of giving everything we had to each other.

With a powerless shudder, I slowed her down, my hand slamming against the leather seat to keep from finishing the moment too soon, from taking the control back from her.

"Miller," she whimpered.

I tugged her feet with my hands, pulling her closer then hooking my arms behind her knees to get a better angle.

Her back arched.

I kissed between her breasts then steadied her pace before filling her to the hilt and watching her lips part on a moan. "Come on, Kins."

"I don't want it to end," she whispered as a tear ran down her cheek.

"Look at me."

She opened her tear-filled eyes.

"This . . ." I moved my hands from her knees back to her hips. "This isn't normal, Kins. This is everything. You." My voice hitched. "Are everything to me."

With a shudder, she bit into my shoulder.

Not exactly the response I was expecting.

And then she moved against me differently.

And maybe I blacked out.

Maybe I just hadn't experienced pleasure like that before in my twenty-two years, but it came so fast I couldn't stop myself from reaching out and meeting her mouth with an open kiss.

I flicked her tongue with mine, then deepened the kiss as she rocked against me.

"Miller—"

I devoured her words with my tongue again, as I felt her tighten around me, clamp down so hard that I couldn't stop my body from meeting her halfway each time.

Her release spurred mine, and I hated it.

Hated that it was over.

That I couldn't stay inside her forever.

That I couldn't trap her in my back seat and have wild sex—preferably not in front of her parents' house—all damn night.

Her head fell against my shoulder. Panting, she slapped me lightly on the chest and giggled. "Good game."

It was so unexpected, both my bark of laughter and her teasing, that I couldn't stop laughing.

"I could win a championship." She teased my lips with her tongue.

I sighed against her mouth. "Remind me to let you wear my ring."

"Naked?"

"Was there really another option, friend?"

"Ah." She laughed. "We're back to being friends?"

"The kind that date, yeah."

"Good thing everyone already thinks we are, hmm?" She shivered against me.

"Yeah." I refused to think about the team, about Anderson, her brother. Shit, I was going to have to tell Jax eventually, because what was happening between us was exploding out of control, and the more time I spent with her the more I realized I wouldn't be able to keep it a secret, and I didn't want to, not anymore. "About that."

"One more week," she interrupted. "And then we can let Jax know . . . he deserves to know."

"And I deserve to play without a broken clavicle, but we can't all have what we want." I swore. "Okay . . . after the first preseason game against Tampa."

She made a face. "Damn Tampa. Five coaches and they still can't win a game? Don't you feel sorry for them? Taylor's completion was horrendous last year, and he only has one good receiver, but Van Austin would rather take selfies than actually condition hard enough to catch a damn ball!"

"Wow." I nodded. "I'm so turned on right now I think I may have to go for round two . . . fucking hot seeing my woman talk about football. Quick, give me my stats."

She rolled her eyes, then fired off all of my last-season stats like she'd been memorizing them.

I kissed her before she got started on Jax.

And ignored the nagging feeling of guilt because when my best friend begged me to take care of his sister so he wouldn't be stressed, I'd had sex with her instead.

And kept it from him.

Good one, Miller.

I was a dead man.

Chapter Twenty-Six

KINSEY

"You ready for this?" I led the rest of the team in some warm-up stretches, giving Emerson a little wink.

I finally saw it.

Why Miller couldn't seem to let Em go.

There was this magnetism about her that was addicting. Hadn't I latched onto her after one day of practice? Her smile lit up the room and just being around her gave me confidence.

I groaned.

Was it wrong to hope that Miller saw similar qualities in me? That when I was by his side he felt better because of it? Maybe I was reaching. Maybe I needed to stop thinking so much.

"Alright, ladies." I moved to the couch stretch for quads and checked my watch. "Full makeup needs to be on before we hit the field for team announcements. Make sure you're ready in a few minutes, and remember . . ." I glared at Lily, the only girl I really had trouble with since she thought it was her right to sleep with every guy on the team. The only problem was she was good, so Coach kept her—well, that and her family was loaded and loosely connected to the Bucks football program. "No talking to the players before the game, they need to focus."

Lily raised her hand. "You mean Emerson can't talk to Sanchez?"

Emerson rolled her eyes. "Nope." She turned to face Lily. "Already did plenty of talking last night . . . and this morning . . . and this afternoon."

The girls laughed softly while Lily scowled.

"Scatter." I moved my hands while the girls all ran in different directions to put finishing touches on makeup and everything else they had to do. Nervous pee, lip gloss. It was cheerleading, and we had to play our part.

I'd actually gotten ready in record time. So had Emerson, and she gave me a knowing look and nodded toward the locker room hallway. "Walk with me."

"Are we about to have the talk?" I grinned over at her. "The one where you tell me to be careful?"

"Hah!" She winked, her bright blonde hair bouncing down her back with each perky step. "Absolutely not. You're a big girl, just like he's a big boy. You seem happy. I'm glad."

"I was happy before!" I tried, pointing around.

"No, you were content before," Em argued. "Now you . . . glow."

"Don't say *glow*." I shook my head. "That's all we need, a pregnancy rumor getting thrown around during our first game."

"Kinsey Romonov!" She elbowed me in the side. "That's not what I meant and you know it, but you're right, I'll watch my mouth."

I stopped walking. "You're not . . . mad?"

Em threw up her hands. "Why in the world would I be mad?"

"He's . . . he was your boyfriend, your best friend—"

"Whoa!" Em held up her hands. "Stopping you right there. Six years ago, yeah, but I have Sanchez now, and even though I love Miller to death and always will, Grant Sanchez is my future. Oh wow, that sounded so wrong even to my ears." She toyed with the giant rock on her finger.

"So wrong it's right?" I grinned.

"He's horribly awesome." She sighed happily. "I only want to kill him half the time, so that's a bonus, and last night he made chocolate cake."

I groaned and patted my stomach. "Next time, save your friend a piece."

"I'm not a monster!" We were nearing the end of the tunnel. "I saved you two."

"This." I grabbed her hand. "This is why we're best friends."

"Thought I was your best friend." Miller's deep voice had me jumping out of my Spanx. "Damn it, already cheating on me, Waffles?"

"Chicken Dinner, I could never do that," I shot back.

Sanchez and Jax were both with them.

While Jax looked ready to strangle anything that spoke, Sanchez was groaning and patting his stomach. "Promise me we get chicken and waffles after this."

"I nominate Em as tribute." I pointed to her with my pom-poms. "She can cook anything."

"Settled." Miller eyed me up and down. "Dinner after the game."

Jax snorted. "Sounds super fun."

"Bring Harley." I crossed my arms.

Everyone around us froze.

He tried to walk past Miller, but Miller grabbed him by the jersey and jerked him back. "Something you wanna tell us?"

"Yeah." Sanchez rubbed his chin. "I thought you guys weren't speaking . . . something about . . . bagging and bailing."

"Holy shit, you slept with her and left?" Miller's shocked expression so wasn't helping Jax's glower.

"Are you guys supposed to be talking to us right now?" Jax pointed out. "Why the hell are you in this tunnel?"

I looked around and paled. "Shit! Em and I were talking, and we took a left. EM!"

She was already running back down the tunnel with me. Even though the players and cheerleaders were like a small family, chatting it up before a game was still frowned upon.

We made it to the right side before most of our teammates had gathered. I wheezed out a cough while Em slapped me on the back.

"So chicken and waffles?"

"Happening," I decided.

"And this Harley situation?"

I sighed. "Yeah, I have no idea. Jax refuses to talk about it, but last night the guy had a hickey the size of Sanchez's ego on the side of his neck so . . ." I shrugged. "No offense."

"That must have been one big hickey." She went with it and wrapped an arm around my neck. "I know you have a lot going on, Kins. Just know I'm here for you, and I think . . . this is going to be a really good year."

"Thank you." I felt my body shudder.

"For?" She frowned, squeezing my body harder.

I shrugged. "Just, being you. An awesome friend."

"Aw." She released me and took in a deep breath, eyeing the field before us; the excitement of the crowd was like an electric pulse, making me dizzy with excitement. Lights flashed in front of us. "Well, thanks for taking me under your wing this last year."

"Like you needed me." I squeezed her hand.

"I really did." She put her head on my shoulder then smacked me on the butt. "Alright, let's do this."

I grinned as the air swirled and shifted around me.

Despite my dad's illness and the situation between Jax and Miller, I had to admit, something felt charged—different.

For the first time in weeks.
I felt fine.
Which should have been the warning I needed.
That what comes up.
Must always.
Always.
Come down.

Chapter Twenty-Seven

MILLER

Preseason Game 1
Tampa vs. Bellevue
Home Turf
Favored Team: Bellevue Bucks

Jax won the coin toss.

The guy seemed to always win the coin toss. We were kicking first and then receiving first in the second half. Part of the Bucks' game plan was to use our defense to make their offense skittish when it came to doing any sort of pass plays, and it almost always worked.

And while playing Tampa? Well, they either fumbled within the first two minutes or an interception was thrown. Luthor was a good QB. He'd been in the game for close to a decade, but he had shit receivers and young rookies who loved the game—but loved the fame just a little bit more.

Rumors ran rampant that Luthor's rookies were known for partying into the season, while the rest of us were focused on winning. They spent all the money they earned faster than most teams.

Then again, it was nothing compared to Miami.

Those guys could take the field drunk off their asses and still somehow find a way to win.

I hated Miami.

Everyone hated Miami.

Thank God we didn't play them unless they made the playoffs or in a preseason game.

Fourth down and my fingers itched to throw on my helmet.

It was hard as fuck not to continuously look in Kinsey's direction, but I knew if I did, I'd lose all concentration, so I focused on the game and told myself there would be plenty of time later.

"You ready for this?" Sanchez flanked my left while Jax stood to my right.

"Been waiting all year."

Fourth down and Taylor, the wide receiver, missed a catch, nearly allowing one of our guys to intercept.

Jax cursed. "The guy needs better receivers."

"Or actual protection." I put on my helmet.

Jax sniffed and looked down at the grass. "You feel like a trick play?"

Sanchez rubbed his hands together. "God, I love football."

I hesitated. "Just what kind of trick play are we talking?"

Jax put on his helmet. "Miller, where the hell is your sense of adventure?"

"Jax got laid!" Sanchez chuckled under his breath. "And we're going to win the championship again."

Jax scowled, but even he couldn't wipe the dopey grin from his face or the fact that both Sanchez and I jumped on him like he'd just said he won a billion dollars and his own private jet.

Close.

He got to see a girl naked.

I smacked his helmet with my gloved hand. "And here I thought you were being an ass because you hadn't gotten any."

"Nah, that's just Jax's pregame routine. Jackassery and constipation." Sanchez grinned. "Trick play . . . wait . . ." His eyes narrowed. "You're not talking about Cherry Coke Me?"

Jax's face spread out into a grin. "Look, they're going to take us out after the second quarter anyway, may as well have some fun."

"Coach!" Sanchez pointed over at Jax. "Your QB just said the F word!"

"Get on the field, you little shits!" Coach yelled back.

"I love it when he gives us compliments." Sanchez grinned while we all ran into the huddle.

Jax took a knee. "Gentleman, let's start this season off right. Most of you are fighting for a spot on this team, so show me what you got, I need good blocking, and let's hope to God Miller actually still knows how to throw a football."

Everyone chuckled while I flipped him off.

"Cherry Coke Me on three!"

Sanchez looked giddy like he was ready to piss his pants while I was thinking about all the horrible things that could happen to me if the blocking went south.

Then again.

I just had to throw a ball.

We got in position.

Insults were thrown.

"I screwed your sister, Jax," one of the defensive ends yelled.

While that was meant for Jax, it was actually messing with me more than him.

Jax counted off.

On three, the ball snapped. I blocked then ran wide right. Jax threw me the ball and took off directly down the middle of the field while Sanchez turned and blocked for him.

Once he was at our forty, I threw up a Hail Mary. It sailed directly into his hands as he ran into the end zone.

Touchdown, Bucks.

I saluted him from my spot on the field and took a bow.

He and Sanchez were standing side by side and did the same thing back.

We got a warning not to celebrate.

And the crowd went wild.

Lost their minds.

It was so loud in the stadium, I couldn't think.

It used to be enough. The fans, the pandemonium, the cheers, but in that moment, all I wanted to do was see the look on Kins's face.

The camera followed me while I made my way back to the sidelines, pats on the back followed, and then I finally found her, locked eyes with her, and winked.

She blew me a kiss.

And that's when Jax smacked me on the back with his helmet. "Cut that shit out."

"Sorry." But I wasn't.

It was going to be a good year.

A good season.

I could feel it.

Coach pulled us out in the second quarter since Tampa had yet to score. It was boring as hell sitting on the sidelines when all I wanted to do was play, but they never wanted to risk their top players getting a stupid injury during the preseason.

"This blows." Sanchez handed me a piece of licorice, I took it and put on my Bucks hat.

"Tell me about it," I sighed, my fingers itching to touch the ball again.

Jax joined us, his face tense.

"What's up?" I frowned while he popped his knuckles and shook his head like he was contemplating murder.

He nodded his head at Coach. "Anderson's blocking well, Coach wants to keep him on, it's one game, and Coach says he's seen all he needs to see."

"That's bullshit," Sanchez spat. "Anderson's—"

Anderson suddenly appeared out of nowhere, helmet off. He grabbed a cup of Gatorade and lifted it up to us like he was celebrating. Meanwhile, I wanted to cut his face off. With a smirk he walked off.

I clenched the bench with my fingers. "He's lucky I don't run him over with my car."

Jax gave me a double take. "You know where to bury a body?"

Sanchez barked out a laugh. "Not sure if this matters but I got a few cousins in New York that claim to be mafia. One's a florist, so I highly doubt it, but I could make some calls."

"Nah, guys." I tried to cool down. "He's doing it on purpose . . . the last thing we need is to get in a fight with him and look like we're the ones with the problem. He's such a cocky little shit. How the hell did you let Kinsey date him?"

"Let her?" Jax wiped his face with his hands. "I warned her, but the more I warned her away, the more she wanted him, so I finally stopped, and then when things got bad, I finally stepped in, and it took more than a few times to convince her that he was the one with the problem, not her."

Rage built into my system until I couldn't take it anymore. I jumped to my feet, only to be grabbed by both Jax and Sanchez and hauled back onto the bench.

"Cool off, man." Sanchez patted my shoulder pads. "She's got you now, alright? He has nothing. Don't give him anything just because you're pissed about something that happened years ago."

Jax froze next to me.

I licked my lips, that guilty feeling returning with a vengeance. "Yeah, you're right."

I didn't look at Jax.

I knew my expression would be more of a confession than an apology about wanting to kill Anderson.

So instead, of giving us away, I stood and started stretching, then went in search of a protein bar. My guilty ass was going to burn in hell if I didn't tell him soon.

I eyed Kinsey across the field.

A few more days before all hell broke loose.

And after Jax got a few hits in—he'd be fine.

Chapter Twenty-Eight

Jax

Harley: Good game! You caught a ball!
Jax: I'm insulted—I'm a football player. I catch all balls.
Harley: Don't leave yourself open to me, QB, I have all the jokes, the ball jokes, that is. Grandma taught me.

I groaned and texted her back really quick.

Jax: Still traumatized she caught us having sex.
Harley: Traumatized? The woman gave me a high five when she came home and proceeded to make a turkey dinner—we don't even have turkey dinner for Thanksgiving. I think I made her life. Though when she asked me about what you were packing, I had to lie, hope you don't mind.
Jax: The hell!!
Harley: And by lie, I mean, I said eh, not too impressive but told her I'd take candids of it later.
Jax: You're insane.

Harley: She's a very dedicated fan. I'm thinking if she actually saw the pictures, she'd probably just have a heart attack and see Jesus—don't you want her to die happy, Jax?

Jax: She's not getting a dick shot.

Harley: Spoilsport.

I was nervous.

Nervous to invite her into my life.

Even though I saw her on a daily basis, going as far as to pick her up from work because I couldn't wait any longer to kiss her.

I was pathetic.

So damn pathetic.

Sex was messing with my brain cells.

And yet, I'd just played the best game of my life, despite the fact that my sister wanted to shank me, my dad was dying, and Miller still refused to look me in the eyes.

I wasn't sure if he felt guilty about abandoning Kins at the house or if there was something else the little shit should feel guilty about. I was afraid to ask. Afraid of the answer. Afraid of having to pick up the mess when he broke her heart—and afraid of what I would do to my best friend if the worst came true.

Rip his heart out.

Stomp on it.

Fire an entire box of ammo in it.

Then tell him to go to hell.

Harley: So why the texting? Shouldn't you be out partying, big star?

I shook my head. Big star? Yeah, right. I rarely went out after games. If anything, I reviewed tape, ate with Kins, and went to bed early.

Big star? More like the most boring man in football.

Jax: Join me for dinner?
Harley: Actual food? You're going to feed me before sex?
Wow, how fancy. Should I wear a skirt?

I rolled my eyes and grinned.

Jax: Just bring yourself, preferably without clothes. Then
again, there will be people with us, so . . . your choice.
Harley: Fine . . . I'll wear clothes. What are we having?
Jax: Chicken and waffles.
Harley: I'll be the syrup . . .

I groaned. The woman was going to kill me.

"She coming?" Miller popped up out of nowhere and slapped me on the shoulder. I almost dropped my phone. I was still thinking about licking syrup off her body, yeah, she was coming—

"If that grin isn't terrifying, I don't know what is." Miller crossed his arms.

I cleared my throat. "Yup, she'll be there."

"Good." Miller stared down at the locker room floor, uncrossed his arms, shoving his hands into his pockets, then slowly nodded his head and went over to grab his bag.

"Everything okay?"

"Course," he called over his shoulder. "Why?"

He threw the bag over his shoulder and turned, his expression completely blank. "What's up?"

Damn it. Nothing good. "Can I catch a ride?"

"Where's your car?"

"I let Harley borrow it for the day. She had a shoot-out in . . ." Miller's grin wasn't helping my attitude, not even a little bit. "Why do I even talk to you?"

"Best friends." He shrugged. "Plus you find me entertaining. So, she's driving your car for work . . . she gonna start packing your lunches too?"

I punched him in the side, just in time for Anderson to nearly collide with us in the hallway.

"Good game." He held out his fist.

Miller looked ready to ram his fist into Anderson's face, but instead, he ignored him and walked the other way while I watched Anderson's smirk widen with every step Miller took.

"Cut the shit before he kills you, Anderson."

Anderson held up his hands. "Hey, I'm trying to be nice."

I snorted. "Try harder."

"Whatever you say, Captain." He shoved by me.

The only reason I didn't turn around was because I saw a flash of Kinsey outside when Miller opened the door to the parking lot.

She jumped into his arms.

The door slammed closed.

By the time I was on the other side of it, Kinsey was gone and Miller was already in his SUV.

I scratched my head.

"You coming?" Miller shouted across the parking lot.

I jogged to the passenger side and let myself in.

"Sorry." I tossed my bag in back while he started the car and peeled out of the parking lot.

I did a double take.

His neck.

Was covered in her lipstick.

It could mean nothing.

A quick kiss on the neck.

I was still pissed, but I did tell them to look like they were dating, and if cameras caught them in time for sports highlights Anderson would see it and know how off-limits she really was. Maybe then he'd move on from his sick fascination with Kinsey and me.

Yeah, I needed to chill out.

"Maybe wipe the lipstick off your neck next time—so I don't contemplate all the ways I'm going to kill you on the way to your apartment," I said in a bored tone.

"Shit." Miller wiped his neck, and the guilty expression was back.

"It won't come off." I drummed my fingertips against my thigh. "The cheerleaders wear that tough shit that takes at least five bottles of makeup remover to get off, she must have just reapplied when she"—I grunted—"did that."

"You sure know a lot about makeup products, Jax. Something you wanna tell me?"

I flipped him off.

And things went back to normal.

I focused on the game.

On the win.

On the fact that I was going to see Harley soon.

I checked my phone again. Nothing from her, but from my dad? Everything.

Dad: PROUD!

A shudder racked my body. I refused to think about what life would be like when my hero no longer existed.

Chapter Twenty-Nine

KINSEY

We cut it way too close. I'd kissed his mouth so hard, and then my lips found his neck. I couldn't stop kissing him, and his hands were everywhere, under my shirt, gripping my hips.

It had been four days of the most amazing sex of my life paired with laughing until tears ran down my face.

Four days of bliss.

Four days of getting to wake up next to my new roommate.

I stopped by the store to grab the ingredients Em said we needed then quickly headed back to the apartment so I could change before my brother made it over.

I was just tossing on some leggings when the door opened.

I peeked around the corner to make sure it was safe.

He dropped his bag onto the floor, took two steps into the apartment, his grin wide. "Kins, stop hiding."

"That was a mighty nice throw, Quinton Miller." I leaned against the hallway wall; my voice carried across the room. Anticipation had my blood pumping so loud that he could probably hear it.

"A cheerleader? Complimenting my throwing skills?"

"Not just any cheerleader, remember, I helped Jax fine-tune his."

Miller appeared around the corner, his face broke out into a grin. "Gotcha."

Hands snaked out around my waist as he tugged me against him.

"This a new look for you? Leggings, bra, no shirt? I have to say I really like it . . ." He thumbed the bra, then cupped my breast.

I slapped his hand away. "We should be next door."

"We should." His mouth descended.

"Mmmm." I leaped into his arms, wrapped my legs around his waist, and met his mouth with as much enthusiasm as I possessed. His fingers dug into my hair, tugging my head down, and our mouths fused. He tasted like peppermint and smelled like spicy clean soap. I inhaled with each kiss, drinking him in.

"A guy could get addicted to your kisses," he whispered against my lips.

"That's all part of my plan."

"World domination with your mouth, who knew?" he teased, pinching my ass and then digging his hands beneath the leggings and cupping it with his warm hands. "We have about five minutes before they come searching, and your brother can't see you in here, or the shit that's taken over my apartment since you moved in."

"I could go back to the hotel."

"You go back to that hotel, and I'll just chase you down and bring you back here."

I bit my bottom lip. "You sure you don't mind?"

"Mind?" Goodness gracious, his grin wasn't just panty melting. That thing could melt the polar ice caps. "Waking up next to you completely makes up for the fact that one of your spiky heels nearly impaled my foot yesterday."

I lifted a shoulder in a shrug. "Maybe you should watch where you're going."

"Your shoes are like a freaking minefield in the master bedroom and the guest room, don't deny it." His breath fanned my neck.

"Aw, is the big bad football player intimidated by shoes?"

He smacked me on the ass and pushed my body against the wall harder, this time meeting my mouth with a punishing kiss, dragging his lips across mine with fierceness that brought tears to my eyes.

"We should go," he whispered against my lips.

"Yup." I didn't move.

He sighed.

"Or . . ."

"I'm listening." He grinned.

"We can do a lot of damage in three minutes."

"Damage." He was already using his left hand to peel down the layers I'd just put on. "Hard and fast damage."

I moaned when he reached for his low-slung jeans and sprang free. I slid down the wall, he turned me around and bit down on my ear.

My head fell back against his shoulder. "Yeah, that kind."

"Thin walls, Kins; don't make any noise."

"It's a penthouse and it has thin walls?"

"You have no idea."

I let out a gasp when he slid into me, then braced myself using the wall for support, all the while trying not to make a noise, but with each thrust I lost more and more of my sanity, finally smacking my hand against the wall as he pumped harder and faster.

"Damn, you feel good." He jerked my hips back against him and held me there. "I think all I'm capable of is hard and fast right now, I'm so close."

I wiggled against him.

He bit back a curse.

"What are you waiting for?"

"A gentleman never goes first."

I started moving despite his protests. "I don't believe I said I wanted a gentleman."

"Kins—"

Swearing, he quickened his movements until my legs felt like they were going to give out on me. And when he lost complete control and jumped off the ledge, I jumped with him.

And screamed out his name.

He clamped a hand over my mouth, as chest heaving, I tried to get my breathing under control.

A knock sounded on our door.

He rolled up my leggings, shoved me toward the master suite, jerked up his jeans, and ran down the hall.

"'Sup, man?" He answered the door, way too out of breath for a guy who worked out for a living.

"You're lucky as hell that Jax was in the bathroom during the show." Sanchez's deep voice echoed off the walls. "Em and I almost had to become exhibitionists so that he wouldn't hear you guys."

"Fuck."

"Get it together, man," Sanchez warned. "The minute he knows you've been fucking his sister, he's going to lose his shit."

"Yeah."

I'd heard enough. Same old story. I quickly cleaned up, grabbed a loose T-shirt, and made my way out of the master bedroom. Miller was waiting by the door.

"You heard?" He scratched his head.

I wrapped my arms around his waist. "Yeah, I heard."

"We'll tell him tomorrow." I kissed the top of her head. "It's going to be fine."

"Thought you said you wouldn't ever lie to me."

He closed his eyes and sighed. "Yeah, well, there's a first time for everything, right?" He held out his hand. I squeezed it then let it go. "I'll go first, you show up in a few minutes, yeah?"

I nodded.

He walked out, shutting the door quietly behind him.

After a few minutes of staring at the door, I finally made my way over to Sanchez's. I let myself in just as Harley was getting off the elevator, thank God. The last thing she needed to see was me leaving Miller's apartment. I wasn't sure how much Jax told her, but from my end, all I'd done was tell her we were dating, which I'm sure she assumed meant a bit of sex but not moving in together.

"Howdy, stranger." Harley gave me a wink.

I met her halfway and gave her a hug. "How's Jax?"

"Eh." She eyed him over my shoulder. "He's okay, I guess."

"Heard that." He moved from behind me then pulled her into a hug. I expected her to hug him back. I expected a bit of shyness, since our last gathering at dinner hadn't gone super well.

Instead, the woman grabbed him by the shirt and led with her tongue, and when I say led with her tongue, it was out before her lips were even touching his mouth.

With a moan, she dragged her hands through his hair and jumped into his arms. My brother, to his credit, caught her and kissed her back with equal fervor.

Sanchez started a slow clap while Miller whistled.

"Grandma says hi." Harley kissed his nose.

I laughed so hard tears formed in my eyes.

"What the hell kind of kinky shit you guys into?" Sanchez shook his head. "Also, can we just talk about the elephant in the room?"

Everyone fell silent. Em poked her head out from the fridge.

Sanchez crossed his arms, his ever-present smirk growing by the second. "Jax, my man, is finally getting laid."

"Atta boy." Miller and Sanchez clinked their beer bottles while Em and I burst into laughter again. See? I could be supportive of his sex life, why couldn't he be supportive of mine? Stupid past. Stupid protective big brother pain in my ass!

Jax flipped the guys off behind Harley's back then slowly lowered her to her feet.

"Is that what's happening every time he lures me into his bedroom?" Harley asked aloud. "And here I thought he wanted my brain more than my body. Well, can't win them all. By the way, congrats on the win today, gentlemen." She winked and grabbed a beer from the bucket and held it into the air.

Jax couldn't take his eyes off her.

It was like nobody else existed.

I sighed, happily noting how Miller was picking up on the same thing as he looked between Jax and Harley.

I gave myself a mental high five for hooking them up and for a few brief seconds contemplated starting my own matchmaking service.

If I could get my brother laid, I could probably plan world domination and become successful!

"Thanks, Harley." Miller spoke first and clinked his beer to hers then made his way into the kitchen. "Em, when's the chicken done?"

She smacked his hand away from the stove. "It's done when I say it's done!" She hit him again.

I tried not to get jealous.

Even after everything they'd been through—they still had a bond I couldn't compete with, something that I knew wasn't mine to worry about in the first place, but there was still that lingering pessimistic thought—what if she and Sanchez broke up for some reason? Would he drop me for her?

No. I was being ridiculous.

"You get used to it," Sanchez said from my left, scaring me so bad I nearly stumbled forward into the dining room table. "The relationship they have."

"Oh." Crap, was I that transparent? I tucked a piece of hair behind my ear.

"Kins . . ." He drew out my nickname. "The guy's crazy about you. Trust me, if there was any indication that he wanted Em again, I'd end his life, so I've got us covered, cool?"

I smiled up at him. "I'm trying to decide if I'm thankful or a bit terrified that you're completely serious right now."

"Em comes before Miller, the game, the team, me—everything. Ergo, I'd end his life," he said in a chilling tone I'd never heard him use before. "Then again, prison doesn't exactly sound like a fun place to hang, but I'd make it look good. Armani model." He winked and struck a runway pose, finally injecting some humor into the conversation.

I patted him on the shoulder. "You'd make orange the new black."

"Hell yes, I would."

We laughed.

Miller joined us, his eyes narrowing. "You two just bury that hatchet?"

"Hatchet?" Sanchez frowned. "No, she's still a skinny little pain in my ass." He said it with a shrug then winked again before walking off. And then like he thought better about it, he turned around and faced Miller. "Then again, didn't she gain some weight in that ass?"

Miller's jaw clenched.

Sanchez threw his head back and laughed. "Looks good on you, Kins."

"Say one more word, I fucking dare you." Miller glared.

"One of my favorite things in the world is pissing you off, Miller. Why would I stop now?"

"So I don't ram my fist through your weak-ass torso and rip your heart out through your stomach?"

"Vivid." Sanchez nodded. "Nice talk, as always."

He joined Em in the kitchen.

"That was graphic." I faced Miller, crossing my arms so I wouldn't reach out to him.

"He knows I'd protect him with my life—unless it came to you or him, then I'd let the zombies get him, but something tells me he's probably got a plan for that too."

We shared a smile.

"Hey!" Jax walked up. "I left my shit in your car. Was gonna toss it in mine since Harley drove it here."

"No problem." Miller tossed him his keys and faced me again. "So, good job with Harley. He's clearly tapping that and completely ignoring the fact that I'm so hard I could pound nails into the granite just from looking at your mouth."

From the heat that swamped my face, I had to be flushing bright red. "You can't say things like that to me."

"Why?" He frowned. "Does it make you uncomfortable?"

"No." Jax left the apartment. I snaked my arms around Miller's neck then placed an open-mouthed kiss below his ear and whispered, "It makes me want to get you naked on the same granite you're so obsessed with."

He let out a moan.

Sanchez coughed.

We separated.

And made our way into the kitchen.

Miller to sneak food.

Me to help.

Harley joined us soon after and was just in the middle of telling us that her grandmother was an advocate of safe sex, and that she had pretended to be a man so she could enlist in Vietnam, when the door to the apartment jerked open.

I staggered back.

Jax's face wasn't just pissed.

It was menacing.

"Jax?"

"No." He jutted a finger at me. "No."

Huh?

His other hand lifted.

A red bra.

My red bra.

My entire body went weak.

Not how I wanted him to find out.

My jaw went slack. I tried to speak but nothing came out. Sanchez eyed me then quickly cleared his throat. "Oh, awesome." Sanchez stepped forward. "You found Em's bra, been looking for that one."

"In Miller's car." Jax's teeth clenched. "And stop the bullshit, Sanchez, I know my sister's stuff when I see it."

Sanchez held up his hands and said under his breath, "Hey, I tried."

Miller hung his head, then licked his lips. "Jax, not here, man. Let's go into the bedroom and—"

Jax launched himself across the room and punched Miller in the face. Miller let him, just stood there and let my brother clock him in the head like he deserved it!

I ran at them, screaming.

Sanchez was able to get between them but was punched in the stomach by Jax, who was trying to get another good hit on Miller.

"Stop!" I yelled.

Nobody listened.

"Jax, STOP!"

He hesitated enough for Sanchez to slam him against a wall and keep him away from Miller. Blood spewed from Miller's mouth and nose, and I was pretty confident he was going to be nursing a black eye for at least a week or two.

I was at his side in seconds, Em brought me a warm cloth.

"What the fuck, Miller!" Jax roared. "Who the hell do you think you are? I asked you to date her so Anderson would leave her alone, not so you could get into her pants!"

Sanchez's eyebrows shot up while Em covered her mouth with her hands in shock.

Harley didn't seem surprised. Then again, it was Harley.

She'd be more surprised if we *weren't* sleeping together.

"How long?" He jerked out of Sanchez's hands. "Damn it, how long, Miller!" His chest was heaving.

Miller dropped the cloth and winced. "The first time was Vegas."

"First time?" Jax's nostrils flared. "Vegas? As in last year Vegas?"

I bit down on my bottom lip and stood in front of Miller. "It was me."

"Move away, Kins. I'm not going to punch him, and it's not like I blame you for him seducing you!"

"Stop!" I clenched my hands into tight fists. "Just stop! It was me! Okay! I was on the couch and I couldn't sleep so I crawled into his bed thinking he was too drunk to notice—"

"You had drunken sex with my sister!" He roared over my head, ready to lunge again.

Oh, this was not going well.

"Jax!" I held up my hands and pressed them against his rock-hard chest. "I made the move, it was me, well, technically it was both of us—"

Jax cut loose with a harsh curse.

I doubled my effort. "But the point is, it happened. Miller helped send me away for my own good and then when you asked us to date again, it was like . . . lighting a match and throwing it on dry wood."

"Wood," Sanchez repeated with a low chuckle.

"Really?" Em elbowed him in the side.

"Let me get this straight, you fucked my sister, then helped me encourage her to leave the country? One of my best friends? You didn't tell me, then proceeded to lie by omission and promised not to touch her again, and just what? Tried not to sleep with her, got naked, and decided 'What the hell, I'm going to do this again because the first time things ended up so well'?"

"You don't know what you're talking about." Miller sneered from behind me. "I liked her, okay? I knew how you felt! How the hell does that make me the bad guy?"

Hearing it put that way made it burn a little less.

"So is that what you do then, Miller? Shit gets hard and you walk away? You listen to people around you? Help me out here, because the other night when she was at her worst, you ran away. You're a runner, so what now? What happens when our dad dies? What happens"—his voice rasped—"if her lupus flares up again? What are you going to do then? I'm sure you know all about that, right? How to treat it when it gets bad? What happens if it does? You gonna leave her for her own good? Help me figure it out, because I sure as fuck don't think you deserved her then and I damn well don't think you deserve her now. Not after what she's been through."

My entire world stopped.

Mouth open.

I couldn't make a sound.

He'd outed me.

In front of everyone.

I don't remember falling to my knees, just that I did.

"Who the hell are you talking about?" Miller whispered.

"Me," I answered. "He's talking about me."

The room shifted.

Warm arms caught me before my head hit something.

A black tunnel.

And then nothing.

Chapter Thirty

MILLER

Lupus.

Flare-ups.

Sickness.

She'd passed out. I caught her before her body hit the floor. The fight between me and Jax long forgotten now that the most precious thing in my life—and his—was momentarily lifeless.

Flashes of my mom collapsing, crumpling into a lifeless heap in front of my eyes.

And the searing pain that split me in two, threatening to never make me whole again, pounded into my line of vision. Not again. Not again.

"Kins?" I gripped her hand. "Wake up, baby."

Jax paced in front of the couch, alternating between wiping his face with his hands and swearing in my direction.

Finally, after a few seconds, though it felt like ten minutes, her eyes flickered open, focusing in on my face. A small smile spread across her features and then fell. She slowly moved to a sitting position.

Jax stopped pacing and knelt in front of her, gripping her hands between his.

She jerked away. "What right do you have?"

Jax shook his head then sucked in his bottom lip, biting down so hard I thought the guy was going to draw blood. "I'm your brother. It's my job. Mine."

"It's your job to tell everyone in this room about my past?" she yelled.

He flinched. "No." His face flashed with anger. "But what the fuck do you think you're doing, Kins? If this was real, if you really loved this guy—" I hated that they were talking about me. They deserved privacy. My heart felt like someone had taken a sledgehammer to it with the goal of breaking it against the only muscle weak enough to shatter on contact. "If you loved him, you'd tell him everything. If he loved you, if you weren't just a hot piece of ass, convenient—"

I growled low in my throat.

"He'd demand to know everything about you . . . You got so sick when you were with Anderson, so sick, and I wasn't there to stop it, you wouldn't let me help you, and now you've put yourself in another hopeless situation."

"That I never asked you to bail me out of," she pointed out, her voice laced with anger and hurt.

Bail? What the hell? Why would she bail? From me? Why would there be any bailing at all?

I dropped her hand.

I had to.

Mine was shaking too hard to be any good.

Jax scowled. "It's my job."

"Who made it your job?" she fired back.

"I did!" he roared, jumping to his feet. "Who was there when your parents left you alone on the dirty floor? Who helped wash the cuts on your feet?" Tears welled in his eyes. "Who held your hand at the hospital when the doctors couldn't figure out what was wrong with you and thought you had cancer? Me! I was there!" Jax pounded his chest. "I've earned the fucking right to protect you—to make sure nothing happens to you, to—"

"Leave," she whispered. "Now."

"Kins . . ." Hurt flashed across his features. "I'm sorry, I shouldn't have said—"

"Go."

"What about him?" Jax nodded to me. Yeah, apparently I was the lucky son of a bitch he was throwing under the bus. Nice.

If he thought I was leaving her. He had another think coming.

She sighed and looked out of the corner of her eyes. "You should go too."

I sucked in a shuddered breath.

"No."

Jax's face went from apologetic to full-on rage.

Kinsey looked down as her shoulders sagged.

"I stay."

"Miller . . ." A tear slid down her cheek. "Just go."

"No."

Jax moved toward me. I braced myself for another hit, but surprisingly he didn't do that, he put his hand on my shoulder and walked off. Harley followed.

The door shut behind them.

Sanchez and Em quietly walked down the hall hand in hand and closed a bedroom door.

The chicken was forgotten.

The waffles.

Funny, that our relationship started with those stupid nicknames, and now, it felt like it was breaking, ending, the very same way.

"You were sick," I whispered hoarsely.

"Am," she corrected. "I *am* sick. I'm in remission, I haven't had a flare-up in years. But I could get sick at any point in my life, hospitalized." Her head tilted to the side, maybe gauging my reaction.

I reached for her hand, she slipped it away.

"Kins?"

"I wasn't going to tell you."

It stung.

More than it should.

Because while I'd convinced myself I was all in, that I was falling in love with her, trusted her, was willing to jeopardize my friendship with Jax and relationship with the team . . .

She'd been, what? Lying to me?

I had to know.

Had to ask.

"You weren't *ever* going to tell me?"

She was quiet.

Too quiet.

When one second turned into five minutes, I knew I had my answer.

I stood, unable to face her. "So all those moments when I walked away and then came back fighting for you, the moments I held you in my arms, and kissed away your tears. I was falling in love and you were . . . what? Just having sex? Just trying to piss off your brother? What the hell was I? A distraction from your dad's condition?"

Her head jerked up. "No! You know that's not true!"

"Do I?" I spread my arms wide. "Because I don't hear you denying it! If you won't even tell me about your past, how the hell are we supposed to have a future?"

Her lower lip trembled.

"Great." I cursed under my breath. "More silence from the girl I'm in love with, the same one who didn't even trust me enough to tell me she was sick! How was I supposed to take care of you if something—"

"Shut up, just shut up!" Kinsey jumped to her feet, and slammed a fist against my chest. "Did you ever think that maybe, for once in my life, I didn't want to be protected?"

I stumbled back.

"You're not Jax! I don't need another Jax! Or a father who calls the doctor every time I get a headache or feel sleepy! I didn't want that with you! Don't you understand! I don't want you to look at me and think I'm weak! That I'm sick!"

"Oh, Kins . . ." I shook my head. "Weak is the last thing I think when I look in your eyes."

A tear slid off her chin.

"You're one of the strongest people I know. A fighter. Menacing. Aggravatingly stunning . . ." I reached for her. "I never stood a chance against you."

"This changes everything though." She wiped her cheeks.

"Only if you let it." I shrugged. "And that's your choice, Kinsey, not mine, not Jax's. Yours." I dropped her hand. "But I need you to know something."

She stared down at the ground.

"I've made mine."

Her head jerked up.

"And it's you." I took a step forward. "I hate that you're sick, but what I hate more is that you think for one fucking second that I would cut and run or worse, turn into the type of controlling prick who makes you feel trapped. Yes, I want to protect you. Because that's what you do when you love someone. And someone like you, someone as special as you, deserves all the good she can get. So while I'm pissed as hell at Jax, I get him, I get why he's upset, I get why he did what he did. And I deserve his anger, because I went behind his back and took something precious, I took you away from what he saw was his job, his protection. In Jax's eyes, I threw you out into the wild and asked you to survive . . . and while nothing bad happened, it could have. And the could-have-been is what scares Jax shitless." I sighed. "I choose you, I just need you to choose me back."

More silence.

Great.

Kinsey reached for my hand. "You really love me?"

I exhaled in relief. "More than I should if I don't want Jax to kill me. Then again, maybe it's the only way to stay alive . . . love you so much he has no choice but to admit defeat."

She smiled for the first time since the fight. "He has good intentions."

I pointed to my face. "Misguided, but good."

Kinsey walked into my open arms and placed her head against my chest. "You're not going anywhere?"

"No." I squeezed her tight. "Not unless you're there with me."

"So this is really real."

"It's been really real since Vegas, I was just too chickenshit to admit it, Kins. I hope you can forgive me for that."

"It's why I called you Chicken."

"Then why are you always the Waffle?"

She grinned up at me. "Because I'm really sweet."

I claimed her lips. "Yeah, you are."

She took a step away from me and walked into the kitchen. "You know, we do have all of this food—"

"Touch the food and you're a dead man." Sanchez came running down the hall. "Oh, and good talk, guys, I really felt the emotion."

Emerson smacked the back of his head and gave us a knowing smile. "He literally only heard the last part, because I had the TV up so loud before that, but I'm happy you guys talked."

"Me too." I kissed Kinsey on the temple, and forced a smile I didn't feel, not because I wasn't happy that she'd actually listened to me. But because it wasn't the ending I wanted. The ending I wanted was Jax approving of us, telling me that he accepted me, accepted what we had, and right now, the guilt was eating me alive and making me feel like shit.

The guy needed time to cool off.

Which meant I had to wait to talk to him again.

I just hoped that our friendship wasn't damaged past the point of no return, because he and Sanchez were literally the only family I recognized, next to Em, and I refused to break up my family.

Even if it was for a good reason.

Kins slid her hand into mine. "You okay?"

"I should be asking you that."

"Your face looks worse than mine."

Pain radiated off my cheek. "I bet."

Sanchez tossed me an ice pack.

I pressed it against my cheek and winced in pain.

"Gotta hand it to Jax"—Sanchez crossed his arms and leaned against the couch—"the man knows how to throw a crazy-ass right hook."

"My cheek's well aware," I grumbled.

Kins shrugged. "He has a black belt too."

All eyes fell to her.

"You're shitting me, right?" Sanchez smirked. "Good ol' Jax is a fighter? Huh, would have never guessed."

"I swear he could have made it in the UFC," Kins added, "but he loves football more."

I knew the feeling.

"Well, hopefully he gets his head clear before next week. We're playing Seattle, and as much as I'd love to say it's going to be an easy game, we all know the Sharks put up a good fight."

Kinsey nodded seriously. "I'll talk to him, it's going to be fine."

Lie.

I saw it in her face.

Her body language.

Nothing was going to be fine.

Chapter Thirty-One

"He's not talking to me."

I was watching the away game with Dad, ready to punch through a wall. Jax was playing like a complete moron, and Miller was saving the game by way of blocking—a technique that the other team's offensive line was not implementing at all, leaving their quarterback vulnerable to the Bucks' defense.

Dad patted my knee. "He's just upset, honey, give him some time. You remember, he's seen you at your worst, helped you through it. Show him a little grace. It's your turn to help."

My shoulders sagged. "He doesn't want my help."

"He does. He just doesn't know it."

I swiped a cookie from his plate and took a bite. Ever since the whole cancer and lupus thing came out, I'd been on pins and needles, waiting for Miller to ask me for details.

What was lupus?

How long had I been sick?

Would I get sick again?

How long had I been in the hospital?

But he didn't pry. I knew he was waiting for me to talk about it, but I didn't want to, because talking about something made it real. Besides, I was so emotionally spent from worrying about my dad that talking about my own health made me feel like I was going to have an anxiety attack.

I sighed again.

Dad turned up the volume. "You gonna sigh during the whole game?"

"Sorry," I grumbled.

It was tied three to three. Seattle had a crazy good team, but I knew ours was better. The battle between the Bucks and the Sharks went back all the way to the 1940s, and because we were in the same division, we almost always had to play them twice before playoffs.

Both times, I held my breath the entire game.

Their defense was intense.

My eyes were drawn to Anderson. I shivered. The guy had basically ignored me for the past few weeks, and I had Miller to thank for that, but there was always that lingering fear that he'd corner me, say something mean, or just bring me back to that helpless place that I was so terrified I'd never get out of. He was an emotional bully—he fed on the weak, and being cornered by him left me feeling afraid, and I was done with that feeling.

The Sharks tight end blocked then went into a run. Anderson was there, he jumped up, caught the ball, and made a run toward our territory. Twenty, thirty, forty yards.

Touchdown.

I didn't cheer.

I hated him.

He jogged off the field like a freaking peacock, then stopped when he got next to Miller and said something that was probably offensive.

Miller shook it off and looked away.

But then Jax shoved Anderson in the back.

Oh no.

No, Jax, back off. Back off!

"Aw hell," Dad swore. "Your mama's not gonna be happy about that."

The cameras caught everything. Miller grabbed Jax to keep him from hitting Anderson, and Jax turned on him. Sanchez moved between all of them and ended up receiving the sucker punch from Anderson.

Miller went to help Sanchez, when Jax shoved past them and landed three huge blows to Anderson's face.

The coach pulled him away.

I covered my mouth with my hands. *Jax, what are you doing?*

Three yellow flags were thrown.

And within seconds, Jax and Anderson were thrown out of the game.

Dad flipped off the TV.

We sat in silence.

Finally, he got up and stretched. "You want a cookie?"

"A cookie," I said flatly. "Jax just got kicked out of the game, and you ask if I want a cookie."

Dad offered a shrug. "They're still warm."

"Dad!" I threw my hands in the air. "Look, I know stress is bad because of the cancer, but you can't just ignore the fact that Jax, Mr. American Football, just got in a fistfight!"

"Sure can." He grinned. "It's about time that boy dealt with all of this."

"But—"

"Anger will always win out, Kinsey. Can't hide your feelings forever." Dad's voice lowered. "And that boy has been keeping in so much anger, for so long, that it's no shock at all he's lashing out. He's angry at you, angry at me."

"Why would he be angry at you?"

"Oh, honey." Dad stepped toward me then lowered his body to my level. "Because he can't be angry at the cancer, he needs something tangible to be angry at, something in front of him, so he's angry at me, he's angry at you, but mostly he's angry at himself. That boy always did have a hero complex. He was lucky, grew up being able to save everyone from everything or at least he thought he did. And now . . . now his world is crumbling. All he's got left is football, the very last thing to be angry at—and look, he's lashing out at that too. Now, do you want a cookie?"

"But, what are you going to do about this?"

Dad looked from me to the dark TV. "Absolutely nothing."

"But—"

"Kins, the cookies are cold by now. I hope you're happy." He walked off, leaving me alone in the living room, wondering if my brother was done saving everyone—was he done saving himself?

Chapter Thirty-Two

Jax

I let the hot water pelt my back like tiny little needles. It didn't make the pain go away.

Nothing did anymore.

I'd failed my dad.

I'd failed Kinsey.

I'd failed my team.

Fail, fail, fail, fail.

"We need to talk." Miller.

I wasn't in the mood for him.

We lost the game.

And it was my fault.

All of it.

I couldn't bring myself to look at my phone for fear that Harley straight-up dumped my sorry ass for being such an embarrassment, or worse, that my father would send me a text that was the opposite of proud.

And Kins.

My heart clenched.

"Yeah, okay." I grabbed a towel, wrapped it around my waist, and followed him into the locker room.

Sanchez still had his gear on, so did Miller.

The rest of the team was gone.

The hell?

"This . . ." Miller held his hands wide. "Is an intervention."

"We were going to make signs." Sanchez grinned. "But I couldn't find any markers, and I knew you wouldn't take us seriously if I used the pink crayon from one of Coach's kids."

"And you think I'm taking you seriously now?"

"We both went to Coach, told him what Anderson said." Miller crossed his arms. "He was out of line."

I nodded, still remembering the words so clearly, the phrasing. He'd done it on purpose, and I'd fallen for it.

With a touchdown like that, I think I should celebrate by fucking your sister, or have you already been doing that this whole time behind Miller's back?

Anger surged through me.

She was my sister.

My baby sister.

I'd never looked at her like—bile bit at the back of my throat—like *that.* I'd never wanted people to even know she was adopted so they couldn't use her against me, or make her feel bad about herself, but that was Anderson for you.

He was a manipulative tool who fed off others' pain. And seeing Miller with Kinsey had finally pushed him off that ledge, the one that I knew he would fall off the longer he went without getting what he wanted, and what he wanted was Kinsey. I knew he would slip up, I knew his true colors would show, I just didn't expect for him to drag me down with him.

"And?" My voice was hoarse.

"He's off the team." Miller shrugged. I visibly relaxed. "It helped that I told Coach about his past with Kinsey."

"You did what?" I roared. "You had no right to tell Coach about that!"

Sanchez pressed a hand to my chest and shoved me back. "Actually, since he loves her, he kind of does. This is what love looks like, man, it protects, not by keeping everything hidden but by being honest."

I blinked at him. "Are you shitting me right now?"

"I love her." Miller's eyes met mine. "I'd do anything to protect her."

"It's not Coach's business. It's nobody's damn business!"

"You can't fix everything!" Miller shouted, "God, look at you! You're a mess!" He got right up in my face. "Not only are you the best quarterback in the league, but you're family, and you're wrecking everything because you can't see past your own damn pride! Yes, I love her. But you can still love her too! And yes, it sucks that your dad is sick, but at least you have time with him. You've got a team that's counting on you to lead them! You wanna be a hero? Then act like it! Starting now." He shoved me against the wall. "Swallow your pride, apologize to the team, and go talk to Kinsey. Get your shit figured out and realize that life isn't about memorizing every single play. Life isn't perfect, you can't always plan for things. Sometimes they happen, and all you can do is react in a way that's worthy of the way your little sister looks at you every damn day, the way your team looks at you, the way we look at you."

Sanchez sighed. "For the record, most the time I look at you like you're a giant prick."

Miller grinned.

I bit down on my lower lip to keep from doing something insane like laughing in such a tense situation, but I couldn't help it. A laugh escaped, followed by another.

Until all three of us were wiping tears from our eyes.

Brothers.

They were my brothers.

The laughter died down.

I looked at Miller, really looked at him, and it was like our responsibilities shifted, like I'd given him that piece to take without even realizing that I needed to let it go.

To let Kinsey go.

"You really love her?"

"Yeah, man." Miller nodded. "I really do."

"And if she gets sick—"

"I'll make her soup," he interrupted with an irritated sigh. "I've got this. You just have to let me take it, man."

I nodded, not trusting my voice.

Sanchez crossed his arms and shook his head. "Guys, I know this was one of those moments . . . so, there's only one thing left to do." He wrapped his arms around both of us amidst the cursing and yelling between me and Miller.

"What the hell do you boys think you're doing?" Coach yelled, the door slamming behind him.

"Hugging it out, Coach!" Sanchez yelled. "You want in?"

"Sanchez."

"Yeah, Coach?"

"You're a pain in my ass!"

"Was that a yes?"

Coach rolled his eyes and mumbled, "I'd punch him if I didn't need him so bad."

"Heard that," Sanchez yelled.

Coach shook his head at us, and then offered a smile in my direction. "You done acting like a little shit?"

"Yes sir."

"Good to hear it. No practice tomorrow, and gentlemen, if I walk back in here and see you hugging again—you're all running."

"Nothing wrong with brotherly love, Coach!"

"Uh-huh." He walked back out of the room.

We'd broken apart already.

I took a seat in one of the chairs and grabbed my bag. "Now what?"

"Now, you start groveling." Miller patted me on the back. "Starting with your sister."

Chapter Thirty-Three

Miller texted me to meet him at home. It still brought a smile to my face to think about that. Home. We were living together.

He said he loved me.

And he texted home.

I grinned and opened the door to the apartment, then nearly ran in the opposite direction when my brother stood up from the couch and very slowly started walking toward me until I really looked at him.

I'd never seen him look so broken.

So tired.

So done.

"Kins—" His voice caught.

I rushed into his arms, too preoccupied with how horrible he looked to be angry. I held on to him for dear life while he kissed my forehead over and over again.

With a sigh, he touched his forehead to mine and braced my shoulders with his hands. "You were four the first time."

Tears filled my eyes. "Jax, you don't have to do this."

"Four," he repeated, ignoring me. "I saw the tree slam into your house. I'd never been so freaked out in my life. My parents were gone, and I knew you were alone. I ran like hell, thankful to God that your front door was open. And when I finally found you. You were"—his voice shook—". . . you were sobbing in the corner, your feet cut up from the shattered windows."

Tears filled my eyes at the memory. I'd been so afraid. So desperate for someone to hug me, to tell me everything was going to be okay.

"You looked like an angel," I whispered. "I asked you if that's why God put you next door, to look after me."

"And I said yes." Jax closed his eyes. "That I'd be your savior every day, every night, until the day I died."

"You carried me."

"I carried you through the storm," Jax added. "And I remember so distinctly promising myself that I wouldn't let anything hurt you. And for a few years, once the adoption went through, once you were really a Romonov . . . everything was perfect. And then you got sick and you were so helpless." He shuddered. "It was stupid, but I remember at the time hating myself, blaming myself for carrying you through the storm, wondering if maybe that's why you got sick."

"Oh, Jax." I shook my head. "One storm doesn't make people sick."

"I was so scared, and once the doctors told us it wasn't cancer but lupus, and that you were going to be okay, I promised myself again that I'd make sure nothing would hurt you—nothing would touch you." His voice cracked. "And in my mind somehow, I'd helped save you again just like I promised." He paused. "You were, you are, my best friend."

Tears slid down my cheeks.

"But I couldn't protect you from Anderson." He swore. "His abuse caused your body to attack itself, and when we found out you were getting flare-ups again, I blamed myself. You met him because of me. You trusted me, therefore you trusted him. I should have seen how badly he was treating you. I should have fought like hell to get you away from him." His fists clenched.

"Jax." I cupped his face. "You can't save the world."

"I can try."

"No." I shook my head. "You can't."

"Clearly." His smile was sad. "Because it seems every time I try, I mess up even more than before."

"Hate to break it to you, brother, but you are human."

He scowled. "Bullshit, you've always said I look like Captain America."

"Doesn't mean you have superpowers even though I secretly always believed you did. It was my fault too, Jax. I put you in that position, not realizing how much pressure it put on you. You saved me from Anderson, and when you sent me away, you were trying to save me again, but this time . . ." I swallowed the lump in my throat. "This time it didn't work because I'd found someone who treated me not like I was about to break, but like I was unbreakable."

"I never meant to treat you that way."

"I know." I hugged him. "I know you didn't do it on purpose, Jax."

"The bastard loves you, and I can't make him stop."

I laughed against his chest. "Let me guess, you tried and he said no?"

"Something like that." His laughter joined mine. "I'm sorry, Kins, so sorry. For telling everyone about your illness, for being overprotective, for—everything."

"Don't be." I shrugged. "You wouldn't be you if you weren't an overprotective asshole with a God complex."

He pinched my side. "Very funny."

"Dad said you'd come to your senses."

Tears filled Jax's eyes. "He knows me well."

"Because you're him." I smiled. "Don't you see? You are just like him, protecting everyone and everything around you, fighting for what's good, what's right. You're his son, and I know he couldn't be more proud of you."

"He's dying," Jax whispered. "And we can't stop it."

"No." I hugged him tighter as my heart squeezed in my chest. "But we can live . . ."

"You still remember, huh?"

"You told me it was my only job."

"Live."

"And look at me now." I pulled away from him. "Miller said something that helped me. He said it's not going to be okay, not today, not tomorrow, not during the funeral . . . he said he couldn't lie to my face, that it *was* going to hurt, but he said eventually, it does hurt less, and that one day, the hurt won't be as intense. So even though it hurts right now, and I'm sure it's going to get a lot worse . . . I'm looking forward to that day, when it's all a little less."

"Wow." Jax shoved his hands into his pockets. "No wonder you fell in love with the guy. Brutal honesty."

"I needed to hear it."

"I think I did too."

The door to the apartment opened. Miller slowly walked in, looking between us like he wasn't sure if a fight was going to break out or if we were finally okay.

"You sucked today," I said, shattering the moment. "You both did. Maybe try not to get into a fight next time and keep your heads in the game." I pointed at Miller. "Your blocking was good, but you're better than that, and you know it." I turned to Jax. "And don't even get me started on your throws. Almost every time you took at least four seconds and barely made it out of the pocket. You're faster than that, stop dancing around and get us a win next week!"

"I love it when she talks dirty." Miller winked at me.

Jax groaned and plugged his ears before walking to Miller, punching him in the stomach then patting him on the back. "Welcome to the family. Remember, I sit at the head of the table during family dinner, the leather recliner is mine when we have a non-game week, and if you even think about stealing the last chocolate chip cookie, I will end you."

"I love your mom's cookies."

I groaned behind my hands.

Jax and Miller both chuckled, did a weird man hug, and my brother left.

Miller grinned at me. "So, how'd it go?"

I held out my hands. "It was good to talk about everything, including all the things I probably need to talk about with you, but haven't."

Miller nodded. "I always figured you would when you were ready, I know it can't be easy."

"No, it's not." I could still feel the glass in my feet, the tubes poking out of my body while my blood was transfused. "But—"

The door jerked open, admitting Jax, his face ghastly pale. "Kins, Mom just called, we gotta go."

"What?"

"It's Dad."

Chapter Thirty-Four

MILLER

Everything in life comes full circle. Everything.

I gripped Kinsey's hand as we made our way down the hospital hall, the same hall we'd walked through two weeks ago for the Homecoming Dance. Staff walked by us, a few stared.

I'd texted Sanchez and Em the minute we hopped into Jax's car. If it was bad, he needed his family—all of his family.

Jax handed me his phone to text Harley too, and when she responded, all I could do was stare at the phone and shake my head. That woman . . . was just what he needed, because her first response was to gather the team.

She understood that his team was family just like Kinsey was his family even if she wasn't blood. If you were lucky enough to be in Jax Romonov's life, you were there for an eternity, maybe that's why it had been so hard for me to go behind his back, because I loved him like the brother I never had.

When Jax walked into the waiting room. It wasn't to face this thing alone.

It was to battle with his brothers by his side, the way it was supposed to be. Every single team member was there, some with their family members by their side, and then there was Coach, tears in his eyes as he walked up to Jax and pulled him in for a hug.

Harley was standing next to Coach, holding a plate of cookies.

Her smile was big, hopeful.

Jax reached for her.

She met him halfway.

Once they were done kissing, he turned to me. "You call the team?"

"Nope." I pointed to his girl. "That was all her. Apparently, she's the queen of group texts, who knew?"

"I did." Jax straight-up rested his head against her neck, breathing her in for a few seconds before straightening.

Kinsey's hand was shaking in mine when her mom got up from her seat and shuffled toward us.

Her eyes filled with tears as she shook her head slowly and whispered in a hoarse voice, "It's probably best that we say good-bye."

Kinsey froze next to me. I sucked in a breath. "I don't understand."

"He fell."

My blood chilled.

"I called the ambulance. They got him here, and . . ." Her chin quivered. "The cancer's spread into his lungs. The doctors have given him a week at most."

"But—" Kinsey stumbled away from me toward her mom. "We were supposed to have more time. He was supposed to be healthy just a little bit longer, right? Isn't that why you guys stopped chemo?"

Jax was at her side immediately, hugging her to his chest as she sobbed softly against him.

My fingers itched to jerk her back against me, to comfort her like only I knew how.

"Oh, baby." Her mom joined them in a hug. "I don't know why it happened this way, just that it did." She swiped her fingers under

Kinsey's eyes where tears glistened. "He wants to see you . . ." Her gaze locked on mine and Harley's. "All four of you."

Stunned, I could only nod my head and try to keep myself from breaking, so that Kinsey would have something solid to hold on to, when all I wanted to do was run.

And in that moment, I felt like the person Jax had always accused me of being.

The guy who ran.

The intensity of the fear that chilled my body was so intense I started to get dizzy, and then Kins grabbed my hand.

The anxiety left.

And in its place, peace.

My mom had always joked that I was her anchor in life—and I'd always joked that if I was an anchor I must be really heavy, and the exchange almost always ended with me telling her she needed to feed me more if she had such high expectations.

We'd laugh.

She'd pile my plate high, and we'd share a meal together.

"This way." Kinsey's mom led us away from the group and down the hall.

"Hey! Hey! Mr. Miller!" a small voice yelled in my direction.

I stopped walking and looked down to my right. Marco was barreling toward me without crutches.

He slammed against my leg, his arms wrapping around my thigh as though he was trying to squeeze me to death. "I knew you'd come back! I told my mama you'd come back, and she didn't believe me! I even told my nurse!"

I smiled despite the sadness at being there for all the wrong reasons, and knelt down so I was at eye level. "Well, look at that, you're right! And I see you're not using any crutches." I held out my fist.

He knocked it and giggled. "Yeah, well, I remembered what you said." He leaned in and whispered, "About my heart being like a lion."

Tears filled my eyes. "Oh yeah?"

He nodded vigorously. "And guess what?"

"What, little man?"

The rest of the group had stopped to watch the exchange; even the nurses' station seemed frozen in time.

"One night, I got really sick. Mama said I had an infection, and I almost died and guess what!"

"What?" Damn, I could talk to this kid forever.

"There was an angel! She had eyes like yours." He touched my face and frowned. "And cheeks like yours! And a dimple right here." He giggled. "And she said she knew you and that you would be really sad if I stopped being a lion! She asked me to *rawr* and I did, I *rawred* so loud, Mr. Miller! And she said that one day I was going to be just like you! Isn't that so cool? And, oh boy, the music she sang was so pretty." He started to hum.

My blood completely chilled. It was the same song my mom used to sing to me at night when I was a child.

"Almost forgot!" He giggled again. "She told me I was going to be okay, I just had to wake up, and fight, and so I did, and when she faded away, her little bracelet on her arm made a jingling noise. It had a heart and a red football—what football is red?" He shrugged.

The kind I gave my mom when I was six.

The kind she wore on her wrist until her death.

The kind I could have sworn I buried her wearing—when I was asked to get clothes for the casket.

I sucked in a breath and stared at the kid.

Tears filled my eyes, I almost couldn't get it out. He shook his head.

I grabbed his hand and held it. "That bracelet must be magic."

A tear slid down his cheek. "I figured it was something cool, because the minute I woke up . . . Mom said I got better, you think she healed me? My destiny angel with the bracelet?"

"Yeah, Marco," I whispered hoarsely, "I think she did."

"Cool." He nodded, his eyes bright with blissful innocence. "I thought so, Mr. Miller. Thanks for coming back to see me."

I made a promise to never let a week go by without seeing the kid. "Hey, you think it would be okay if I came by next week? You still gonna be here?"

"Nope!" He rocked back and forth on his heels. "I'm gonna be better, so I can go to your game against San Francisco!"

"Sounds like a plan."

One of the nurses stepped forward. "Okay, Marco, it's time for dinner. Why don't you say good night to your new friend?"

Marco wrapped his arms around me again and whispered, "Thank you for showing me how to *rawr* loud, Mr. Miller."

I could only nod, my voice was a wreck, my throat felt like it was on fire. He disappeared around the corner, and I turned to the nurses' station. "Can I get his mom's number, please?"

"That's against protocol." She smiled sadly. "But if you give me yours, I can pass along the information."

I quickly jotted down my name and number then turned to Kinsey. She was crying.

I imagined it was because of her dad and the whole situation just reminding her that even though Marco was okay—her dad wouldn't be.

I stared up at the group.

Jax licked his lips and said in a hushed tone, "Something tells me you knew someone with a bracelet like that."

I smiled. "My mom."

Kinsey covered her mouth with her hands.

Her mom let out a sob before reaching for me.

And this time.

This time I held her tight. As tight as I could.

Panic didn't overwhelm me.

I didn't think about running away.

I didn't think about the pain or the road ahead.

I just held her.

And she held me back.

And then I was joined by Kinsey, Harley, and Jax.

Minutes went by.

And then, as natural as ever, my family broke apart, and walked with heavy hearts toward the room that said "Ben Romonov."

Chapter Thirty-Five

KINSEY

My dad didn't look like himself.

He was more pale than normal, and his lips were drawn back against his teeth like he was having trouble sucking in air and couldn't quite get enough moisture in his mouth to lick them—or maybe he was just so exhausted he didn't want to bother. What I was looking at was not my father.

It was a shell.

And in that moment.

I wanted for him to have that peace.

I wanted for him to be free.

I wanted for him to let go.

Because my father was gone.

Amazing how death sneaks up on a person, how it changes even the shell of the body, making the person unrecognizable, maybe it's the fact that the soul's finally releasing its tendrils around the human heart, maybe it's the soul that gives up first and realizes that this was never the plan, to live with sickness—but to live free from it.

Dad smiled up at us. "Anyone bring any cookies?"

Harley handed over the plate and winked.

"You keep this one, son." Dad grabbed a cookie and lifted it to his nose and winked at Harley. "Smells like heaven. You add—" He coughed a bit. "You add extra butter?"

Harley grinned down at him. "The trick is extra brown sugar and a bit of love."

Jax's eyes filled with tears as he gripped her hand.

"Mmm." He lifted the cookie to his lips and took a small bite. "The sugar's easy to taste, but the love? That stays with ya, doesn't it, Harley?"

"Yeah." Her lips trembled. "It really does."

She touched her stomach.

I frowned briefly then looked up at Jax.

His hands followed hers.

Like he was protecting her.

Shielding her body?

Or maybe I was just being hypersensitive and overemotional.

I wasn't sure if he was actively doing it or just doing it because that's where her hands were at; my dad noticed too, his eyes doing that little calculating thing that meant he was thinking.

My mom got busy straightening his pillows. He grabbed her hand and kissed it. "Give me a few minutes with my kids."

Miller and Harley started to leave.

He cleared his throat. "All my kids."

Miller froze.

Harley let out a little gasp.

"Sit." Dad didn't have to ask twice.

All of us found spots around his bed, Jax sat on the corner, and I sat in Miller's lap while Harley found the only other chair in the room and pulled it forward.

"Now." Dad grinned. "That's much better. So, Jax, it seems like you've been keeping yourself busy off the field."

"Dad—"

"Good for you, son." He peered over at Harley. "He treat you right?"

Jax cursed under his breath.

"At first yes, then no, and now yes." She winked. "We're happy. So happy . . . even though he snores like an elephant and doesn't flush the toilet."

"Right?" I chimed in.

Dad cackled while Miller stifled a laugh behind his hand.

"Thanks, Harley." Jax rolled his eyes, then a smile formed behind his lips before he reached for her hand.

"You kids will need each other." Dad nodded. "Kinsey, you and Miller are going strong still, I see."

I grinned. "Yeah, well, I kind of love him."

"I know." Dad shrugged. "Even when you tried not to."

I licked my lips and nodded.

"Miller?" Dad frowned. "You done being a pansy-ass?"

Jax laughed.

"Yes sir." Miller smiled wide. "I can safely say my pansy-ass days are behind me . . . I just had another reminder before we came in here that it's better to have the heart of a lion. I had that heart once—before my mom died—and I think I finally just got it back." He squeezed my hand. "And I have Kinsey to thank for that . . . and a certain little boy who's walking out of this joint in a few days."

"Hah." Dad placed half of his uneaten cookie back on the plate. I quickly grabbed the plate and set it on his tray for easy access.

"Jax, I'm not dead yet. Try not to get into any fights this week, I'll be watching. And Miller, you need to block a bit harder, give my son a few more seconds to throw to ya."

"Yes sir," they both said in unison.

"Now . . ." Dad crooked his finger, and we all leaned in. "Listen carefully . . ."

I held my breath.

"My body is giving up. But my soul is a fighter, so when I leave this earth, I want you to remember that even though my body's broken, gone, dust, my soul's free." Tears filled his eyes. "You're going to take shots of whiskey after my funeral. And I want cookies. Anyone brings your mom a lasagna, you throw it out! No casseroles either! I want joy! I want to go out the way I came in, buck naked and screaming. I want balloons, celebration, and I want to be buried with my fork." He winked.

"Your fork?" Miller just had to ask.

"You've never heard that story?" Dad grinned. "A husband and wife were both dying. He said if he was to die first, he wanted her to bury him with his fork, you wanna know why?"

"Because he liked pie?" Miller guessed.

"Nope!" Dad's grin widened. "Life is the main course, son . . . and after life? Well, that's the dessert, and I'm not showing up to heaven—my dessert—without my fork. Makes absolutely no sense. A man has to be prepared about these things."

I rolled my eyes even though tears still filled them while Miller burst out laughing and nodded his head. "Alright then, a fork it is."

Jax and he shared a look.

It was one of brotherhood. Of shared sadness.

Of shared grief.

In all my life, I'd never seen my brother touch another guy other than my dad. I wouldn't call him cold. He was just reserved, controlled.

But when Miller held out his hand to Jax on the bed.

Jax took it.

He squeezed.

Jax didn't let go.

And suddenly I was so thankful that Miller was in not just my life, but Jax's.

"Alright, no more sadness," Dad announced. "You kids scatter so I can get some sleep before Paula comes in here and fluffs another damn pillow."

We all said our good-byes.

I kissed him on the forehead.

"You did good," he whispered.

"Yeah, I did."

We were almost out the door when Dad said, "Miller, a word, son."

Jax slapped him on the back.

Reluctantly I released his hand, shut the door, and waited.

Chapter Thirty-Six

MILLER

"Something's been bothering me," Ben said in a casual tone. "Wanna know what it is?"

"I'm sure you're going to tell me regardless, so go ahead." I took a seat and offered him a polite smile as I leaned down and folded my hands to keep from doing something stupid like grabbing his and crying like a little boy over the fact that the woman I loved was losing her dad and the only thing I could do about it was watch.

"You talked with Kinsey and Jax, naturally they talk to their mom, and their mom talks to me." He shrugged. "We're talkers."

"Everyone but Jax."

"Hah!" He laughed. "He's more of a thinker." He took a deep breath. "Your mom . . . Kinsey says she died suddenly."

I'd literally only talked to Kinsey about my mom a handful of times. Suddenly guilty, I nodded.

"Did you ever mourn, son?"

I shook my head. "No, but I'm getting better."

"Not good enough. Not for me. Not for her. It's okay to hurt here." He touched his chest. "And to remember them here." He pointed to his head. "But to let it cripple you, turn you into the opposite of the man she wanted you to be . . . I'm not saying that's what you're doing." He gave a weak shrug. "But, that's not fair to you, not fair to the life she gave you. I think, before you can fully love my little girl, you need to let go of the only other woman who's ever truly held your heart."

Stunned, I just stared at him.

"And that woman was your mama." He shrugged again. "I know nothing about your past relationships, but I'm assuming that none panned out quite the way you wanted them to—and with Kinsey, well, I see forever in my girl's eyes, so I want you to do me a favor." He leaned forward. "When she lets me go, you let your mama go too. You mourn together. You cry together. You grieve together. I think maybe we were put in your life for a reason. I think maybe this is your chance to move beyond something that happened to you when you were too young to understand, too young to deal with it."

Tears filled my eyes. I looked away.

"And when you're done grieving, I need you to ask Paula for her mother's ring . . . so you can put it on my daughter's hand."

"I haven't asked yet."

"You will."

"I will." I sniffed. "You know I will."

"So, you gonna ask permission? Or do I need to beat it out of you?"

I laughed through my tears. "Ben Romonov, may I have the honor of marrying your daughter?"

He looked at me straight in the eyes and whispered, "The honor is all mine."

I didn't mean to move.

Just like I didn't mean to wrap my arms around his frail body and squeeze.

And when the tears came.

He hugged me.

And said something that I'd been dying to hear for the past six years since my mom's death.

"She would be so proud of you."

Chapter Thirty-Seven

Jax

Miller and Kinsey went to grab a bite to eat while I made sure my mom had everything she needed for the night. She refused to leave his side. I didn't blame her, couldn't blame her since I wanted to do the same thing.

But according to my dad, I had rough practices and an even tougher game later that week, and since I made a promise to win and stop getting into fights, I knew it was time to go.

I held Harley's hand and walked her all the way to my car.

I wasn't sure what to say.

Words seemed so . . . inappropriate in this kind of situation. *Thank you for making cookies for my dying dad* didn't quite cut it either.

Thanks for holding my hand when all I wanted to do was break.

Thanks for being you.

Thanks for not running away.

I clamped my lips together the entire ride back to my apartment. Not even thinking that she might want to go home.

Thankfully, Harley didn't protest. Simply dropped her purse onto the countertop of my pristine granite and then reached for my body.

She pressed her head against my chest and whispered, "I know you're not okay, so I'm not going to ask if you are. . . but what can I do to help you prepare for practice tomorrow? The game this week? Laundry? Cook? Clean?"

I grinned down at her. "You know how to do laundry?"

She pinched me in the side. "I know how to do a lot of housekeeping things. For example . . ." I exhaled while she moved around to my washer. "I know that this is the start button, I know that if I use cold water I can get stains out of the chocolate variety, and I know that even when a person's sad, they still need food."

I nodded. "Soup. You said you were soup people."

"Butternut squash people, to be exact." She winked and then in a husky voice added, "With a dash of bacon."

"I don't think *dash* has ever sounded so sexy."

Harley hummed while she familiarized herself with my kitchen, and when she realized she'd need to go to the store, she kissed my cheek, grabbed my keys, said she'd be back, and then left me alone with my thoughts, with my sadness.

I took a shower then walked around my apartment like a zombie. Out of my control. All of it.

What the hell was I going to do without my dad?

It broke a piece of me.

It severed my heart.

And made me feel like I was just one second away from cracking; all my life I'd looked to him, and now I felt lost. Out of focus. Afraid.

Damn, I was so afraid.

And I wondered if I'd ever be the same without that man in my life, without his words of encouragement, without his crude jokes and ability to demolish an entire tray of cookies.

Lost in thought, I lay down on the couch.

It felt like minutes later when I was getting softly woken up.

Harley stood over me with a bowl of soup and the best-smelling bread in the entire universe.

I ate, and then I had another bowl and then I told her that if I wasn't already half in love with her—the food would have done it.

She sucked in a breath.

I cursed the magic food.

"You mean that?" she asked in a small voice. "I mean we've only known each other a few weeks."

"Yeah, well." I put the bowl down. "Kinda feels like longer when you go through shit like this together, huh? It either kills a relationship or bonds you more."

Her smile was weak and then she got up and left.

Shit. I messed up. Again.

Within seconds, she emerged from down the hall and handed me something.

Frowning, I looked down at the plastic stick in my hand.

Two blue lines crossed a little window.

Two.

Blue.

Lines.

"I suspected," she whispered. "I was afraid to tell you—"

I devoured her next words with my mouth, lifted her onto the table, and braced the side of her face with my hands. "You're pregnant?"

"Yeah." She gulped. "Remember that first night?"

"I think it's impossible to forget."

It was only the second time I'd seen her blush. "I was afraid it was positive, afraid you'd run, and then all of this happened." She sighed. "I pushed the suspicion back, thinking my body was just under an insane amount of stress, and then you came back and we were happy, and I thought, *Oh great, just one more thing on his plate.*" Her eyes met mine. "One more thing you can't control."

Our foreheads touched. I let out a long sigh. "You know, if there's anything this last year has taught me, it's that some of the best things in life can't be helped or controlled."

Tears filled her eyes.

"Like you," I whispered against her lips. "Like our baby."

"Our baby," she repeated with a smile.

"Yeah." I kissed her softly on the mouth. "Ours."

"Are we telling your dad about this?"

I nodded my head and laughed. "He's going to kill me, call me an idiot, and then try to live just a little bit longer to feel that baby kick."

"I hope so." She touched her flat stomach.

"Thank you." I lifted her off the counter and carried her over to the couch, careful to lay her down so that I was holding her, not heavily pushing against her frail body.

"For getting pregnant?" she teased.

"Sorry to break it to you but that's all on me . . . it just . . . God, Harley, it felt so good to be in your arms, to have nothing but you surround me, I've never felt that way about anyone before, I think the first time I've ever fully relinquished any sort of control was that moment in your arms."

She sniffled.

I looked over her shoulder. "Is the unbreakable Harley crying? Should I tell Grandma?"

She elbowed me in the stomach. "That was really sweet."

"It's true." I kissed her neck. "So I guess you could say that the very first time I lost control—I wasn't given one gift." I pressed a hand to her stomach. "But two."

She turned in my arms and kissed my mouth, her hands tugged at my hair and then my shirt.

Clothes were off in seconds without our mouths ever leaving one another.

And then, I was home.

In her arms.

And I had to imagine that this was exactly how it was supposed to happen for me, because in that moment, it seemed impossible for it to be any other way.

Chapter Thirty-Eight

Preseason Game 2
San Francisco vs. Bellevue
Home Turf
Favored Team: Bellevue Bucks

Coach stomped into the locker room, took one look around, and cleared his throat. "Men, normally I wouldn't be giving a speech before a preseason game, and if I did, it would center around playing your heart out to secure a spot with this program. But today, after this last week, I feel like some words are warranted." He turned his attention to Jax. "When one of us hurts, all of us hurts, that's what brotherhood is about, we suffer together, we stand together, so when we walk out there, I want to see unity, I want the world to know what type of team they're cheering for. This goes beyond football. This, men, is life. You never know who may be watching, who may need to see their heroes stand tall. Play like heroes today, and you'll win."

Nobody made eye contact.

Probably because it was one of the best speeches any of us had ever heard, and every damn one of us had tears in our eyes.

Jax stood.

We followed.

And then he did something I'd never seen him do before—he reached for Sanchez on one side, then looped his arm through mine.

The rest of the players followed suit as we linked arms all the way down the tunnel and out onto the field.

Screaming made it hard to focus on anything but the fact that when the world saw us walk tall out onto that field.

They saw unity.

Hope.

They saw a brotherhood.

And I'd never, in all my life, been so honored to be a part of it.

Jax, in that one second, solidified himself as the only leader I wanted to follow, and I knew I wasn't the only one who felt the exact same way, that I would rather take the hit than have any harm come to him.

So when we won the coin toss.

When our defense shut them out and it was our turn to take a spot on the field, I turned to him and said, "Trick play?"

He threw his head back and laughed. "Does this mean you wanna throw again?"

"They won't be expecting the same thing again."

"Nope."

"Your dad's watching."

The huddle grew silent.

Sanchez was the first to speak. "Double Dr Pepper on two."

Jax looked up at him and nodded.

Sanchez bumped his fist and ran to his position on the field.

When the ball was snapped, I ran toward Jax, blocking the center before Jax turned on his heel and threw the ball to Sanchez.

Sanchez caught it while I followed Jax's route, hitting everyone in his path with as much violence as I could muster.

I knew the exact moment the ball was sailing toward Jax, his eyes lit up, his focus was trained. One guy stood in our way. I took him out so hard that he flipped onto the ground backward.

Jax caught the ball.

Made the touchdown.

And saluted Sanchez.

And in that moment, it was more than football to me.

More than a game.

It was something I'd never forget.

Something I would teach my kids and their kids and whoever the hell would listen to me: that life isn't always about the big moments, but the smaller ones that lead up to them, the truly important parts of your life are the ones that you a lot of times want to ignore, they're the pain, the agony, the anxiety, the bad.

But they have a purpose.

Everything does.

That big moment was incredible.

The moments building up to it, painful.

And yet I could stand there and look around the stadium and whisper to myself, "It may hurt, but it's good. Life is good."

"Mr. Miller, Mr. Miller!" Marco was waiting for me in the locker room right along with his mom. "You played so good!"

"Thanks, man." I gave him a high five just as Sanchez walked around the corner.

Marco's eyes bugged out of his head. "Grant Sanchez! Best receiver in the league!"

"Hey, look at that, he knows my official title." Sanchez winked down at him then knelt. "You have fun today, my man?"

"So much." Marco did a little dance. "Hey, can you sign my football?"

"I'd sign a thousand footballs for you." Sanchez shrugged like it wasn't a big deal when we both knew it was.

I slapped him on the back and then grabbed Jax so Marco could meet him.

Jax was already on his way over to me. "The infamous Marco, good to see you again."

"Oh, hey!" He pointed at Jax. "You were at the hospital too. Are you sick?"

"Nah, man"—Jax knelt down—"but my dad is."

"Oh." Marco's smile fell. "When my daddy died he told me that it's really important to eat your vegetables."

Jax's eyes widened. "Wow, really? I'll have to make sure to do that."

"Know what else?"

"What?"

"He said to treat every day like it's your last because you never know if it will be. I bet your dad is doing that right now, huh? I bet he watched your game and was so proud and screaming and yelling like I was. I bet he cried too. Because that's what dads do when they get proud, they cry."

Jax's eyes filled with tears. "I believe you on that one, buddy." He put his hands on his hips. "You know, you're pretty smart."

"Duh." He rolled his eyes. "My mom always says so."

"Well then." Sanchez chuckled while Marco's mom blushed, you could tell she'd been through a lot. Her face was tired. Exhausted, really.

"So." I split my gaze between him and his mom. "The guys and I thought it would be really cool for you to have season tickets, what do you think about that?"

"Really?"

"Yup! Only on one condition. You see those boxes way up high?"

He nodded his head vigorously.

"You have to sit up there where it's nice and warm, and you have to promise to eat as much food as possible."

"I'm in!" He clapped his hands while his mom mouthed a *"thank you"* to us, and wiped at some of her tears.

Life without a husband, with one child sick, I couldn't even imagine.

And then it hit me. All this time I'd been focused on myself and on what I couldn't offer Kinsey rather than what I could offer. I'd been angry over my past, irrational over my mom, over losing Em even, and yet this little kid was giving me a run for my money, humbling me to such extremes that I wanted to punch myself.

When they left, I was still thinking about it.

When I got home, Kinsey was there waiting with a glass of wine.

I blurted out, "Do you think I'm selfish?"

She frowned. "What? Where did that come from? You're one of the most selfless people I know!"

"No." I shook my head. "I wish that was true. I think when it comes to you especially, I'm the most selfish man alive."

"Miller—"

"Hear me out. I want you all to myself. I wanted you when I shouldn't have wanted you, when I sure as hell didn't deserve to touch you, to take your heart, and then to promise you nothing but sex? To promise to protect you from Anderson and take you for myself? All of it. Selfish. Horrible. That's not the guy I want to be for you, Kins. I can't be him for you. I want you—but I need to want you in the right way, where if you walked out that door and said you wanted nothing to do with me, my feet would stay planted to this ground in order to honor what you really wanted."

"You done yet?"

I sighed. "Yes. Maybe. I don't know."

"You, Quinton Miller, next to my daddy and brother, are one of the best men I know. You are kind. Smart. Giving. Inspiring. You love with your whole heart even when you're afraid it's going to break all over again, and when I needed you most in my life, you were there. You know, when I was little, Jax was my hero. He was . . . everything. I placed him on a pedestal and got pissed when he tripped off it."

"Stupid Jax," I teased.

"Right? I learned a thing or two about pedestals, about perfection. Eventually you fail, and when you fail, you fall really hard, Miller. I don't want perfect. I just want you. I want us. I want what we have, this burning violent uncontainable thing between us. That's all I need. As far as you being selfish? Good. Because it means that you want me solely for yourself—and that works out great for me, I've been yours since that first kiss in Vegas."

"I love you."

"I love you too." She said it slowly, without taking her eyes off mine.

I kissed, tasted her, craved her so much that it was impossible for me to stop kissing her.

"Hold my heart, Quinton Miller. I'm sorry it hurts so much right now. You deserve a heart that's not mourning."

I sighed. "Aw, Kinsey, my heart never stopped mourning, maybe our two hearts can help heal each other."

She nodded.

"I was wrong."

"About what?"

I slowly pulled her sweater from her body. "It's going to be okay. It gets better. When you're with someone you love. It gets better."

Her eyes filled with tears as she nodded and placed a hand on my heart. "I know."

Chapter Thirty-Nine

His kisses were like a drug. His hands, possessive, just the way they'd always been since that first time.

When his tongue circled around my belly button, I almost kicked him in the face.

"You're beautiful." Miller's mouth covered mine. "So beautiful."

"You sure you're not too sore? You did get hit a lot today."

"You're worth it." He winced a bit as he hovered over me.

"Nope!" I crawled out from underneath him and walked naked all the way over to the shower, turned on the hot water, and pointed. "In, now."

"Bossy," he grumbled, standing up and sliding off his pants until all I saw was mocha-kissed skin and abs, so many abs I was dizzy. "See something you like?"

"Somethings." I shrugged. "Plural." He stopped in front of me. My hands found his chest and then he was kissing me against the wall, lifting me into the shower, teasing my tongue with his. Hot water pelted against my back, wetting my hair as pieces stuck to my face.

"Love you." His head fell as he nuzzled my neck, breathing me in before bracing a hand above my head and pulling me in to him.

My breath quickened when he thrust in and out. Steam billowed between us as we made love.

Love.

That's what this was between us.

And in my mind's eye it suddenly clicked into place.

Saved by the prince.

Protected by the king.

Given to the knight on his white horse—the one who claimed to have a broken heart—only to find out that it matched the very one I held in my chest.

Love . . . would be stronger than death.

I would make sure of it.

"Love you," he said again and again. I was lost in the sensation of his strong body, of the way he made me feel strong. "So much."

Epilogue

The funeral was three weeks later.

Not one.

Three.

I'd like to think that he fought a little bit harder because he wanted to see grandchildren. Cancer had spread everywhere until it was impossible for him to breathe without help.

And when it was time.

We were all with him.

Even Sanchez and Em.

The team was in the waiting room.

My family.

Six years ago, I'd lost my family, I'd lost everything.

And now?

I had around eighty people I called brother, a few I called sister, several I called friends.

One I would soon call fiancée.

I cried.

I had promised him I'd let myself.

I cried for him. I cried for my mom. I cried for Kinsey and Jax.

I cried for me.

For all those times I held the tears in for fear of looking weak in front of my dad, for fear that once I let go I wouldn't stop.

And when dirt was thrown onto his casket.

I smiled.

Because he was at peace.

"Cheers." Jax walked up with a bottle of whiskey and seven shot glasses, each of us took one and waited for him to pour. Once he was finished, he faced the grave and said, "To the best man who ever lived— may you live some more . . . and may there always be chocolate chip cookies."

"And football," Kinsey added.

"Whiskey." Harley handed her shot to Sanchez, who took it.

"And Eddell." I beamed, saying my mom's name. "Say hi to my mom, she'll be the one making the cookies."

Paula pulled me in for a side hug after she took her shot. I looked down at her and smiled. "So about that ring . . ."

We didn't win the championship.

We lost by a field goal.

I was too nervous to be pissed.

In minutes, I was going to be asking my girl to marry me, and all I had to show for it was a dirty uniform and a ring in my palm.

She was just starting to run off the field when I crooked my finger in her direction.

Frowning, she jogged up to me. "Hey, what's up? Are you okay? Did you get hurt? I'm so sorry we lost—"

"I can still win," I interrupted.

"Oh?" She grinned as people started moving around us, giving me the space I needed to drop down to one knee.

And suddenly the rest of the team was surrounding us.

Em walked up to me, and gave me the biggest hug. "She'll say yes, I promise. I'm so proud of you, and she would be too, ya dumb football player."

"Cheer hard, cheer-tator," I teased back, using her nickname from high school.

She joined Sanchez's side and I got down on one knee.

Kinsey gasped when her mom stepped forward with roses and a plate of cookies. Naturally, we had to celebrate once my woman said yes, and I figured she'd want a piece of her dad with us.

"Kinsey Romonov—"

"Yes!" She jumped into the air amidst hoots and hollers as well as laughter.

"Baby." I laughed. "You gonna let me finish?"

She'd actually knocked me on my ass.

"Oh." She braced her hands on either side of the grass, then leaned down and kissed me on the mouth. "Yes, I'll marry you."

"You stole my sentence."

"Talk faster next time."

"Kins—"

She huffed out a breath and smiled.

"Will you really marry me?"

"Yes. I only said yes three times." She kissed me across the mouth and said it for a fourth. "Yes, Quinton Miller . . . best tight end with a tight end in the league, I'll marry you."

My team all burst out laughing.

Yeah, I wasn't going to get rid of that nickname for a very long time. Thanks, Kins.

Mine.

She was mine.

I just hadn't known it.

She helped me to my feet while the crowd around us cheered, a few of the Dallas players came over to congratulate us, and my team lifted her into the air and cheered.

They walked off with her.

I stayed back.

Em reached for my hand.

I squeezed it tight. "Well, best friend, definitely not how I would have written the story."

She laid her head on my shoulder. "Me neither." I wrapped my arm around her. "It's better. This is the way it was supposed to be."

"It's everything it was supposed to be."

She nodded.

"Thank you for being you, Em."

"I'm so proud to call you friend, Miller."

Full circle.

Just like I said.

Everything.

Everything comes full circle.

That's life.

And mine?

Was just getting started—all because she said yes.

Acknowledgments

Thank you, GOD, for this amazing job. I honestly wake up every day pinching myself and wondering how I'm able to do what I love! I'm so honored and blessed to have incredible publishers, readers, bloggers, just PEOPLE in my life who make this job so amazing. I can't even call it a job, it's a passion, it's something I do because I love it so much.

Thank you, Erica, for being the best agent around. I can't even describe how much I think about you and the impact you've had on my life. I want to give you to every author out there yet feel so selfish about you at the same time (hah-hah).

Skyscape, one of the best publishers in the world: I'm daily honored to work with you and hope to keep writing stories until you tell me no. ;)

Thor and Nate: thank you for being so understanding and helping inspire some of my best work!

The Rockin' Readers: GAH, you guys are the best family EVER!!! I'm so lucky to have you and your support. I know that at a drop of the hat I can ask for help and you'll be there ASAP. It's so encouraging to have a group of readers that are family to me and I'm so blessed with you guys. Thank you!

To my awesome publicist (Nina!) at Social Butterfly PR and to JILL, oh gosh, JILL (my sister!): I think I would actually just be rocking in a corner without you two! Thank you for keeping me sane, for making all the things work, and just for being so awesome!

Liza, Kristin, Jessica, Lauren, Michelle—EVERYONE who worked on this book with me: I'm so thankful for your input and hard work! Thank you so much.

And bloggers: I love you. I really do. I would not be able to do what I do without you guys. Thank you for your constant support and help with all the things!

I hate these because I always forget people. It really does take a village and I'm so thankful for mine!

HUGS,

RVD

About the Author

Photo © 2014 Lauren Watson Perry, Perrywinkle Photography

Rachel Van Dyken is a *New York Times*, *Wall Street Journal*, and *USA Today* bestselling author. When she's not writing about hot hunks for her Regency romance or New Adult fiction books, Rachel is dreaming up *new* hunks. (The more hunks, the merrier!) While Rachel writes a lot, she also makes sure she enjoys the finer things in life—like *The Bachelor* and strong coffee.

Rachel lives in Idaho with her husband, son, and two boxers. Fans can follow her writing journey at www.RachelVanDykenAuthor.com and www.facebook.com/rachelvandyken.